ALL YOUR PUCKING SECRETS

A. RIVERS

To my husband,
For believing in me and
challenging me every day.

CONTENT WARNING

This book contains reference to sexual assault, bullying, domestic violence, emotional abuse, financial abuse, and use of alcohol as a crutch. It also has a hero who veers toward being morally grey. If any of these trigger you, please proceed with caution.

1
____

ECHO

The moment my friend Cassie utters the word "hockey player," I mentally shut down. I watch her lips move as she, Anita, and Ryan exchange gossip, but I don't hear a thing they say.

"Echo?" Cassie nudges me with her elbow. "Are you even listening?"

"Of course," I reply automatically. "Hot jock. Hockey. Salacious details."

"Uh-huh." She doesn't look impressed.

"Leave her alone," Ryan says. "You know she doesn't care about sports. Or guys."

I hide my wince. It isn't that I don't care about those things; more like hockey has some terrible associations for me. And as for overly handsome hockey players...well, I've had enough of those assholes to last a lifetime.

"But she cares about me." Cassie pouts. "Don't you, sweetie?"

"I do," I say. "Sorry. I'll try harder to listen."

Ryan leans back in his stool at the coffee bar and meets my eyes, his expression concerned. I force a smile in response. I've never told any of my friends why I don't share their enthusiasm for jocks, but somehow, Ryan has always seemed to understand that it's more than just a personal preference.

"Good." Cassie opens her mouth to resume her story, but a waiter interrupts her.

"Oat milk flat white?" he asks.

Ryan accepts the drink.

"Skinny caramel mocha?"

I take it, then empty a sachet of sugar into the coffee while the waiter delivers the rest of the drinks. I stir and scoop up a spoonful of foam. If you ask me, frothy coffee is ten times better than any muscle-bound hockey player ever could be.

I glance across the counter toward the entrance, and everything inside me freezes. My stomach tightens, and I struggle to draw in a breath.

There, leaning against the column beside the sliding door, is the man primarily responsible for my aversion to hockey players.

Tyler Kinsey.

His eyes meet mine, the pale blue so intense I can barely stand to hold his gaze. Meanwhile, my heart hammers wildly against the inside of my ribcage, trying to break free.

What the hell is he doing in a coffee shop in Newbury, Oregon? He should be at a big-name college with all his rich friends. Not slumming it with us.

I glare so he won't get any ideas about coming over here.

"I told you," Cassie murmurs. "I know hockey players aren't your type, but even you have to admit he's hot."

"Wait, what?" I tear my gaze away from his and turn to face my friend.

She looks at me like I'm crazy. "The transfer student. Tyler. Totally gorgeous."

My eyes fly back to him, then skitter away as I realize he's still staring at me. Cassie is right. He looks incredible. But then, he always did. He's like one of those poisonous butterflies: so pretty that you can't tell how lethal he is until it's too late.

"Um…" I try to summon a response, but my heart is beating harder and harder, and it's all I can do to hear anything outside my own pulse.

My throat constricts and it feels as though I'm breathing through a thick layer of fabric, my lungs laboring with the effort.

"Whoa." Ryan's hand lands on my back, and he pushes gently, guiding my head downward, toward the bar. I rest my forehead on the wooden surface and count as I inhale.

One, two, three, four.

Exhale.

One, two, three, four.

"You're okay," Ryan says, rubbing my back. "Just keep it up. In and out."

I finally get a handle on my breathing, and my airways relax. I straighten, my lips trembling.

Tyler Kinsey is now a student here.

The man who tore my heart to shreds and discarded me like used baggage has followed me to my refuge.

It's wrong. He shouldn't be allowed here. Not when I've carved out a life for myself that doesn't revolve around him, or what happened in high school.

I scrunch a napkin in my hand, twisting it over and over. Cassie and Anita are talking in whispers, looking at me as though I might be on the verge of a meltdown.

Honestly, it wouldn't surprise me if I am.

The lights overhead are too bright, and I blink rapidly. My throat begins to tighten again, and I count out my breaths until it relaxes.

"All good?" Ryan asks, his hand dropping from my back.

I glance toward the door, where Tyler was a moment ago. He's standing tall now, a few steps away from the column he was leaning against. He cocks his head, a question in his eyes.

Oh, God.

Is he going to come over here?

I shove back from the bar leaner and slide my feet to the floor, my coffee forgotten.

"I think I need some air," I say.

Anita drains her drink in a few mouthfuls. "I'll come with you."

"No." If she does, I won't be able to avoid Tyler without it being obvious that's what I'm doing. "I'll be fine. Really."

She doesn't look certain, but she nods and holds up her phone. "Call if you need, okay?"

"I will."

I hurry out of there before anyone else offers to accompany me. Knowing Ryan, he'd be right on my heels if he had any idea what was going on. Thank God I've never spilled my past to him. And thank God there are two ways into and out of the coffee shop.

I'm outside the building in a matter of seconds. I don't know where I'm going, but I know I can't linger in case one of my friends—or worse, Tyler—decides to follow me. I duck behind the library and jog down the alley and around the corner, emerging into an open courtyard.

Looking around, I don't see anyone to be wary of, so I slow my pace as I cross campus. My dorm is a couple of blocks away, and I try to ease my breathing as I walk toward it.

A cool breeze stirs my hair, and I shiver. Damn. I left my sweater in the coffee shop. Hopefully, one of the others will bring it for me later. I shoot Ryan a quick text, knowing he's the most reliable. Anita or Cassie would most likely "borrow" it and I wouldn't see it again for weeks.

The dorm looms ahead. Occupying almost an entire block, it stands eight stories tall and is a mishmash of chrome and brick. I make a beeline for the door, only to stop dead at the sight of Tyler standing a few yards in front of it.

He stalks toward me.

TYLER

My body thrums with anticipation as I close the distance between us.

Echo Dean steals my breath, just as she always did. I scan her greedily, eager to see what changes the years have wrought. She's just as beautiful as ever. Slender, with dark hair, and luminous hazel eyes magnified by glasses.

She wraps her arms around her waist and glances over her shoulder, as if debating whether to make a run for it. There's no point. I'll catch her. I'm bigger, faster, and more determined.

She must realize that because she slumps and stops walking. Nerves twist and turn in my belly. I wish I could yank her into my arms and shield her from the world, but if I tried, she'd no doubt kick me in the balls.

"It's nice to see you again," I tell her.

"Nice" is an understatement. Being this close to her after so many years is like standing in front of the gateway to heaven. Except I've done too much sinning to be allowed through.

"It's the opposite of nice to see you." She shudders, her narrow shoulders hunching as if she's trying to will herself into nonexistence. "I wish you'd stayed away."

Staying away would be like stabbing myself in the heart

with a dagger. I'm not strong enough to do it. Her words hurt almost as much, even though I deserve them and more. If I want her back, I'll have to weather everything she throws at me and come through the other side.

"I couldn't," I say.

She sucks in a sharp breath, and then clutches her throat, as though she's having trouble breathing.

"Are you okay?" I ask, placing my hand on her back.

When she flinches away, I feel like someone has flayed me open. I release her immediately and stuff my hands in my pockets, so I won't touch her again by mistake.

"Breathe," I say. "Take it slow."

I recognize the signs of a panic attack. My mother was prone to them, although she seems to be over that now. Amazing what time and death can do.

She struggles to calm her breathing. Her lips move, forming words, but there's no sound accompanying them.

"That's it," I croon. "You've got it. Keep going."

She raises her head, and her eyes are blazing. Without saying anything, she plants her hands on my chest and shoves so hard that I fall back a step.

"Leave. Me. Alone," she pants raggedly.

"You're struggling. I can't in good conscience leave you."

Her eyes flash with temper. "When has your conscience ever stopped you from doing anything?"

She's still breathless, but she seems to be getting herself under control.

"Why are you here?" she asks, straightening her back like a warrior. God, she's so fucking strong.

"I transferred to Newbury," I tell her. "I've had a gaping hole in my life without you, and I want to win you back."

I know it won't be easy, but surely, it's not impossible.

She wrinkles her nose like she's smelled something rotten. "You're fucking crazy."

She tries to dart around me, but I block her path.

Her upper lip curls. "Stay the fuck away from me. If you come near me again, I'll get a restraining order against you, and that won't look good to the NHL."

I stiffen, taken aback by the fact she's willing to go to such extremes so quickly. But then, I've done a lot of damage to this girl. Maybe even more than I thought. I won't let her attitude put me off though. I'm not going to fall at the first hurdle. Not this time.

"You do whatever you have to do," I say. "I know I fucked up, but I have no intention of going anywhere."

She can trash my career prospects if it makes her feel better. I'd love to play in the NHL, but being with her matters more. The NHL was always my dad's obsession, not mine.

"Why?" She looks baffled, and a little shell-shocked. "Why do you think you can waltz back into my life after all this time?"

I open my mouth but don't have the chance to respond before she continues. Never mind. The question was probably rhetorical anyway.

"Haven't you done enough damage?" she asks, her tone weary.

"I don't want to hurt you," I say.

I never did. But having good intentions doesn't always pay off. When it comes to Echo, all the good intentions in the world mean nothing in the face of what happened.

"I don't care what you want." She rubs her upper arms, trying to warm herself, as the breeze picks up. "Not everything is about you."

"I know that."

"I don't think you do."

I sigh. "Look, I know you won't forgive me. I don't expect you to. For what it's worth, I'm so fucking sorry, but I know you probably don't give a crap about that, and rightly so. I guess what I'm trying to say is that I'm not going anywhere. Now, can I help you inside? Because you don't look great."

Her eyes turn flinty. It's not an expression I'm used to seeing on her. Another way she's changed.

"No," she says. "You may not."

She starts marching toward the entrance. I fall into step with her.

"Can I call one of your friends to keep you company?" I ask. "I'm not sure you should be alone after having a panic attack."

"No."

The door opens, and a man in a navy uniform—a security guard, perhaps—saunters toward us, his gaze flicking from Echo to me.

"Is this guy bothering you?" he asks her.

She tosses a look over her shoulder at me. "Yeah, he is."

The guard's hand goes to his hip. I doubt he's carrying a gun, but he might have pepper spray or a taser.

"Beat it," he growls.

Despite my frustration, I'm proud of Echo for standing up for herself, and I'm pleased she has protection. I hold my hands up to show the guard I'm not a physical threat, but I don't take my eyes off Echo.

"I'll see you tomorrow," I tell her.

2

____

ECHO

Ben, the security guard, leans closer to me. "You need me to call the police?"

"No." I wrap my arms more tightly around myself. "But thanks anyway."

As he swipes his keycard and we enter the building, warm air rushes down on me from the heat pump above the entrance. I glance over my shoulder, relieved when the door clicks shut, and I can see Tyler still on the other side of it.

Without a keycard, he can't get to me here. I'm not stupid enough to think that he couldn't get his hands on a keycard if he wanted one, but for now, I'm safe. Even if he were to get inside, he doesn't know my room number, and I always keep the door locked.

I learned the hard way how important personal security is.

When we reach the elevator, Ben presses the button.

"See you later," he says as the doors sweep open, and I step inside.

"Bye."

When the elevator doors close, I draw in several slow,

deep breaths before pushing the symbol for the third floor. I ride in silence, grateful that there aren't any stops along the way.

The doors glide open, and I hurry along the corridor, digging in my pocket for the keys before fumbling them. They drop to the floor, and I have to snatch them back up again, nearly getting knocked over by a guy coming out of another dorm room.

"Watch it," he snaps.

I ignore him, and shove the key into the lock, twisting furiously. My hand is shaking, and if I don't get to privacy soon, I'm going to hyperventilate.

Finally, the door opens. I step inside, slam it behind myself, and immediately lock it again. The room is empty, and I thank my lucky stars that my roommate, Martina, isn't around. Unfortunately, she set up a diffuser before she left, so the room smells overpoweringly of vanilla. I don't mind a little scent, but this is too much.

My throat constricts and tears well in my eyes as I stride to my bed and collapse onto it. I curl into the fetal position and let the tears fall. A sob racks my body.

I grab my phone and mess around until it's connected to the wireless speakers. I select my bad mood playlist and turn the volume up loud enough that nobody will be able to hear me crying. Then I shut my eyes and relive the horror of seeing Tyler Kinsey again.

My stomach clenches with remembered fear, and my heart throbs from how much he hurt me. Even though it's been more than three years, the pain lingers on.

I trusted him. I thought he was a good person, but he proved me wrong.

God, did he ever.

I gasp for air, my shoulders shuddering violently. Why is it that he can affect me so strongly after so much time?

Outside, someone hammers on the door.

"Turn down the music!" they shout.

I don't. It's either the music or the soundtrack of my misery. I can guess which they'd prefer. They bash once more, then try the handle and leave. No doubt a passive-aggressive note will be shoved beneath my door soon.

I lie there until I'm exhausted, both mentally and physically. I don't know what it is about crying, but it wears a person out.

I wipe my puffy eyes on my sleeve and check the time. It won't be dinner for a while yet. I grab my phone, drawn to social media in a way I know isn't healthy. Still, I can't seem to help myself. I open the app and search for Tyler's name.

He appears immediately. Another tear leaks out the corner of my eye and I wipe it, the surrounding skin stinging. Tyler's profile photo is a shot of him on the ice, clad in full hockey gear except for the helmet. The number 7 is plastered on his chest.

I sniff and click into his profile. Honestly, I'm surprised he's not one of the many college athletes whose profiles feature photos of their naked chests and abs. As I scroll through his content, I quickly realize that none of the pictures are of him with women, except for a younger blonde I'm pretty sure is his sister.

Strange. I was sure he'd be enjoying all the puck bunnies he could get his hands on.

I roll into an upright position and rest my chin on my knees, still flicking through his feed. None of his photos are all that recent, except for a few featuring what I assume is the hockey team at his former university. From the "C" embroidered on his shirt, I can tell that he was the team captain.

God, he'd screwed them over by leaving in his final year. And he claims to have done it for me.

I snort. Yeah, right. Why would the king of the campus change schools in his senior year because of a girl he used to date in high school?

In secret.

At least, until he humiliated me.

I don't know what Tyler is planning, but he's full of shit, and I'm not stupid enough to fall for it. Not again.

Nothing good comes from Tyler Kinsey.

I need to stay away from him, and for the sake of my mental health, I should talk it over with a professional.

I call my therapist Dr. Rodriguez's office and make an appointment for next week.

Thank God for my scholarship. The benefactor behind it arranged for the scholarship to come with a package of counseling sessions. There's no way I'd be able to afford to see a therapist otherwise, and after high school, I've needed all the therapy I can get.

TYLER

After the security guard stares me down, I return to Full of Beans, the campus coffee shop. Echo's two female friends have left, but the guy, Ryan, is still at the bar.

Just as we arranged.

"How's Echo?" he asks as I pull out the stool beside him and sit on it.

"Not great."

The barista approaches, and I order an americano and slip him some cash.

"About as well as you thought, or worse?" Ryan asks. "It was fucking scary seeing how she reacted to you. Do you really think that was the best way to let her know you're here?"

I wince. Yeah, that wasn't my finest moment.

"I didn't realize she'd have a panic attack," I say.

I'm aware she's seeing a therapist, but I have no idea what her symptoms are, what they discuss, or whether she has a mental health diagnosis. My money only buys me so much access.

"Worse than you thought, then," he huffs. If he weren't such a nice guy, he might let me have it. But he is, so he doesn't. That's the problem with nice guys. They have no follow-through.

Fortunately, I've never had that problem.

"You should probably check on her after you leave here," I tell him, because while I'm not a nice guy, Echo is one of the few things I actually care about. Not that I've done a great job of showing it.

"I will."

He sounds offended by the implication that he needs me to tell him so. Perhaps he thinks it should be obvious, but I never like to take anything for granted. Especially not when it comes to her.

Ryan hesitates, then adds, "Are you sure you want to go through with this?"

I scowl and narrow my eyes. "Have I ever given you any reason to think I don't?"

"No. But so much time has passed since you dated. You're probably different people now than you were then. The connection might not still be there."

"It is," I grind out. "She may have changed, and I sure as hell hope I have, but my feelings for her haven't. I lost her once, and I won't do it again."

Losing Echo tore me apart. If not for the knowledge that, one day, I'd be free to pursue her again, I might not have had any reason to go on. Those days were dark. And yeah, my behavior may have caused the darkness, but when you're raised the way I was, it's hard to see the light.

Ryan holds out his hands defensively. "I get it, man. I get it."

Good, because if Ryan decided to get in my way, he'd regret it. Only one monster terrified me enough to keep me away from Echo, and now that he's gone, I won't allow anything or anyone else to interfere with our relationship.

"But how do you plan to win her over?" he asked. "'Cause from where I'm sitting, it looks like she wants less than nothing to do with you."

I grit my teeth. He's lucky he's been such a good friend to Echo.

Although he has a point. I'm starting at a disadvantage. But I've never let that affect me on the ice, and I won't let it affect me now. Echo will be mine again, even if she doesn't know it yet.

"First, I need her to get comfortable with seeing me around," I tell him. "I'm in one of her classes, so she can't avoid me completely."

"Unless she decides to skip class," he points out.

I shake my head. "She's not that kind of girl."

To my surprise, he laughs. "You're probably right. She won't risk missing anything important, and even if she was willing to risk it, she might turn up just to prove she's not afraid of you."

I like the idea of that—it's something the Echo I used to know would do—but I get the feeling she *is* afraid of me now. Or, if not afraid, then at least apprehensive about being near me.

Is it purely because of how I hurt her, or is there more to it than that?

"I hope I can convince her to talk to me, at least in passing," I continue, deciding to focus on my plan. I can mull over her potential fear of me later. "I know that might not work though."

"Yeah, she can be pretty stubborn," Ryan says. "I'd have a backup plan, if I were you."

"The backup plan is to shower her with meaningful gifts." We used to be incredible together, so surely, with a few well-placed gifts designed to remind her of that time, I can soften her toward me.

Ryan snorts. "They'd better be some gifts."

"They will be." I've already got the first one on order and it should arrive here soon. Regardless of whether gifts become necessary, she deserves them.

The waiter appears with my coffee and slides it across the bar. I cup my hands around it and inhale the rich scent, then blow across the surface.

"So...you never told me what you actually did to Echo," Ryan says, bracing himself as though I might attack. "I know you broke her heart—that was easy to work out—but there must be more to it than that. She was a mess when she first moved here."

I keep silent. If Echo has chosen not to tell Ryan what happened, then I'm certainly not going to.

"It's not my business to share," I say.

He arches an eyebrow. "It kind of is."

"Then let's just say that I don't feel like sharing."

"Fair enough."

Despite his obvious dissatisfaction with this answer, I sense his respect for me grow.

"But let's just get one thing clear," he adds, holding my gaze: "No matter how rich and powerful you are, no matter how big your muscles are, or the fact you could probably kick my ass, if you hurt Echo again, I'll make sure you regret it."

I nod, my respect for him also jumping up a notch. Not

that it was low to begin with. And as for me kicking his ass...
He could probably hold his own, but he's a baseball player
and I'm a hockey player, so yeah, it's safe to say I've got a few
pounds on him and more experience with my fists.

"If I hurt Echo again, you won't have to make me regret
it," I tell him, meaning every word. "Because I'll self-
destruct. I can't exist in a world where I cause her more
pain. I refuse to."

3

—————

THE PAST

TYLER

My arms burn as I finish another set of bicep curls and drop the weights onto the bench, the crooning voice of Dan from Imagine Dragons blasting through the speakers. As I grab my bottle and gulp water, something crashes elsewhere in the house. I flinch.

Then, ignoring the crash and hoping like hell that nothing bad is happening, I check the whiteboard leaning against the back wall. I have another set to do and then I'm onto tricep dips.

I wrap my hands around the barbells and lift them into position, grimacing when the rough metal rubs against the calluses on my palms. I inhale slowly, relishing the tang of sweat that's always present during a good workout, and begin pumping iron again.

The door beside the whiteboard bursts open and Dad strides through, his phone clasped in his hand. Without a word, he switches off the Bluetooth speaker and brandishes the phone at me.

"What's this?" he demands.

I peer at the phone screen, confused to see my biology teacher's email address at the top.

"An email," I mutter because I've learned that failing to answer my father never leads to anything good.

"I can see that," he snaps, and jabs his finger at the text below. "How the hell did you fail a major assignment?"

My heart sinks. I should have known someone would tell Dad about the 'F.'

"I don't know." I look down at my feet. The truth is, I'm just not great at science, and I'm not interested enough to put in the effort it would take to do well.

"You can't afford to fail." He pockets the phone and steps toward me menacingly. "If you're going to go to Princeton, you need top grades. Being a great hockey player won't be enough."

I bite my lip to stop myself from telling him I don't want to go to Princeton. Any decent hockey college would do.

It won't matter what I have to say. He's been claiming I'll play hockey for Princeton every year since I started high school, and he'll be humiliated if I let him down.

When Dad is humiliated, he's dangerous. But he won't take it out on me. He'll take it out on Mom and Soraya.

"I didn't have much time to work on it," I mutter, edging away from the weights in case he decides to throw one.

He puts his hands on his hips. "You had the same amount of time as everyone else."

Not true. But as soon as I open my mouth to protest, I close it again.

"Didn't you?" he demands, his voice rising.

"I've been busy with extra training since Shaw was injured," I say, knowing even as the words emerge that I should have kept quiet. Dad won't care if I've had to get a new winger up to speed. In his mind, I should be able to do that while getting straight As.

"You know I have trouble with biology," I add defensively, hoping to distract him from my guff.

Dad taps his chin, his expression cold as the Arctic. "You know who else has trouble with biology?"

I tense. This isn't good. I don't know what's coming, but I can tell I won't like it.

"Me." He grins, as if it's all a big joke. "In fact, I'm so bad at biology that I might forget how frail your mother is if I see anything beneath a 'B' from you again. Wouldn't it be a shame if something were to happen to her?"

I grit my teeth. My fists clench at my sides. I wish I could plant them in his face, but even though he's older than me, he's still just as strong—and a whole lot meaner. There's a reason I don't fight back. The few times I tried, it didn't end well.

"I'll work harder on the next biology assignment," I say.

"Fortunately for you, I've already spoken to your teacher, and he's agreed to allow you to write a new essay and resubmit it." He sounds smug. "I've also hired a tutor to help you with it, but she won't write the essay for you."

I barely manage not to wince. If Dad has gotten me a do-over, chances are it was because someone within the school administration put pressure on Mr. Harding. He's absolutely not the type to let people start over.

As for the tutor... Knowing Dad hired her makes me nervous. She'll probably be reporting back to him on my progress, which means I can't stretch the truth.

I stride to the squat rack and start loading the ends of the bar as dread swirls in my gut. I can't be benched from the hockey team, but I don't understand why Dad cares if I just pay someone else to do my assignments. Half the guys on the team do that.

"Are you listening?" he snaps.

"Yes, sir." I finish loading the bar because I can't bring myself to face him.

"Good. I expect you to do your best. It took a lot of doing, but I managed to persuade the top student in class to tutor you."

Translation: he shelled out a lot of money.

"Thank you," I say, knowing it's expected of me.

Then the rest of what he said sinks in. The top student in class. I have no doubt who that is, and I hate the idea of her learning that I'm stupid enough to need help. He probably told her about the 'F' too.

"Aren't you grateful?" he demands.

"Of course." I turn and contort my face into the closest thing I can manage to a smile around him. "I appreciate you looking out for me."

"You'd better, after the lengths I went to for your worthless ass."

Some people might flinch if their father called them worthless to their face, but it's not even the first time he's said it this week.

"Nothing less than a 'B'," he says, echoing his earlier words. "You start tomorrow."

I nod, and he pivots and stalks out of the room.

A shiver ripples down my spine. I've always considered the home gym to be my sanctuary. Any time he enters, it puts me on edge.

Crash!

I jerk at the unexpected noise and bite my tongue. The metallic tang of blood fills in my mouth. I glance at the ceiling, listening carefully, but apart from muffled voices, nothing seems amiss.

I rinse my mouth out to get rid of the bloody taste.

Please let no one be hurt.

My instincts scream at me to go and check, but I can't. If

I do, it will only be worse. So instead, with my insides tangled in knots, I take the weight of the squat bar on my shoulders and lift it off.

My thighs and ass burn as I perform the reps. I'm on my second set when there's a light knock at the door.

"Come in," I call.

My sister appears around the corner. Her usually golden skin is waxen, and a furrow is etched between her eyebrows. I position the bar over the rack and slot it back into place.

"He's gone," Soraya says, wrapping her arms around herself.

"Thank fuck." The house is always a better place to be when he's not here. "Is everyone all right?"

She rubs her lips together. "Yeah. He just smashed one of the vases on the shelves in the foyer."

"Typical. How's Mom?"

Her upper lip curls. "She's already cleaned it up. She's shaken, but you know how she is."

I grunt in acknowledgement. I love Mom, but sometimes I want to grab her and demand to know what's going on in her head. I don't understand why she stays with Dad. It's sure as shit not for us. If she cared about us, she'd have gotten us out of here years ago.

"So, you're getting a tutor?" Soraya asks, dropping her arms to her sides as I position myself beneath the squat bar again.

"Seems like it." I'd rather not think about it. I suppose I'll have to soon, since she'll be here tomorrow.

"Who?" she asks.

"Dad said it's the top of the class, so I'm guessing Echo Dean," I reply.

She bites her lower lip and her forehead crinkles. "The scholarship girl?"

"Yeah." A pint-sized super-brain with holey jeans and

threadbare sweaters. Cute, but wary of me and my friends from the hockey team—especially our first-line winger, Eric, who's been low-key pursuing her for months.

"I mean, at least he chose someone who could use the money," Soraya says.

"I'm pretty sure she's scared of me," I admit.

I'm also pretty sure I've done nothing to alleviate that. Girls like her and guys like me don't mix. It's best that way.

ECHO

I clutch the textbook to my chest as I walk down the drive toward the Kinseys' massive house. All of my instincts tell me I shouldn't be here—nothing good comes of contact with the school's elite—but I need the money.

Apprehension tightens my chest as I approach the imposing front door. There are windows everywhere and the back of my neck prickles, telling me that someone is watching.

Or maybe I'm just paranoid.

After all, keeping my head down is how I've managed to get through three and a half years at a school that prioritizes wealth and social connections above all else. It's bad enough that Eric Weston has started harassing me—I don't need to be on anyone else's radar.

Shuffling the textbook to one arm, I raise my hand and knock. There's no doorbell, and I can't help wondering whether anyone will actually hear me. I almost hope they won't.

Unfortunately, a moment later, a lock clicks, and the door handle turns and moves inward. The woman inside has to look up to me—not something that happens often. A furrow forms between her eyebrows and she tucks a lock of salon-blonde hair behind her ear.

"Mrs. Kinsey?" I ask.

"Oh, yes." Her voice is breathy, with a thread of surprise. "You must be here for Tyler."

"I'm his tutor," I say, bouncing the textbook meaningfully. I don't want anyone thinking I'm here for anything else. That's how rumors get started, and rumors draw attention. All I want is to get through this year unnoticed so I can focus on college.

"Of course." Her frown makes it clear that it hadn't crossed her mind I might be here for any other reason. I'm tempted to be offended, but instead, I decide to be an adult and chalk it up to the fact that Tyler isn't allowed to have serious girlfriends—a well-known fact he takes advantage of to sleep around without commitment.

Mrs. Kinsey steps aside. "Please come in."

She lowers her eyes, and I study her surreptitiously. She has angular cheekbones and hollow cheeks that suggest she hasn't eaten enough for a while. I suppose she's pretty, in a fragile kind of way, but her sunken eyes and defensive posture speak volumes about the type of man her husband is.

I follow her inside, through a foyer with a high ceiling and polished wood floors. My worn-out runners slap against the wood, and I cringe. I probably should have taken them off.

Mrs. Kinsey stops in the doorway of what looks to be some kind of living room, decorated in shades of brown and gray. It doesn't look like it would be to her taste. She seems more the type to prefer pastels.

"Take a seat," she says. "I'll get Tyler."

"Thank you."

I remove my shoes before stepping onto the carpet,

which is lush and soft beneath my toes. I carry my textbook to the corner sofa and sit, nerves stewing in my gut.

I don't want to be here.

In fact, I'd prefer to be almost anywhere else. Especially since Eric is bound to find out I'm tutoring Tyler and he'll somehow use it against me. Ever since he decided he wants to sleep with me, he's been alternately pursuing me so doggedly it makes me uncomfortable and then tossing insults when I turn him down.

But Mr. Kinsey offered me too much money to refuse the tutoring job. When you've scraped for every cent like Mom and I have and know how it feels for hunger to gnaw at your insides because you haven't eaten, it's difficult to turn down lucrative offers.

Even if I'm certain I'll end up regretting my choice.

There are footsteps on the stairs and then Tyler appears in the doorway, his handsome face twisted in a scowl. He looks about as pleased to see me as I am to see him.

"You're here already?" he asks.

I glance at my phone. "Your Dad said to be here at two. Was that wrong?"

"No." He doesn't elaborate, but he does slowly make his way over to me and lowers himself onto a cushion far enough away that I can't help wondering if he thinks being poor and nerdy is contagious. I stiffen, not used to being even this close to him.

"So, you've been given the chance to redo your biology essay on animal reactions to external stimuli and how they regulate their environments," I say to distract myself. "Have you been assigned a particular animal for the do-over?"

The way he stares at me makes me uncomfortable, so I drop my gaze to my hands.

"Mice," he says gruffly.

"Okay, great. We can definitely work with that. So, what

you need to do is find a particular stimulus that interferes with, or forms part of, a mouse's natural patterns, then explain their reaction."

He snorts. "We can't do anything if you won't even look me in the eye. I'm not that terrifying, am I?"

With difficulty, I raise my eyes and meet his gaze. "I'm not scared of you."

He cocks his head. "Then why are you so fidgety? You're like a cornered cat with its fur puffed up."

My nostrils flare. "First, that's an insulting comparison, and second, I get enough of being pushed around at school. I don't need it on the weekends too."

One of his eyebrows arches in a way that's absolutely infuriating.

"You get pushed around?" he asks, his tone slow and deliberate. "Really?"

"Yeah." Every part of me wants to fold in on myself but I keep my back straight. Somehow.

He watches me, his pale eyes unreadable. "By who?"

"Everyone." I roll my eyes. "It's not like I get beaten up like some people do, but pushed around? Yes. Both physically and otherwise. You wouldn't believe how many rich assholes at school try to get me to do their homework, run their errands, or—like your buddy Eric—sleep with them when I've made it clear I'm not interested."

"Huh."

I don't know why I'm surprised by his confusion, which seems to be genuine. He's probably never paid the least bit of attention to me.

"Okay." He intertwines his fingers and rests them on his lap. "How's this? If you help me pass this assignment, I'll make sure the hockey team leaves you alone."

"Including Eric?" I don't see how he can control his friend, but I'd love for him to try.

"Yeah."

I study his face. His expression doesn't give much away, but I think he means it.

"All right, then." I make an effort to hold his gaze and smile. "Let's do this."

An hour later, I have to admit that I'm impressed. Tyler is a better student than I expected. He's made a solid start on the assignment and, unless he goes off the rails, he should have plenty for me to review next time I'm here.

He walks me to the door, although I get the feeling it's more to make sure I don't go wandering around his house than out of politeness.

"Remember what I said," he says as I step outside. "If I pass with at least a B, I'll talk to the guys."

I nod. "I'd appreciate that."

He closes the door. I turn and start down the drive, carrying my textbook. I'm halfway to the street when I hear raised voices and glance over my shoulder. I freeze. Two figures are silhouetted in one of the windows, and as I watch, one shoves the other.

I draw in a ragged breath and close my eyes for a moment. When I open them again, the figures are gone.

I hesitate. If someone is hurt, they need help, but they were there and gone so fast, I can't be certain of what I saw.

4

———

ECHO

I move with the stream of students into the lecture hall and climb the stairs to sit near the back on the right-hand side, facing the podium where the professor will stand. As I open my backpack and pull out a notebook and pen, someone sits beside me.

I don't look up, instead soaking up the sense of relief that comes with regaining a sense of normalcy.

Class is normal. Note-taking is normal.

I only have two semesters left before I finish my undergraduate degree. Not that I intend to be done with academia yet. To become a therapist, I need a few more years under my belt.

The person beside me clears their throat. I glance over, expecting it to be Ryan, who's also in this class, but my features freeze in place.

It's not Ryan.

In fact, this person isn't a friend at all. He makes himself comfortable next to me, spreading his muscular legs too wide and leaning back as if he hasn't a care in the world.

Tyler Kinsey.

That goddamn bastard.

"What are you doing here?" I demand, pulling as far away from him as I can without leaving the seat. I won't let him chase me away when I was here first. Unfortunately, Tyler has the sort of presence that occupies a lot of space, especially with those strong shoulders and arms that I definitely shouldn't be noticing.

His lips soften. He isn't smiling exactly, but his expression is warm. My eyes instantly narrow. He's up to something; I just haven't figured out what yet.

"I take this class," he says, setting a tablet on the pull-out desk and switching it on.

"So, take it from somewhere else." The further from me, the better.

He looks completely unconcerned. "I'm happy here."

"Well, I'm not happy with you here. Get lost." I huff and catch a whiff of menthol. Great. He still smells the same as he always did. Part of me wants to breathe him in and reminisce while the rest of my mind is screaming at me to run.

"How are you?" He doesn't move. "Were you okay last night? I was worried about you."

My jaw drops. The absolute nerve of this guy. Asking if I was okay as if he wasn't the reason I was very much not okay.

"That's none of your business," I tell him.

"But I'd like it to be," he murmurs, and my tummy flips over at his low, husky tone. The same one that used to drive me wild. "I care about you, Echo. I know it's been a long time, but I want—"

"I don't care what you want," I hiss, wary of speaking too loudly and drawing attention. "Leave me alone."

He gives me a hurt look, as if I'm the unreasonable one between the two of us.

I'm perfectly reasonable. I cut someone who hurt me out

of my life and moved away from a town that had treated me unkindly as soon as humanly possible. All of that was logical. He's the one muddying the waters.

Tyler hefts his backpack onto his lap and opens it, the zipper loud enough to grate on my frayed nerves. He reaches inside and draws out a small gift box, which he offers to me.

I ignore him.

"Come on, Echo. Take it."

When I don't respond, he reaches for my bag as if to slide it inside. I snatch the bag away and shove his shoulder, annoyed when I'm tempted to keep my hand on the firm muscle and savor it for a moment.

"I want you to have this," he says quietly. "Think of it as a peace offering."

"If you put that anywhere near me, I'm going to throw it across the room," I say through gritted teeth.

His nostrils flare. "Why are you so stubborn?"

"How about I'll tell you that when you tell me why you're bothering me after three blessed years of never having to see your awful face?"

To my surprise, he winces.

"I told you," he says. "I'm here for you."

"And I don't believe you." Once upon a time, I would have, but I've learned that Tyler likes to play games. He enjoys hurting people. The only reason he's here is because it benefits him for some reason—and I'm sure it's not that he's been pining for me since we graduated high school.

Fortunately, at that moment, the professor arrives. It's only then that it occurs to me that this isn't the sort of class Tyler should be taking. It's behavioral analysis, which is a prerequisite for my psychology degree, but I doubt it's relevant for the business degree he intended to study toward.

That means he's here only to mess with me.

As the professor begins speaking, I force myself to pay attention by jotting down a summary of everything he says in a form of shorthand I developed myself. I got tired of people trying to cheat off me, and now they never can.

After a few minutes, Tyler's knee bumps against mine. Sparks sizzle up my thigh and I do my best to ignore them.

"Do you still want to be a doctor?" he asks under his breath.

The guy in front of us turns and glares. I mouth a silent apology.

"Echo?" Tyler prompts.

"No." Back when we were together, I'd intended to go into pre-med, but that changed after The Incident.

"Then what?" he asks.

I pretend not to hear. He leans sideways, getting way too far inside my personal space, making it difficult to breathe without inhaling his masculine menthol scent.

"What degree are you studying?" His breath gusts over my ear and goose bumps race down the back of my neck.

"Back. Off." My pen snaps, and I gasp. I hadn't realized I was clutching it so tightly.

"Here."

I glance sideways. Tyler is holding out a pen. It's an expensive one, with a brand name along the side, inlaid with what looks like gold. Because who wouldn't have a gold pen?

With a sigh, I take it from him. He doesn't seem to need it and I do, so it only makes sense. For a moment, I'm tempted to steal it just so he'd feel some of the frustration coursing through my veins, but then I'd be stuck with a reminder of him, so it's best if I don't.

I resume notetaking until Tyler's foot nudges mine.

I'm tempted to stomp on it.

"How's your mom?" he asks.

I don't react.

"Does she still live in Charlesville?" he persists.

I glare at the front of the class, refusing to turn toward him.

"Ignoring me won't make me go away, Echo. I told you; nothing can drive me away from you again."

At this, I huff. Drive him away? As if he wasn't the one behind the wheel when he left me in his dust.

Everything bad that happened to me during our fateful senior year was because of him.

Well, everything except The Incident.

Even I can admit he had nothing to do with that. Nevertheless, his presence brings me back to that time in my life. To the days and weeks I'd dearly love to escape.

His shoulder bumps mine. "You okay? You don't look great."

"I'm fine," I snap, loud enough that several people turn toward us. One shushes me.

His questions continue for the. Entire. Lecture.

"Hey, Echo, why won't you tell me your major?"

"Hey, Echo, have you been back to Charlesville recently?"

"Echo, are you still in touch with anyone from school?"

And on and on and ON.

By the time the closing minutes of the lecture are upon us, I'm ready to stab him through the neck with his fancy pen.

I'm struggling to listen to the professor, who's saying something about a group assignment.

"...teams of four, randomly assigned. You'll find your team in the class page on the university's study app."

I automatically reach for my phone and open the app.

"The group assignment is worth thirty percent of your final grade," the professor continues.

Damn. That's a lot. I hate group assignments. It's so easy for one or two people to be stuck doing the majority of the work while the others reap the rewards.

I scan through the class list until I see my name. Beside it is the letter S. I scroll to see who else has an S beside their name. The first is someone I don't know. And the second...

Is Tyler fucking Kinsey.

TYLER

I lean over Echo's shoulder to see what's upset her. It takes a minute to compute. When I realize, it's all I can do not to pump my fist.

Fuck, yeah.

We're in the same group project team. What a great opportunity to prove to her that I've changed. She won't be able to avoid spending time with me. Even if we do most of the work individually, we'll still have to communicate with the group and probably meet to go over it.

This assignment is a golden opportunity.

Echo tilts her face toward me. "Who did you pay off to make this happen?"

I grimace. I shouldn't be surprised that's what she thinks of me. Honestly, I have used my money to my advantage a lot over the years, so she's not totally off base. If I'd thought of this, I'd have made it happen.

"No one," I reply.

"Uh-huh." Her expression says she doesn't believe me.

"It's true."

"Shh," someone hisses from behind us.

The professor clears his throat, drawing our attention.

"I'm ending class fifteen minutes early. But—" He holds up his hand as people start talking excitedly over him. "I want you all to spend that time getting together with your team for an initial meet-and-greet. Understood?"

There's a murmur of assent. I see Echo's jaw tighten. She really doesn't like this. It grates on me. I need to take advantage of the chance to get close to her, but I also never want her to be unhappy.

It pisses me off that getting my way means upsetting her. I'd be tempted to bow out—after all, I don't need this course for my degree—but I can't. It's an unexpected lifeline, and I won't let go.

As people stand and push their way to others to form their groups, Echo takes the stairs down to the front of the lecture hall. I follow close on her heels, unwilling to let her out of my sight until after this team meeting is finished.

"Professor," she calls as she draws near to him. "Excuse me."

He turns toward her. "Yes?"

"I need to change groups," she says.

Ouch. Straight to the point.

But the professor is shaking his head. "I'm afraid that's not possible, Miss..."

"Dean. But it's extenuating circumstances," she protests.

I grin to myself. I love hearing big words coming from Echo's perfect little mouth. It reminds me of a time when I took that for granted.

The professor's bushy eyebrows pinch together above his glasses. "How so?"

Echo hesitates. She glances at me and then back to the professor, as if trying to figure out how to make this sound like more than petty relationship drama.

"He's my ex," she says finally. "It ended badly."

The professor's eyes sharpen. "Did he abuse you?"

"Not physically."

I wince at this response. I wouldn't consider what I did to her any kind of abuse, although it certainly wasn't nice.

"Were any police reports filed?" the professor asks.

"No." Echo deflates.

"Do you have a restraining order against him?"

"No." This time, she glares.

The professor steeples his hands, apparently uncon-cerned. "Then I'm afraid you'll just have to figure out how to work together. Consider it a bonus lesson in behaving like an adult."

Echo stomps away from him. I follow behind, hiding my amusement—and relief. Concealing my emotions comes easy to me. A by-product of growing up with Dad.

I check the app on my phone to see who else is in our team. Not that it makes any difference to me. The only people I've met since transferring are the hockey guys, and as far as I know, none of them take the behavioral analysis class.

My phone vibrates and a message pops up on the screen via the university app.

Elle: Meet outside the lecture hall, to the left, near the stairs. I'm wearing a blue dress.

Ahead of me, Echo also sees the message and taps a response.

Echo: Be there in a minute. Brown hair, black top, glasses.

I don't bother contributing. Echo is the only reason I'm taking this class, and she knows I'm coming. I don't give a shit about anyone else.

We exit the lecture hall and turn left. A few yards from the base of the stairs stands a thin blonde in a powder-blue dress that barely covers her thighs. Doesn't this girl know it's not that fucking warm out? Or does she just want everyone to admire her figure?

Echo makes a beeline for the girl, and I'm right on her heels. Just before we get there, an Asian guy who's even taller than me—but half my weight—stops beside Elle. He sends Echo a lazy grin.

"Hey, Echo." He speaks with a confidence that says it's not the first time they've met, and everything in me wants to shut that shit down fast. "Group work buddies again."

"Jin." Finally, Echo smiles. It's a fucking shame it's directed at another guy. "I'm so glad we're working together."

I clench my teeth and thrust my hand at the interloper. "I'm Tyler."

Jin's dark eyes slide from Echo to me and his eyebrows lift, but he takes my hand and shakes it firmly. "Did you recently change majors? I've never seen you in any of our classes before."

Elle raises her finger, a sly smile twisting her glossy lips. "You're the transfer student on the hockey team. The new first-line center."

"That's right." I glance at Jin to see if he's impressed, but his expression is impossible to read.

Elle sashays forward, rolling her hips in a way that's probably supposed to tempt me, but just comes across as overdone.

"Elle Summers." She holds her hand out, and based on her stance, I'm not sure if I'm expected to shake it or drop to my knees and kiss it.

I don't do either. It's obvious from the invitation in Elle's eyes that she'd like more from me than a study buddy and I have no intention of letting her think she has a chance. Nor do I want Echo to believe I'm interested.

Eventually, she reclaims her hand and turns up her

nose. Beside me, Echo makes a huff that could be amusement. Jin's lips twitch.

"So." Elle fingers the hem of her skirt. "We've met. I see no reason to waste another ten minutes chatting. Why don't we set a time to get together later in the week, after we've had a chance to review the assignment properly?"

"Sounds good," Echo replies. "How about Thursday?"

Jin opens his phone. "Morning or afternoon?"

"Morning," Elle suggests. "I have a lab in the afternoon."

They all turn to me.

I shrug. "Thursday morning is fine."

Even if I have class, I'll find a way to make it work. Nothing is more important to me than spending time with Echo.

Nothing.

"Done." Elle weaves past me and Jin and takes a few steps toward the door, but then her gaze returns to catch on me. "If you decide you want someone to show you around, send me a message."

I nod. "Thanks, but I won't."

She stalks away, clearly unhappy with the response.

"Are you in the child psychology class now?" Jin asks Echo.

"No." She shakes her head. "I'm taking that next semester."

He looks disappointed. "I guess I'll see you later then." He tips his head toward me. "Nice meeting you."

He leaves, and Echo follows close behind. I fall into step beside her.

"So, if you're not going to be a doctor, are you going into psychology?" I ask, trying to make sense of the classes she's taking.

She ignores me.

"Echo. Please." My voice drips with desperation, and I

don't even care. "I know I fucked up. I'm trying to do better. Give me something."

She stops walking, and I lurch to a halt, too. She turns and wraps her arms around her waist. The gesture is defensive, and a thread of loathing tugs in my gut. I hate that she feels the need to be on guard with me. Even if it's completely understandable.

Echo's green-and-gold-flecked eyes burn as she stares me down. "If you really want to do better, then listen to me when I ask you to leave me alone."

"I—"

She scoffs. "Yeah, that's what I thought."

She brushes past me. As she goes, I slip the small box into her backpack for her to find later.

A shoulder slap takes me by surprise, and I whirl around, finding one of the guys from the hockey team standing behind me.

"Did you strike out?" he asks, his mouth turned down sympathetically.

"No." I refuse to admit defeat. "The game is only just beginning."

5

____

ECHO

Getting drunk is supposed to make you feel better, right?

Not that my therapist agrees, but most of my friends do. Yet, somehow, bathing my mind in beer is only making me more irritable and confused.

I lunge for the ping-pong ball, catching it on a bounce, and stand, swaying as I aim at a cup on the other side of the table. Loud dance music throbs around me, making it difficult to concentrate. I throw...and miss.

Hayden, one of the frat guys on the other team, grabs the ball and returns fire. Unfortunately, it lands in a cup on my side of the table. I fish the ball out and down the beer, wincing at the bitter taste. I pass the ball to Anita, my partner, for her turn.

"What do you think it means?" I ask Anita as she tosses the ping-pong ball neatly into one of Hayden's cups.

I've just finished explaining to her about the jewelry box I found in my bag earlier in the week. Inside, nestled on a bed of velvet, was a beautiful silver pendant shaped like a shooting star. I'd almost had a panic attack when I opened it. Then I nearly cried.

Damn Tyler for getting under my skin like this. I don't want to remember the time when we meant something to each other. It's best left in the past.

While Hayden drinks, Anita turns to me, flicking her auburn hair away from her face. "If one of my exes gave me an expensive necklace, I'd assume he wanted me back."

My lip curls. "That's not it."

He might say it is, but I know better. He's playing games, and once again, I don't know the rules. What I do know is that I'm returning the pendant next time I see him. There's no way I'm holding onto it. Not when I don't understand what he wants from me or what the consequences of keeping it might be.

Hayden's partner Rock—real first name unknown—misses his shot. The ball bounces off the end of the table and I chase it, bending clumsily to retrieve it from the manicured lawn and apologizing when I bump into a blonde in a minidress.

We're out in front of the Kappa Delta Psi sorority house for one of their famous Kickoff parties. No, it's not anything sports-related, just an excuse to start the year with a lot of alcohol and indiscriminate hookups. I don't usually go, but Anita caught me at a weak moment.

I take my turn, unsurprised when I miss again. I'm terrible at this game. Anita is the pro.

"It's a shooting star. Did I tell you that?" My voice slurs, but no matter how carefully I try to enunciate, I can't seem to help it. "He used to call me his shooting star because he said I was the light in his darkness."

Anita's plum-red lips press together and her expression melts. "Aww, that's so sweet. He definitely wants you."

"Well, too bad."

Hayden sinks the ball again, and again, I have to drink.

"Why?" she asks. "Was whatever he did really so horrible?"

Emotion wells inside me, climbing up my throat and threatening to choke me. For a moment, I can hardly breathe.

"He stopped my sparkle," I tell her. "He pulled me into the dark with him, and now I'm a black hole. Everything sucks and there's no light to be seen."

Her eyebrows arch. "Morbid much?"

"Echo, with the greatest respect, could you stop talking about your dating life and play properly?" Hayden calls across the table.

Anita and I both glare at him, but he just shrugs in response.

"Fine," I huff, and pass the ball to Anita. She misses. We continue back and forth for another few minutes. I drink once more, and somehow manage to sink a ball so Rock has to drink, too.

When he sets the cup down, he surprises me by looking straight at me and saying, "If a guy gives you a gift, he's into you, even if all he wants is sex."

"Huh." The word pops out of me before my brain connects to my mouth. Rock is a quiet person. Stoic, too. I'd never have guessed he was paying attention to our conversation.

We finish the game without further discussion of Tyler. We lose soundly, despite Anita's best efforts. When we make way for the next team, Anita wraps her arm around me to steady me.

"Should we get you some water?" she asks, her forehead wrinkling with concern.

"Probably," I admit. My vision is blurry, and my bloated stomach is screaming for relief.

"So, tell me more about your ex," she says as we wind

between groups of people, making our way across the lawn and past the Roman-style pillars at the sorority's entrance.

"There isn't much to tell." It's a lie. I've seen more of who Tyler Kinsey really is than anyone else. Or at least, I thought I had until he tore the rug out from beneath me.

She snorts. "Liar. What's his name?"

I zip my lips. I don't want to tell her when she and Cassie have already gossiped about how hot the hockey-playing transfer student is. If she knows it's him, she'll keep digging until I give her at least some of the juicy details. Unlike Cassie, whose favorite topic is herself, Anita loves knowing everything there is to know about everyone else.

"Nope. I won't tell you." I raise my chin to demonstrate my determination, but the effect is lost when I stumble, and she has to catch me.

"Come on. We're nearly there." She leads me into the kitchen, where a couple of guys are standing beside the fridge, drinking beer from the bottle.

She finds a clean glass in the cupboards, then fills it from the tap and offers it to me. I sip from it as she steps around the guys and selects a red vodka drink from the fridge. She cracks the top and slings her arm around me again.

We walk down the pink-and-white hallway to the living room, which is crowded and overly warm despite the open window.

"Just give me a name," she pleads, guiding me to a spot by the wall near the door.

I send her a look of disbelief.

"Just a name, I swear." She grins and takes a drink. "No need to be so suspicious."

"No names. But he was someone from high school."

"I figured." She releases me and leans against the wall. "Unless you've been seeing someone in secret."

We drink in silence for a few minutes, and slowly, Anita's pretty green eyes light with unholy glee.

"What?" I ask, uneasy.

"Your ex..." Her eyes are fixed somewhere behind me. "Does he happen to be a hot blonde hockey center?"

My breathing stutters. I follow her gaze to find Tyler staring at us from the sofa on the other side of the room.

"We need to go," I say, straightening. The water has sobered me a little, and I manage not to trip over my own feet.

Anita is only a step behind me. "What's wrong?"

I shift closer to her and lower my voice. "He really hurt me, okay? I can't be here when he is."

She nods, and relief makes my knees weak.

"I need to use the bathroom," she says. "Let's head there first and then we can go."

"Can't you hold it until we get home?" I ask. Anita and I live in the same dorm. "It's only a fifteen-minute walk."

Surely, I should be the one with the overactive bladder after everything I've drunk.

"Trust me, no. It's not a number one." She takes my hand and leads me back down the hall to a door with a poster of Marilyn Monroe in a white dress attached to the front. "Wait here. I'll be a few minutes."

I rest my back against the wall and turn toward the end of the hall, where people are entering through the foyer. A group of laughing jocks split in two, with half heading for the living room and the other half going to the kitchen.

A moment later, one of them—a solidly built guy with dark hair and a beer bottle in his hand—reemerges. He glances my way, then does a double take. A cocky grin tugs at the corners of his lips and he saunters toward me in that dude bro way I really hate.

"What's a pretty girl like you doing all alone?" he asks,

getting way too close into my space. His beer breath wafts over me and his pupils are pinpricks. Is he on something?

I jab my thumb toward the bathroom door. "I'm waiting for a friend."

He shuffles closer, caging me between his forearms. "I could keep you busy while you wait."

"I'm not interested." I draw in a shallow breath. The air between our bodies seems to press in on me, heavy as lead.

He chuckles. "Sure, you aren't."

He grips my hip tightly enough to bruise and flattens himself against my front. Black spots dance in front of my eyes. My thoughts go fuzzy, and I sense myself beginning to detach from my body. I fight to stay in the present, but memories are snatching at me with clawed hands, dragging me back to the past.

TYLER

Echo is drunk.

She never used to get drunk. Is this because of me, or am I giving myself too much credit? It's been three years since I saw her. She could have changed during that time.

It's been a couple of minutes since she left the room with her red-headed friend. Anita Wagnor, twenty-one years old, training to become an elementary school teacher. I made a point to look up both of the female friends Echo had been in the coffee shop with the first time I spotted her. I want to know who she's surrounding herself with these days.

I get up from the sofa I've been lounging on, discard my beer bottle even though it's barely been touched, and head for the hall. Several people reach for me, but I dodge their hands and pretend not to notice. For some goddamn reason, the students here seem fascinated by me.

I guess that's what happens when you're a rich hockey god who turns up in senior year and doesn't like to talk about the past.

"Kinsey!" one of my teammates calls out.

I nod to him but don't stop. I need to set eyes on Echo again, just so I know she's okay. It's obvious she wasn't expecting to see me here.

The instant I enter the hall, I stop abruptly. Echo is here, all right, but she isn't okay. A guy twice her size is towering over her, with one of his hands on her hip while the other rests against the wall, a beer bottle dangling from his fingers. She's cringing away from him, making herself as small as she possibly can.

I see red.

Why the hell does that asshole think it's acceptable for him to put his hands on her?

She's obviously freaking the fuck out. Her chest rises and falls rapidly as she sucks in breaths, as if she can't get enough oxygen, and her eyes are squeezed shut.

I storm up the hall, grab his hand, and tear it off her. I shove him. He stumbles back, opening up more space between him and Echo. She drops to the floor, her arms covering her head as she curls into a ball.

"What the hell?" he shouts, too loud for the confined space.

I get up in his face and shove him again. "She clearly didn't want you anywhere near her," I snap. "If you touch her again, I'll rip your fucking arm off and club you with it."

He holds his hands out, palms toward me defensively. "Is she your girlfriend or something?"

I stare at him, hoping he can read the scorn in my expression. "No, but does that even fucking matter? You were scaring her. That's unacceptable."

His eyebrows furrow in a way that tells me he doesn't get it. "She's all yours. Too much drama anyway."

He pushes past me and stalks away, muttering under his breath. I kneel in front of Echo. She's rocking back and forth, clasping her head. I shift position, trying to put myself in her line of sight, but her eyes are glazed and unseeing.

"Echo," I say hesitantly. "Baby, you're safe."

My gut twists. It feels like barbed wire is tangled in there, drawing tighter with every passing second.

I've never seen her like this.

Even when things got bad for her at school—as they inevitably did after she made a serious accusation against one of the undisputed kings of the senior class that ended with him in prison—she'd never shut down so completely. At least, not that I'd seen.

She whimpers, and helplessness swamps me. What am I supposed to do? How do I help her fight something that lives inside her mind?

Shit, how much have I missed over the past three years?

I thought I'd been keeping a good eye on her. I believed I knew what I was dealing with, but this... I'm not prepared for this.

Her eyes snap to mine. "Go away."

Even having her pissed off at me is a relief, because at least in this moment, she's mentally present.

"I can't leave you," I tell her. "Not like this."

Trembles wrack her body.

"We need to warm you up." I try one of the bedroom doors, but it's locked. The one next to it is open. "Come on."

When she doesn't move, I wrap my arm around her. She flinches and buries her face in her knees. I let go, horrified by her reaction to my touch.

"Let me get you warm," I say. "Please, baby."

This time, she allows me to guide her to the bedroom.

She lowers herself onto the bed. I lift the end of the bedspread and fold it over her. She's not looking at me again, and her breathing is still too fast.

"Breathe with me," I urge. "In." I draw in a deep breath, counting to four before releasing it. "And out." Inhale. "In." Exhale. "Out."

At first, she can hardly hold air in her lungs, but after several breaths, the pressure seems to ease, and she mimics my breathing pattern more easily. She's still despondent, and self-loathing curdles inside me. I'm partly to blame for why she's like this. I wish I could fool myself into believing otherwise, but that would be a lie.

She loved me, and I helped to break her.

"What are you doing?"

My head snaps up. Anita is standing in the doorway, scowling.

"Did you hurt her?" she demands, rushing to the bed and pushing me aside. "Echo. Honey. What's wrong?"

"I didn't do anything," I say. "Some asshole was coming onto her pretty aggressively and it scared her. I chased him away, but we need to get her out of here."

She glances at me, her eyes tight at the corners. I don't know if she believes me. From the suspicion painted across her face, Echo must have said something to her about our shared past.

"I'll get her home," she says, then turns back to Echo. "Can you stand up, honey?"

To my surprise, Echo complies, wriggling out from beneath the bedspread and getting to her feet. Her movements are sluggish, and she keeps herself angled away from me.

"Can I come with you?" I ask. "I need to make sure she's okay."

Anita purses her lips. "No. Maybe you really did help

her, but all I know for sure is that she didn't want to see you and now you're here and she's upset."

I slump. I get it. She's being a good friend and looking out for Echo. If only she knew I'd slice my veins open before I hurt Echo again.

6

———

THE PAST

TYLER

"You're not trying hard enough!"

I pump my arms and legs faster, driving my feet across the long, narrow lawn that runs along the side of the house. My lungs burn and my muscles quiver. I'm afraid they might fail at any second and I'll crash onto the wet grass and skid through the mud on my belly.

I reach the end of the lawn, pivot, and run back toward the starting point.

"Faster." Dad claps his hands briskly. "Get a move on. I didn't raise a pussy."

Rain streaks down my face as I arrive at the starting line he set up earlier, pivot, and take off again. He's had me out here doing shuttle runs for half an hour now. I don't know how much longer I can keep it up.

Unfortunately, this is what happens when we lose a game. This time, he blamed my lack of explosive cardio training for the failure. I tried to point out that it's a team game, but he didn't listen. He never does.

A muscle in my thigh seizes and my steps falter. I try to

mask it by pretending to slip on a muddy patch—of which there are plenty. I drag in a lungful of air, wishing I had time to appreciate the scent of rain on the concrete.

"I saw that!" Dad yells. "Keep going. Half-ass isn't good enough."

I sprint to the end of the yard, then return to the start, nearest the driveway, where he's sitting beneath an umbrella, with a cup of coffee nestled on his lap.

Asshole.

I stop beside him and grab the towel slung over the arm of the chair, then mop my face with it.

"Did I say you could take a break?" he demands, his eyes flat.

"My tutor will be here soon," I puff, struggling to catch my breath. "I need to work on that biology essay."

I bend, my hamstrings protesting, and wrap my hand around the water bottle on the ground. I slug the water back, desperately thirsty despite the fact I'm soaked to the skin.

A muscle ticks in Dad's jaw. "You should have thought of that before you let your fitness slide. I want twenty more, and don't even think about slacking off."

Anger heats my insides, combating the chill that's long since settled into my bones.

"I can't do everything." A sense of helplessness consumes me. "It's nearly impossible to get the grades you think I should and keep my fitness and skills in peak condition."

Dad laughs, but the sound is all edge and no humor. He gets to his feet and, before I have time to react, he smacks me across the face. My head snaps around and the metallic tang of blood fills my mouth. A searing pain flares in my cheek and I raise my hand to it, gently probing the area.

Fortunately, he hasn't split the skin.

I stare at him, seething. Fuck, I wish I could punch the smug expression off his face.

"Laziness and excuses won't win you a Stanley Cup." He shakes his head and stalks away.

I watch him go, and a flicker of movement in the corner of my eye catches my attention.

My heart sinks.

Standing on the driveway, a backpack slung over one of her shoulders, is Echo Dean. Her eyes are wide, her lips parted, and a dozen emotions flicker across her face. I know in an instant that she saw everything.

"What are you looking at?" I demand.

Her mouth falls open. "N-nothing," she stammers.

"Better fucking not be."

I can't have rumors spreading about Dad hitting me. I can't stand the idea of my classmates looking at me with pity or disgust. I'd become a laughingstock. Then, somehow, Dad would find a way to blame me, even though he's the one who acted like a child where someone could see.

I know I shouldn't let him get away with what he does. I'm a big guy. Strong. I shouldn't be a victim. But I can't protect Mom and Soraya all the time, and no one else will ever back me up against him. He's too adept at talking his way out of situations, paying people off when that fails.

"Are you ready for our session?" Echo asks hesitantly.

I wave at the cones set out on the lawn. "I have to do another twenty."

I hate myself for giving Dad what he wants, but he'll no doubt be watching, and he'll find a way to make me regret it if I defy him.

"O-okay." She nibbles on her lower lip, visibly nervous. "I'll wait inside."

"Thanks."

I watch her go. She probably wishes she wasn't here. I do, too. Now I have to turn myself inside out wondering what she thinks she knows—and what she intends to do about it.

I spit out a mouthful of bloody saliva and launch into another sprint. Thanks to the brief break, I'm able to force my body to move.

The rain picks up, and if not for the fact my muscles are screaming and I'm dreading dealing with Echo, I might actually enjoy this now that Dad isn't supervising. His presence makes everything worse.

When I'm done, I take a few extra minutes to carefully stretch my legs and glutes. I'm going to need to repeat the exercises later today or I'll be miserable at training tomorrow.

I empty my water bottle down my throat, peel off my T-shirt, which is plastered to my torso, and stomp over to the front door. On the doorstep, I remove my muddy shoes and wipe the souls of my feet on the mat.

Inside, I do my best not to drip on the floor as I make my way toward the living room, where Echo is likely waiting. Mom appears from the direction of the bathroom with a fluffy towel clutched in her hands. She scans my face, her teeth catching her lip as she notices the bruise forming on my cheekbone.

"Here." She offers me the towel. "Use this to dry off. There's a change of clothes inside."

"Thanks, Mom."

Why won't you stop him?

The unspoken question hangs in the air between us. She just smiles awkwardly and leaves.

I take the towel, set the jeans and T-shirt aside, and dry

myself. Then, with a quick glance toward the living room to make sure I'm out of Echo's sight, I strip off my shorts, towel off my bottom half, and pull the change of clothes on.

I toss the towel into the bathroom, knowing Mom will take it to the laundry, either out of guilt for not saying anything to Dad about hitting me or out of fear of what he'll do if she doesn't maintain a pristine show house.

I stride into the living room, where Echo is waiting on the sofa. She looks up and her gaze searches mine.

"Are you okay?" she asks, her fingers toying with the edge of the textbook on her lap.

"Fine," I bark.

She flinches, and guilt flashes through me. I can't show any weakness now. Not after what she witnessed earlier.

"I needed motivation, and Dad gave it to me," I say, hoping to explain it away without any future questions. "If you mention a word of this to anyone, I won't help out with my teammates like I said I would. I'll make sure your life is hell."

Her porcelain skin blanches. Her eyes drop to her knees, and for a moment, I think that's the end of the matter, but then her gaze lifts and she determinedly thrusts her chin forward.

"It isn't okay for parents to hurt their children." Her voice is shaky. "No matter what the reason."

A breath gusts between my lips. For some reason, her certainty soothes a hidden pain inside me. Logically, I know it isn't right that Dad hits us, or that he controls every aspect of our lives, but he makes it seem inevitable. As if it's just the way things are. It's nice to know that not everyone believes that.

My silence must worry her, because she starts skimming the pages of the textbook, running her finger over the end of the paper, her gaze no longer on me but staring into space, somewhere past my shoulder.

"I won't say anything," she adds. "But you deserve better."

I grunt as her words land with the precision of an arrow. How can she say that to me when I just threatened her? How can she look at me and see someone worth protecting?

I don't know how to respond, and unease is slithering up my spine.

"I'll be back in a minute."

I get the hell out of there.

ECHO

I fold over the corner of the textbook, trying to make sense of everything I've seen and heard since I arrived at the Kinsey's house this afternoon.

I'm having a hard time merging my idea of who Tyler is with the fact I saw his father strike him and he didn't retaliate or even seem shocked by the blow.

Come to think of it, the way they each behaved gave the impression the encounter wasn't out of the ordinary for them, and I don't know what to do with that.

Tyler is an outgoing, confident guy. Or at least, that's how he comes across at school. It's difficult to believe he'd let his father hit him.

Let.

I roll my eyes at myself. As if victims of domestic violence are somehow at fault. I know better than to think something like that. Victims come in all shapes and sizes, and just because they're physically capable of fighting back doesn't mean they aren't still being abused, or that there aren't other ways to control them.

Whatever the case, Tyler is obviously afraid I'll tell someone.

I won't. I can't do that, especially knowing how much his reputation probably means to him. But I want to help him. How can I when he's clearly determined to pretend I never saw anything and that nothing ever happened?

I run through options in my mind. If I was looking at this in black and white, the most reasonable thing to do would be to tell the police. But Tyler would never forgive me, and despite the tentative truce we reached during our last tutoring session, I believe him when he says he'd make my life hell.

Is there someone I could quietly mention it to? One of the teachers, perhaps? Or maybe the coach? Tyler is the star center on the ice hockey team. Surely, he has a good relationship with his coach.

But what if I did and then word got back to his father? Mr. Kinsey seems like the type of man who's very involved in his children's lives. It's possible the coach wouldn't believe me.

I can't risk it.

I grit my teeth, frustration making me edgy. I'm supposed to be smart. My teachers are always telling me so. Mom, too. Why is it so hard to figure out what to do?

My eyelid twitches, reminding me that I was up late studying last night. I need coffee. Tyler could probably do with one too, after all of that running in the rain. I don't know when he plans to return, if at all, so I don't know how much time I have, but keeping him caffeinated won't take long and it seems like the least I can do.

I place the textbook on the coffee table, straighten, and tiptoe into the foyer. Tyler is nowhere to be seen, but his mother is leaving a room opposite me with a damp towel slung over her shoulder.

"Excuse me, Mrs. Kinsey?"

She jumps, apparently not having noticed me.

"Oh, Echo." Her hand flutters over her chest. "You gave me a fright."

I wince. "I'm sorry."

But now my mind is working overtime. I know some people are just jumpy, but the way Mrs. Kinsey's eyes are darting all over the place makes me wary. Perhaps Tyler isn't the only member of the family that Mr. Kinsey has laid his hands on.

"Does Tyler like coffee?" I ask, studying her features for any evidence of violence. She's wearing enough makeup that it's impossible to tell if her skin is discolored beneath. I scan her arms, but she's wearing long sleeves, and her capri pants cover her legs to mid-way down her calves.

I don't see any damage on the skin beneath the hem, but there are plenty of places it could be hidden.

"Um, yes. He does." She glances at the hall as if she'd like nothing more than to disappear down it.

"I'd like to make him one before we start, and maybe a snack, too. I saw him running outside. He must be hungry. Is that okay? Could you show me where the kitchen is?"

"I suppose so." She sounds uncertain, which only increases my certainty that Mr. Kinsey takes out his temper on his whole family.

We each stand there for a long moment, unmoving.

I clear my throat. "The kitchen?"

"Oh." She jolts in surprise. "Yes. This way."

She leads me down the hall and into a kitchen with large windows that overlook the back lawn. An island with a marble countertop occupies the center of the space, and all of the paneling is dark wood. Slightly outdated, but no doubt expensive.

Mrs. Kinsey gestures to a fancy coffee maker on the island. "Have you used one of these before?"

"No, ma'am." I'm liable to break it if I try.

She hesitates, then glides toward it. She's surprisingly graceful, for a shadow of a woman. She moves like a dancer.

"There are mugs in the cupboard on the other side of the island and a box of protein bars on the shelf above the counter at the end of the room. Why don't you get those while I make the drinks?" she suggests.

"That would be great. Thank you." I don't want to lose all my tutoring money as soon as it arrives just because I don't know how to work a coffee maker.

While she presses buttons and the machine comes to life, I search for mugs.

"Are you having one?" I ask.

"No, but you're welcome to," she replies.

I withdraw two mugs and slide them across to her, then go to the shelf at the end and search for the protein bars she mentioned. I find a stash of them—nearly four boxes—and pull one out. Then, after consideration, I grab another. I don't want a hangry jock on my hands.

That done, I hover awkwardly while Mrs. Kinsey makes coffee.

"How do you like yours?" she asks.

"Whatever is easiest." I definitely have preferred tastes when it comes to coffee, but I'll drink anything with caffeine in it.

A couple of minutes later, Mrs. Kinsey passes me two flat whites on a tray, along with a sachet of sugar, just like I'm at a coffee shop. I thank her, add the protein bars to the tray, and return to the living room, grateful not to encounter Mr. Kinsey on the way. Now that I know what he's like, I don't want to see him again.

Tyler is sitting on the sofa, scowling at the textbook,

which, to my surprise, he's actually opened. I don't know why he's using mine when I'm sure he has his own, but it's not like it hurts anyone, so I keep quiet.

"Here." I lower the tray of coffee onto the table and push the protein bars toward him. "Coffee and a snack."

He gives me a searching look. "What's this?"

I squirm, self-conscious. I hadn't thought about how this might look beyond assuming he'd probably like food and a nice, warm drink. Now, I can't help but wonder if he suspects this is my weird way of flirting with him.

"I thought you might be hungry, and I wanted coffee, so I asked your mom to make us each one." That's all he'll get from me.

I sit beside him and smooth my jeans self-consciously. Where his are artfully distressed by design, mine have tiny holes in the knees because I've worn them through. They're slightly too baggy on my slim frame.

They make me look like exactly what I am: someone from a working-class family. I'm not ashamed of that, but it's yet another way I'm different from my wealthy classmates.

I glance up and draw back, caught off guard by Tyler's face so close to mine. He's gazing at me, his pale blue eyes intent on my mouth. My breath hitches. If I didn't know better, I'd think he was about to kiss me. But then he shakes his head and blinks, and the intensity vanishes.

"Thanks." He picks up his coffee and swallows a mouthful.

"No problem." I reach into my open backpack and pull out the small case where my tablet lives. Mom can't afford to buy me a laptop, so I make do with this and my phone. "Show me what you're up to."

Together, we go through his notes. He's done more than I expected, and not once does he ask me to finish the essay for him, which I appreciate. While he revises a paragraph where he'd gone off on a tangent, I debate whether to bring up the elephant in the room again.

In the end, I wait until we've nearly wrapped up before raising the topic.

"If you ever need to talk, I'm here," I tell him.

His expression closes off. "There's nothing to talk about. Thanks for your help, but it's time for you to go."

7

———

ECHO

"Are you sure you don't want company?" Anita looks worried, and after what happened over the weekend, I get it.

"No, I'm fine. I'll see you tomorrow." I turn my key in the lock and let myself into my dorm room, a little surprised when she doesn't try to follow me in.

Honestly, it's a miracle she's letting me out of her sight. She's been like an overprotective mama bear. Even though I refuse to explain what's behind my occasional panic attacks, I'm sure she's noticed enough context clues to guess.

I step inside and a wave of vanilla-scented warm air greets me. Martina must have left her diffuser going and the heater on before she went to class. I shut the door, flip the lock, and cross the room to my bed, where I stop short.

There's a wrapped bundle on my pillow. I never get any mail, so I have no idea what it is or whom it's from. Come to think of it, mail isn't delivered to dorm rooms. We have to collect it from a cubby hole downstairs. So what's up with this?

I tiptoe closer, threads of anxiety spooling in my gut. The package looks to have something reasonably thick inside. There's nothing written on the back. I turn it over, but the other side is also blank.

My gut tightens. The package is the size and shape of a book, but I didn't order one recently, and no one has offered to loan me anything, so there's no reason for it to be here. I briefly consider that it might be Martina's, but the way it's displayed on my pillow leaves no doubt that it's intended for me.

My guess is that someone delivered it by hand and Martina placed it here for me to find.

Tentatively, I sit on my bed and place whatever it is on my lap. It's sealed, so I gently tear the paper wrapping open. The rip is uncomfortably loud in the quiet room.

I reach inside and brush my fingertips along the spine of a book. I grip the edges and slowly draw it out. The book is bound in faded blue leather, with black lettering on the spine and front. The title reads: *A Collection of Poems from the Romantics*.

A slip of paper falls from inside the cover and lands on my lap. I pick it up and, as I scan the familiar handwriting, my chest begins to tighten.

I don't have the words for how I feel about you, but these guys do. ~Tyler

There's an XO printed beside his name and the letters are wobbly, as if he was nervous when he wrote them.

I bite my lip. It's a gift. I should have expected him to send another after slipping the necklace into my backpack the other day.

If he's trying to make it more difficult to hate him, he's succeeding.

He knows how much I love poetry, and there's something about old books that's absolutely magical. Their slightly musty scent, the delicate pages, and the knowledge that dozens of others have pored through them over the years. I can never help wondering who they were, where they lived, and what their lives were like.

Against my better judgment, I open the book and read the small print on the inside cover. My eyebrows fly up. It's a first edition. I close the book and scan the exterior. It's in excellent condition.

This can't have been cheap. My stomach hardens, my softness toward him vanishing. It would be just like Tyler to think he could buy my forgiveness. That said, he chose an excellent way to do it. I gaze at the cover longingly. I can't keep it. That wouldn't be right.

But damn him for knowing just how to press my buttons. Especially now, when I'm still emotionally tender from my experience at the Kickoff party. I don't want to be reminded of him, or of the fact that he supposedly saved me from a creep and comforted me during a panic attack.

I don't know what to make of that, so it's best if I don't think of it. In order to keep him out of my head, the book has to go, and so does the necklace. If he refuses to take them back, I'll just have to give them away or donate them. The library is always looking for rare editions.

It doesn't matter how much I want it for myself. My peace of mind is more important.

Metal clinks on metal as a key turns in the lock, and then the door swings open. Martina breezes into the room, a wide smile on her face. Her plump cheeks are rosy, and she pauses to breathe in the scented air. She glances at me and notices the book in my hands and the discarded envelope.

"Oh, good," she says. "You found your gift."

"I did." And now I feel like a kid with their hand caught in the cookie jar. "Did someone give this to you?"

"Mmhmm." Her glossy pink lips adopt a sly slant.

"Who?" I don't have the mental energy to play guessing games as she'd probably like me to. I know Tyler sent it, but

I'm curious if he delivered it himself. If so, it means he knows where my room is, or at least what my roommate looks like.

She rolls her eyes. "You're no fun. It was that hockey transfer student. Tall, blonde, built like Thor. I wouldn't mind seeing his hammer—if you know what I mean."

"Thanks." I bite my tongue. For all that she's a shameless flirt, Martina means well, so there's no point snapping at her just because Tyler is throwing me off my game.

"So, what is it?" she asks, coming closer.

"A first edition collection of poems by the romantics." I hold it up to show her. "Do you want it?"

She looks at me like I'm crazy. "Girl, no. If a guy like that wants to woo you, you let him." She frowns, then adds, "Unless you're dating someone, or identify as part of the rainbow spectrum that isn't interested in men."

"I'm straight," I tell her, amused by the speculative gleam in her eye.

She throws up her hands. "Then what's the problem? If you ask me, that's a pretty romantic gift."

It is. That's the problem.

Tyler is being annoyingly thoughtful about trying to buy my forgiveness.

"I don't want it," I say. "Tyler and I have history, and it's not the type I want to remember."

Her deep brown eyes shine with sympathy. "I'm sorry. I didn't know. I don't have any use for a poetry book. You know I'm not much of a reader."

I sigh. "You could sell it."

"Or you could return it to him and say, 'Thanks but no thanks'?"

Damn, I hate the fact she makes a valid point. Tyler's family has money, but his father always kept him on a tight leash, so I don't know how much he has personally or whether he can afford to throw it away. I should give him the chance to resell or return the book before I get rid of it.

"Maybe," I mumble, my mind already busy trying to work out where I could track him down. I've given no thought to his living situation here.

Mostly because I've been doing my best not to think of him at all.

Is he in a dorm?

No, that doesn't seem like his Dad's style. He'd insist Tyler be in a fraternity or else live in an expensive apartment off campus.

I open my social media and search his name, frustrated that he pops up immediately because I've already cyberstalked him several times. I don't need to be reminded of my weakness.

I scroll through his information, looking for any hint of where he might live, but the sparse details don't give me much to work with.

"You could wait for him after practice."

I flinch, surprised that Martina managed to sneak up on me. She's hovering over me, watching me behave like the kind of stalkery ex-girlfriend that guys warn each other about.

"What?" I ask, her words not making any sense.

She shrugs. "The hockey team has practice today. If you want to give the book back to him, you could catch him as he leaves the ice."

"That's...a good thought." I don't ask how she knows the hockey team's schedule. Sometimes it's better not to know. "Any idea what time they finish?"

TYLER

I stride into the changing room, inhaling the familiar aroma of cold sweat and menthol. Hockey gear has a distinctive scent that comes from working up a sweat in such a cold environment, and then never drying properly. The only thing I can compare it to is damp socks that have been worn for a couple of days straight.

It's nasty, but it also reminds me of one of my favorite things in the world, so I don't hate it.

Half the team are already undressed or in the showers. I sit and remove my skates before stripping off my gear. I wrap a towel around my waist and I'm heading for the showers when Ruiz, one of the second-line wingers, calls out to me.

"Kinsey!"

I turn toward him. "What?"

"I'm going to visit my girlfriend after I'm dressed," he says.

"Good for you." Why does he think he needs to share this with me?

He rolls his eyes good-naturedly. "She has a super-hot roommate. I'm a happily taken, man, but this girl is fire. Why don't you come and meet her?"

Ah. There it goes. These guys seem to have made a game out of trying to hook me up.

"Not interested." I turn away and enter one of the shower cubicles, slinging the towel over the divider between my shower and the next one over.

"You never get any action!" Ruiz yells from behind me. "Your balls are going to shrivel up and die, man. Do them a favor."

A few of the guys laugh. Someone whistles.

Calmly, I shout back, "There's only one woman I'm interested in."

There's an explosion of whispers in the locker room.

Until now, I've been tight-lipped about my intentions, but perhaps that isn't the best way to go. I crank the shower on, tuning them out, and quickly wash, then shut it off again.

As I'm drying, a voice rises above the others again. "Is it that girl you were with the other day?"

I scowl and push the cubicle door open. Matthews, the guy who witnessed Echo shooting me down, has joined the others and is looking my way. I narrow my eyes at him, then sweep my gaze around all the horny fuckers who might find it funny to get in my way.

"Yeah. Echo. And if any of you even look at her sideways, I'll make you regret it."

None of them deserve her. I don't either, but I don't care. She's mine, and that's all there is to it.

"Calm the fuck down, Kinsey," Ruiz says.

I ignore him. "She's off-limits."

None of them reply. Perhaps they're all too busy wondering if I'm secretly psychotic. After a long minute, Matthews strikes up a conversation with our captain, Anaheim, about the first game of the season. Gradually, the murmur of voices returns. I dress, sling my duffel bag over my shoulder, and leave without saying goodbye.

As I exit the arena, the cool breeze sends goosebumps skittering over the exposed skin of my face. My mind travels to Echo. Has she found my gift? Does she like it? Even if it only softens her toward me a tiny bit, I'll take the win.

A handful of cars are dotted around the parking lot. I hurry past the glass-paneled stadium walls toward my vehicle, a black Audi in last year's model. I'm halfway there when movement in the corner of my eye catches my attention.

I glance over my shoulder. Echo is beelining across the concrete, her gaze locked on me. She's carrying the book I sent her, and resting on top of it is the jewelry box containing the shooting star necklace.

"What are you doing?" she demands, her eyes sparking with fury.

I frown. That's not quite the reaction I've been hoping for.

"Leaving practice," I say, deciding it's in my best interest to play dumb.

Her glare intensifies and she waves the gifts in my direction. "I mean with these."

I raise my chin. "I'm wooing you the way I should have back then."

"W-wooing me?" she stutters, blinking rapidly, having apparently not expected that response.

"Yes. I want you to have nice things. You deserve to. I didn't treat you as well as I should have in the past, but I'm going to make it up to you."

If it takes my last fucking breath, I'll make sure she knows how much she means to me.

"You...what?" She shakes her head and thrusts them toward me. "Just take them. I can't keep them."

"Why not?" I ask.

She opens her mouth, then closes it. Her lips press together, and she huffs through her nostrils.

"I just can't," she says. "I won't accept gifts from you. Take them back."

I slide one of my hands into my pocket and use the other to hold onto the strap of my duffel bag, so neither of them are free to take anything from her.

"They're yours." My tone is firm. "You can sell them and use the money to pay for something you actually want if that's what you'd prefer, but whatever happens, I'm not taking them."

She nervously runs a finger along the wire arm of her

glasses. "You can't just give me random gifts. These must be worth hundreds of dollars."

Thousands, actually.

I shrug. "It's my choice what I do with my money. I choose to spend it on you. What you do with my gifts is up to you."

Her eyelashes flutter, and is it just me, or do her glasses seem to be fogging up? "Why won't you just let me go?"

My heart squeezes, and my insides roll nauseatingly. The anguish in her voice makes me want to be sick. My lips part but no words emerge.

Her shoulders slump. "Haven't you done enough to me?"

Oh, fuck. Fuck. She's going to cry.

If she keeps this up, I might cry too. My throat is tight, emotion choking me.

"That's not what this is," I whisper, barely audible.

She steps back and tucks the book underneath her arm while she uses her other hand to remove her glasses and wipe the lenses.

"Is this all some kind of twisted game to you?" she asks.

"No." I reach for her, but the second I touch her arm she recoils so much that she stumbles. "I love you."

Three little words I've never said to anyone else. Not Mom. Not Soraya. Sure as hell not that asshole who tried to mold me in his image.

"I've always loved you, even if I haven't shown it well."

She scoffs and swipes at her eyes. "Yeah. You have a unique way of making me feel so loved."

I bite my tongue so hard I taste blood, and it reminds me of the first day I ever wanted to kiss her. After she saw how my father treated me and somehow looked past my threatening bluster to react with kindness.

"You're the only girl I've ever loved," I tell her. "I haven't been with anyone since you. I haven't even kissed anyone else since the day we broke up. I know that doesn't make things right, but I want a second chance, and I can explain if you're willing to listen."

She puts her glasses back on, and the air between us chills ten degrees. I can tell by the way she's doing it that those glasses represent a barrier between us that she's fortifying with every breath she takes.

"You expect me to believe you haven't been with any of those puck bunnies that fawn all over college athletes?" Her words drip with venom.

"I haven't." I understand why she might doubt me, but it's the truth.

A flicker of pain crosses her features. "Or Whitney?"

"I wasn't with her like that. I never cared about her. Please, let me explain." My fist clenches around the strap, and a rock sits heavy in my gut. It feels like everything rides on this moment.

Echo looks me straight in the eyes. "I don't believe you."

Then she leaves, taking the broken remnants of my heart with her.

8

———

TYLER

Sipping my flat white, I watch Echo across the coffee shop. I arrived at Full of Beans early for our group project meeting and positioned myself strategically just inside the door, where I can see her, but she's unlikely to see me.

Students buzz around the brightly lit interior, making small talk and tapping on their laptops at the coffee bar, while seated in clusters around the tables. There's too much chatter for the environment to be great for studying, but several people have earbuds in, so I guess they've found ways around it.

Echo is sitting by herself at a rectangular wooden table. Her laptop is open in front of her and she's reading something on the screen, scrolling down every now and then. Her eyebrows pinch together, a faint groove forming between them, and she pauses to scribble on the notepad to the right of her keyboard.

I tip my coffee cup up, draining the rest of the flat white. The coffee is creamy and rich, just how I like it, but it pales in comparison to Echo.

Everything does.

Sometimes I wish I'd realized that before shit went down. I've wondered a hundred times how I could have done things differently. But at the end of the day, it doesn't matter. I made choices, and now I have to live with reality.

In this case, my reality is that Echo has been showing up for class a few minutes late to avoid me, and racing for the exit as soon as class ends. I could follow her back to her dorm or arrange to intercept her, but I've been trying to respect her wishes as much as possible without abandoning my plan.

I've given her a little space, but I won't give her too much.

As I continue to observe her, I notice that I'm not the only one doing so. At a table two over from hers, a pair of guys in jeans and death metal T-shirts are surreptitiously checking her out. The way they're leaning close to each other to talk, flicking their gazes to her every few seconds, makes me think they're discussing her.

I shift on my seat and tug my ball cap lower, angling my head to shield my face. The stockier of the two guys stands and makes his way over to her. When he's hovering beside her table, Echo glances up at him and smiles.

She *smiles*.

My jaw tightens. This asshole gets to bask in the warmth of her smile when it's all I can do to persuade her not to flee from me every time I get near her.

I understand why, but it grates.

Echo's lips aren't moving, so I assume the guy is doing the talking. His back is to me so I can't see his expression. After a moment, she replies to him. He swaggers away from her, toward the line at the counter. I wonder if she told him her coffee order.

Oh, hell no.

I wait until Echo refocuses on her laptop before leaving

my post by the door and joining the line. Luckily, no one else has joined, so I'm immediately behind the asshole whose been trying to flirt with my girl. I tap him on the shoulder.

He swivels around. "What?"

"Are you buying a coffee for the girl over there?" I ask softly. "Glasses, brunette."

"Yeah." He grins. "She's cute, right?"

"She's mine," I growl. "If you so much as lay a finger on her, I'll break it."

His eyes widen. "Whoa. What the fuck?"

I inch closer to him. "I'm completely serious. Leave now and don't ever talk to her again. Don't even fucking look at her."

He scowls. "You're crazy."

I incline my head in acknowledgement. "Probably. But I'm not joking around."

He sizes me up and seems to realize that I'm bigger and meaner because he steps out of the line and defensively holds up his hands.

"I'm going. But you need to get a grip, man."

Yeah, I do. I'm going to get myself arrested before I win her back at this rate, but I can't bring myself to regret my actions as my competition scurries out the side door. Echo doesn't even look up. She hasn't realized he's gone.

I stay in the line, regretting the fact I didn't ask him what sort of coffee she wanted before sending him packing. We never did anything in public, so all I know about her coffee preferences is that she used to like adding a shot of chocolate to her drink when we used my family's coffee maker.

When I reach the front of the line, I order a skinny mocha. Then, tugging my cap low again, I shuffle around to wait for the drink, doing my best to stay out of her line of sight. I'm more exposed to her here, and it won't be long before she realizes her admirer has vanished.

But then something happens that I could never have prepared for. The girl who was in front of Coffee Guy in the line receives her cream-topped drink and sidles over to Echo. From here, I can hear every word she says, and it makes me wish I could disappear in a puff of smoke.

"It was so hot how your boyfriend chased off that other guy," she tells Echo.

Echo looks around, obviously confused. Her gaze sweeps past the counter and, failing to land on her admirer, returns to the girl who's approached her.

"My boyfriend?" she asks.

"Yeah." The girl cocks her hip. "He was all, 'Grr, she's mine, back off.' Very alpha male, and hot A.F."

Echo scans the counter again, and this time her gaze snags on me. I look away, hoping she didn't see my face properly, but no such luck. In two seconds, she's on her feet and stomping toward me. The girl leaps out of her way, startled.

"You." She jabs her finger at me but doesn't make contact. "What right do you think you have to do that?"

I shrink against the counter. She might be nearly a foot shorter than me, but that doesn't make her anger any less terrifying because she's literally one of the only things in the world I give a damn about.

"I can do what I like," I say, but it comes out sounding like a question.

Her eyes form hazel slits. "What part of 'leave me alone' do you not get?"

"I, uh, can't do that," I respond sheepishly.

"Why not?" If looks could kill, I'd be six feet under.

"Because we have our group meeting in—" I check my watch. "Five minutes."

Her nostrils flare and she grumbles, but must realize she's not going to make any progress on that front because she changes tack.

"That class is the only reason we have to talk to each other," she says. "I don't want to hear about you interfering with my life again. No gifts, no chasing people away, and—"

"Skinny mocha?" the barista says behind me.

Cringing, I turn and take the drink from her, then pass it to Echo. "Sorry, I'd already ordered it."

She glares at me, and then the coffee. She snatches it from my grasp. "This doesn't mean anything."

I nod agreeably. "I'm sorry for upsetting you. I just..." I know I'm about to make a fool of myself, but she deserves the truth, even when it's uncomfortable for me. "I can't stand to see you with anyone else, and I hope you'll agree to hear me out eventually. Trust me, you'll want to hear what I have to say."

Confessing the truth wouldn't change the past, but it could alter our future, if only she'd stop being stubborn for long enough to find out.

"I wanted to talk things out years ago." Her tone is steely. "But instead, you hurt me badly."

Everything inside me aches, right down to my soul. I was an idiot. A stupid, impulsive kid who'd been backed into a corner. I'd paid the price, but Echo had too. In many ways, the price she paid was steeper.

"You weren't polite enough to grant me the privilege of not seeing you with someone else, so why would I do that for you?" she asks.

ECHO

My chest feels like it's been scraped open. My heart is a

raw, bleeding mess as I stare at Tyler. Even years later, the memory of seeing him with Whitney festers like an unclean scab.

"I—"

Before he can finish the sentence, Jin rolls up, a friendly smile in place.

"You beat me here," he says, coming to a stop in front of us. "Do we have a table?"

I nod and jerk my thumb toward the table I claimed earlier. "Over there."

Jin's forehead creases. He glances from me to Tyler and back again. "What's with all the tension?"

I silently will Tyler not to overshare. So far, he seems not to have any compunction about letting everyone know what he wants from me. It's so different from the way we used to hide our relationship with polite smiles and feigned indifference that I don't know how to react.

Tyler's eyes, which have always reminded me of ice—so pale and cool—search mine. "We were having a heated discussion about the ethics of operant conditioning on an unknowing subject," he says.

Even as relief flows through me, I gape at him, stunned by the words that came out of his mouth. He must have been paying better attention in class than I'd thought.

"Oh." Jin seems to accept this at face value. "Personally, I don't think it's ethical, but there can be circumstances in which it might be the best approach regardless of its questionable ethical standing."

"Agreed," Tyler says quickly, waiting until Jin is facing away before he mouths, "This isn't over."

I ignore him, hating the little flash of excitement in my gut. I shouldn't want him to fight for me. There's nothing to fight *for*. We were broken a long time ago. Yet part of me can't help being drawn to him, even if I can't afford to indulge that secret desire.

"There's Elle." Jin waves to the final member of our group, who's appeared in the doorway.

Elle's gaze skims over Jin and she gives a half-hearted wave. She barely acknowledges my presence and aims the full wattage of her porcelain-pink smile at Tyler, who shifts from one foot to the other uncomfortably.

I sip my mocha, enjoying the chocolatey flavor, even if the sweetness of the caramel syrup I usually add is absent. Considering Tyler and I only ever drank coffee from his parent's coffee maker, he made a solid effort of guessing what I might want.

"I'm looking forward to seeing your first game," Elle says, obviously hoping to entice Tyler into conversation.

He just grunts.

It's ridiculous. I can't make the guy stop talking and leave me alone, no matter how much I want to, and meanwhile, she can't convince him to string two words together. Honestly, if I weren't determined to hate him, it would be flattering.

"Shall we sit down?" Jin suggests.

I pass him my coffee. "Can you bring this over for me? I need to use the ladies' room."

"No problem." He flashes me a grin and saunters to the table.

Elle waits, determined to walk over with Tyler. After giving me a pained look, he obliges. I release a shuddering breath and haul air into my lungs.

Don't panic. Don't panic. Everything is going to be all right.

"Hey, um."

A light touch lingers on my forearm. When I turn, the girl I spoke to earlier is standing beside me.

"So, I'm sorry. I obviously got it wrong before," she says. "I heard a little of what you said to him, and I get the feeling he's not your boyfriend."

I cross my arms and her hand falls to her side. "No. He's not."

She comes closer, moving into my personal space. "Do you need any help with him? It kinda sounded like he's causing you problems."

My eyes fly up to hers, caught off guard. Her irises are so dark they're nearly black, but sincerity glitters from their depths. I swallow, taking a moment to compose myself. I consider her offer for all of one second and then dismiss it. I don't want to rehash our whole sorry story with a stranger. Even my friends don't know what happened.

"Thanks, but I'll be fine."

She purses her lips. "Are you sure?"

"Yeah." I force myself to smile. "Thank you for the offer though. It's very sweet of you."

"Anytime." She hesitantly backs away, visibly torn as to whether to accept me at my word.

I go to the bathroom, where I splash cold water on my face and recite a pep talk to myself in the mirror. I've done this dozens of times before. When I'm overwhelmed, sometimes, all I need is to see my own face tell me I can achieve anything—whether it's actually true or not.

It's going to be difficult to maintain a clear head with Tyler around, simultaneously tempting me and terrifying me, but if I want a good score on this group project, then I'll have to make it work.

I close the toilet lid, sit on it, and bury my face in my hands. I growl my frustration, but the sound is muffled by my palms.

I wish I knew what Tyler's end game is. He says he wants me back, and honestly, the longer I'm around him, the more I wonder if, at least on some level, that isn't true. After all, surely, he wouldn't have bothered to chase away that guy who wanted to buy me a coffee if he wasn't jealous.

The trouble is, he's three years too late.

But isn't it sexy that he wants to stake his territory?

"Shut up," I mutter to the traitorous voice in the back of my mind, even though it's right, in a way. Back in high school, I longed for Tyler to announce to everyone that we were together, but he never did.

"Now it's too little, too late."

I stand, wash my hands, dry my face, and return to the table, where Tyler has somehow maneuvered the seating arrangement so he's beside the seat I left my laptop at. Elle and Jin are opposite. Jin's eyes twinkle mischievously, but Elle doesn't look the slightest bit amused.

I sit and open a new document.

"Our assigned topic is the use of operant conditioning in elementary schools," I say. "We need to address methods, pros, cons, and ethics. Who wants what?"

"Why don't you take ethics?" Jin suggests. "Since you and Tyler have such strong feelings on the subject."

There isn't much I can do to argue, and honestly, I don't have a preference, so I nod. "Okay, unless anyone objects?"

"I'll take the cons," Tyler says unexpectedly.

"You will?" Elle sounds surprised he's doing more than sitting back and riding the wave. I'm not though. Tyler is smart and hardworking...when he wants to be.

"Yeah."

"Then I'll do pros." She smirks. "Perhaps we can bounce ideas off each other."

Jin rests his elbow on the table. "Sounds like I've got the methods. Should we go around and each say what our vision is for the project?"

Tyler rolls his eyes, but we agree.

Twenty minutes later, our roles have been fully assigned and we're in a good position to get started. I've logged into the library's online search function to begin sourcing research papers we can use as references. Both Jin and Elle have also got their laptops out. Tyler is using his phone.

He's also touching me at every opportunity.

Any time he leans forward, his body brushes mine, sending sparks skittering along my nerves. When he stretches, his knee nudges mine, and heat races to my core. He leans closer to murmur something about positive reinforcement and his breath stirs the fine hairs near my ear, making me shiver.

I want to scream. But the worst part is, while I know it's all intentional, none of it is blatant enough for me to call him out. Elle must have noticed because she keeps sending me death glares, but Jin seems completely oblivious.

"What's with the stars?" Jin asks.

I frown, confused, and he gestures toward my notepad. Horrified, I realize I've been doodling shooting stars in the margin. I stop immediately and keep my head low, refusing to acknowledge Tyler even though I can feel him burning a hole through me with his stare.

"It's nothing," I mumble.

At least I'm not wearing the necklace. I haven't been able to bring myself to get rid of it yet. Not when so many complicated emotions are entangled in everything it represents. But I won't wear it, especially not where he might see.

Another half-hour later, we decide we've done enough for one day. I pack my laptop into my backpack, along with my notepad, sling it over my shoulder and hurry out the nearest exit, surprised when Tyler doesn't immediately follow me.

I'm halfway back to the dorm when I slip one of my cold

hands into my pocket and stiffen as my fingers brush the corner of a folded piece of paper. Slowly, I draw it out.

The paper has a ragged edge from where Jin ripped it from his notebook to give to Tyler, who hadn't brought anything to take notes on. It would seem he didn't use the paper for our assignment.

Echo,

I haven't given up on you. I won't ever give up on you.

I'm letting you have some time to process, but we will talk about the past. We need to have that conversation. Both of us. So we can put it behind ourselves and move on.

We need closure.

~ Tyler XO

9

THE PAST

TYLER

Sweat trickles down the back of my neck as I stare at the last question on the pop quiz that Mr. Harding surprised me with after school. The ticking of the clock seems abnormally loud in the otherwise silent classroom.

I chew on my lip. I'm pretty sure I know the answer, but if I get this wrong, it could ruin everything.

If I'd only known about this goddamn test, I might have been more prepared. I was only supposed to be collecting my grade for the essay I was allowed to resubmit, but when I arrived, he sat me down, put the test in front of me and told me to get started.

I should have seen this coming. Mr. Harding isn't the kind of teacher who likes giving second chances. He was probably bullied into letting me redo the essay and this is his way of getting back at me for it.

The clock continues to tick.

Sweat soaks the hair at the nape of my neck.

I put pen to paper and fill in an answer for the final question, then I read over everything I've already written. My stomach churns and I regret having chugged down a protein shake before coming here. The liquid sloshes around in my gut, making me feel ill.

Ping! Ping! Ping!

The timer on Mr. Harding's phone goes off. He uncrosses his legs from where he's leaning against the desk, crosses to me, and reaches for the paper. I grab at it, desperately trying to recheck the last few lines, but he tuts.

"Time is up, Tyler. That's it."

I grit my teeth as he takes the paper back to his desk. He sits and picks up his red pen, holding it poised above the test as he goes through it. He frowns and makes a note, then glances up at me and back at the paper. I wriggle in my seat. What if I got it wrong? What if I only thought I'd gotten my head around this stuff?

How much does this pop quiz even count for? He hasn't said. For all I know, he could be making it up as he goes along. My instincts tell me he is, and I want to protest, but considering he's giving me special treatment already, I keep my mouth firmly shut.

"Hmm. Interesting." He jots something at the top of the page and circles it, then raises his head. "Not a bad effort, Tyler. Nine out of ten. You lost half a point each for incomplete explanations of questions two and seven. You were on the right track but didn't quite get there."

All of the tension I've been holding in my body releases at once.

"I did well?" I ask, unnecessarily.

His nose scrunches, a line of irritation forming between his eyebrows. "I just said that, didn't I?"

He gets to his feet, grasping the pop quiz in one hand and a file holding a few sheets of paper in the other. He passes them to me. My gaze skims past the test since he's already told me my result and settles on the essay. Circled in the top right-hand corner of the front page, beside the title, is an A minus.

I close my eyes as relief overwhelms me. Tears prickle at the backs of my eyes but I refuse to let them fall.

"It was an excellent essay," Mr. Harding says gruffly. "So much better than your previous one that I felt the need to make sure you hadn't gotten someone else to do it for you."

My eyes fly open. "You don't think—"

He chuckles. "Relax, Tyler. I'm satisfied that the essay is your own work, and I appreciate you taking this opportunity seriously. I hope you know that it's out of the ordinary for me to allow students to improve their grades and it won't happen again, no matter who tries to pull strings on your behalf."

I nod. "I understand, Mr. Harding. Thank you. And I swear, I did all the work myself. I had a tutor who helped, but she just walked me through it."

"Ah, yes. Miss Dean." His expression is almost fond. "You owe that young lady."

"I know." I clasp the file to my chest.

He shoos me. "Go on. Go home and break the news to your dad."

"Yes, sir." I hurry out, choosing not to mention the fact that I plan to inform Dad of my new grade by text message. It may be good news, but I find it's best to avoid him whenever possible, and I have better things to do tonight.

I exit the school building and circle around to the parking lot, where I stop dead. Echo is sitting on the ground next to my car, enthralled by something on her phone. She glances up, catches my eye, and waves. My feet lurch into motion, carrying me toward her.

"What are you doing here?" I ask, inwardly wincing as I realize it sounds like an accusation.

She clambers to her feet and puts her phone in her

pocket. "I wanted to be here when you got the news. How did it go?"

I scowl. "He made me do a pop quiz."

"And...?"

I can't hold back my smile. "I got an A minus on the essay and a 90 percent on the test."

She high-fives me. "That's great! I knew you'd do well."

"Yeah, well." I shuffle from one foot to the other, then run my fingers through my hair, remembering too late that it's sweaty. "It's all because of you."

She shakes her head. "You did the work. You put in the time. It's your grade."

Warmth floods me and, before I have time to think it through, I've pulled her into a hug. I freeze, my face buried in her hair, and slowly let her go.

I clear my throat, my cheeks heating. "Sorry about that."

She laughs. "I don't mind random hugs. I'm glad you're happy."

I am, and despite what she claims, it is largely because of her. If I'd screwed this up a second time, I might be benched, or Dad would find a way to take it out on me. She seriously saved my ass.

"You wanna grab some takeout to celebrate?" I ask impulsively.

She studies me cautiously. I can tell she's torn. She probably intended to go home as soon as she'd seen me and, considering how hot and cold I've been toward her, I can see why she might not want to spend more time with me. Especially if she's not getting paid for it.

"My treat," I add. "I was planning to get a burger and fries and watch the meteor shower."

At the mention of the meteor shower, her face lights up, as I'd thought it might. I love watching the stars and don't usually like having company while I lie on my back and study the heavens, but for some reason, I want her to come with me.

"Just the two of us?" she asks.

"Just us," I agree.

She nibbles her lower lip. "Okay, then."

Triumph rushes through me, much the same as if I'd just scored a goal on the ice. I grab the key fob from my pocket and unlock the Chevy before she changes her mind. I hold open the passenger door for her. She seems taken aback by the gesture, and honestly, so am I. I've never held a door for a girl before.

I head around the car and get into the driver's seat. I breathe in as I buckle and turn the key in the ignition. Trapped inside the car with her, I realize for the first time that she smells faintly of lemon. It reminds me of the cleaning products Mom uses at home, but sweeter.

I drive us to the nearest takeout joint and order a bacon cheeseburger and fries for me and a chicken burger for Echo. I pay despite her protests since it was my idea; I don't know how much money she has but I doubt it's much. Then I take her down to my favorite spot near the lake.

It's only when I turn down the gravel road onto old man Wilson's property that it clicks in my mind that I've never brought anyone here before. Not the girls I've fucked, or the guys from the hockey team. Not even Soraya, one of the few people who gets to see my softer side.

This place has been just for me until now, and I have no idea why Echo Dean is the one to make me change that.

We rumble down the gravel, past fields of corn, to the edge of the lake. Echo is quiet, but every now and then, she shoots a look at me out of the corner of her eye. Perhaps she doesn't understand why I'm bringing her here. That's fair. I don't either.

The road ends abruptly up ahead, where it meets the

water's edge. Apparently, it used to continue on, but the lake water rose to cover it during a massive flood a decade or so ago and never retreated to its former level.

I slow to a halt and shut off the engine. I stare out at the water, which is a mass of black in the descending darkness, and then glance over at Echo. Her face is in profile as she gazes straight ahead and, all of a sudden, it hits me that she's actually quite pretty.

Her nose is small and sharp, and there's a dusting of freckles across the bridge of it. Her hazel eyes shine with intelligence, but there's a warmth there too. Her figure is slim, and she's not very tall, but she's shaped nicely, and everything is proportional.

Perhaps I should have realized she's attractive sooner. Eric certainly noticed, but I never got the appeal.

She turns to me. "This place is beautiful." Her lips quirk. "I bet you bring all the girls here."

"Actually, you're the first."

ECHO

I gawk at Tyler, stunned by the honesty etched into the hard planes of his face, but before I have time to respond, he shoves the door open, climbs out and shuts it firmly. I watch through the window as he goes around the back of the Chevy. Am I supposed to follow him?

I don't know what to make of the fact he hasn't brought other girls here before. When we pulled up, the stunning view stole my breath and I immediately assumed that this is where he brings people to hook up. I'd wondered what, if anything, he expected of me. But then he went and turned what I thought upside down.

The Chevy rocks, the balance of weight shifting as Tyler

climbs onto the flatbed. I should probably see what he's doing, but the inside of the vehicle is warm and cozy, and smells of burgers. I wait a few more moments, but when he doesn't return, I sigh and get out.

I circle the Chevy and come up short, surprised once again. Tyler has arranged a bunch of cushions and blankets on the flatbed, forming a comfortable nest.

"Can you grab the food?" he asks. "We'll have a better view out here."

"Sure." I retrieve the cardboard boxes containing our burgers and a small paper bag with Tyler's fries and bring them around to the flatbed.

Tyler has set a small cooler beside the nest and is settling himself onto a cushion. He holds a fluffy blanket up and gestures for me to join him. I place the food on the flatbed and clamber up, then pick up our dinner and approach him shyly.

I know that for Tyler and his friends, physical intimacy is nothing, but this will be the first time I've been in such an intimate setting with a guy who's not either family or gay. It leaves me feeling vulnerable.

I slip beneath the blanket and try to position myself as comfortably as possible, shifting around until I find the best place to lie. I prop a cushion behind myself, tuck the blanket over my lap, and drag the food closer.

"Thanks for the burger," I say, opening the box labeled CB.

"No problem. Thanks for saving my ass in biology." Somehow, the darkness makes him sound even closer.

"I was paid for it." I don't feel right accepting his praise when tutoring him was a job.

"Maybe so, but I'm not the easiest person to deal with."

"Actually, working with you was easier than I expected." I don't want him to think anything else. Yeah, he was emotionally all over the place, but he tried, and that's all a tutor ever wants.

He doesn't acknowledge my comment, instead reaching into the cooler and pulling out a can of beer. "Want one?"

I wrinkle my nose. "No, thanks."

I'm far from twenty-one and I've never been the type of person who likes breaking the rules.

He shrugs. "Have it your way."

We eat in silence, but it's not awkward. Once I've finished my burger, I set the box aside and rest my head against the cushion, gazing up at the stars. Our hometown isn't large, so it doesn't emit enough light to mess with the night sky. Unless it's cloudy, we always have an excellent view.

Tonight, the stars are as bright as ever.

"What time is the meteor shower supposed to happen?" I ask.

He checks his watch. "Around eight-thirty. It's a little after eight now."

He's still eating, so I relax and close my eyes. Tonight has been full of surprises, but perhaps the strangest part is how normal it feels to be here with him. I was nervous when he invited me, wondering what the catch was, but now my mind is easy.

The paper bag crinkles, presumably as Tyler digs around for the last of the fries, and then he scrunches it into a ball. I open my eyes and watch as he packs the trash into the cooler, beside what remains of a six pack of beer.

He flops back, his arms supporting his head, and angles himself toward me.

"When I thanked you earlier, I meant it." He clears his throat. "I know you were paid to help me, but it felt like you really cared, and that means something."

His eyes gleam in the darkness and, based on the way

he's squirming, I suspect his cheeks are flushed red; I can't tell for sure in the near-dark.

"I do care," I tell him.

Honestly, I care about more than his grade. I can't get that encounter between him and his dad out of my mind. It's been weighing on me ever since. The question, 'Is your Dad abusive?', is on the tip of my tongue, but I don't let it out.

Even if I did, I don't know that he'd answer with the truth. Or at all. He might be angry at me for broaching the subject in the first place, and I don't want to ruin his mood.

"Thank you." His voice is rough, and his fingers brush against mine beneath the blanket. I'm tempted to curl my fingers around his, but I don't want him to think I'm making more of this than it actually is, so I resist the urge.

"I'm serious," he continues when I don't respond. "You gave me hope."

My heart squeezes. Everyone should have hope. The world would be a bleak place without it. I'd have thought a guy like Tyler would have plenty of things to look forward to or to hope and dream about. I'd never have guessed that such a small thing could make a difference to him.

Above us, a streak of white flashes across the sky.

I gasp. "Did you see that?"

He turns to look up and, together, we watch as another meteor burns itself out in the earth's atmosphere.

Dozens of faint lines appear and disappear so quickly that neither of us have time to point them out before they're gone again. Every few seconds, a brighter meteor trails across the canvas of stars, capturing our attention until it fades and falls from the sky.

"It's amazing," I breathe.

His hand nudges mine again and, this time, Tyler's palm slides against mine and clasps firmly.

"They remind me of you," he murmurs.

I tilt my face toward him, only to realize we've shifted closer while we were staring up, and now we freeze, gazing into each other's eyes as we share breath.

"How?" I whisper, afraid to end the moment.

He touches the tip of his nose to mine. "You bring light into my darkness, even if I know it's going to be gone too soon."

My chest swells. I can't help myself.

I kiss him.

10

––––––––

I grip the edges of my notepad tightly and tuck my legs up beneath myself on Dr. Rodriguez's sofa, bracing myself for the question I know she's about to ask.

"You've come a long way since we started these sessions," she says, leaning forward in her comfortably padded chair.

"I like to think so," I agree. "Although some days, I wonder."

"You have," she repeats firmly. "But encountering Tyler isn't something you were prepared for, and now he's not only in your class but also doing a group project with you. How does it feel to see him again?"

"Not good." The words fall automatically from my lips, and then I pause and think the rest of my answer through more carefully. "It's like I reached this point where everything was stable. I know I still have issues with anxiety and panic attacks sometimes, but it's manageable. I was in a routine. It was comfortable."

Her expression is understanding without being sympathetic. I like that. I hate being pitied.

I take my pen from my pocket and begin doodling on the notepad. By trial and error, we discovered that doodling helps distract part of my mind so that it's easier for me to talk about things I otherwise have a difficult time opening up about.

"Now, everything is on edge. I feel like I'm waiting for the other shoe to drop. It's making me more prone to over-reacting."

"That's understandable, given your history." She smiles and adjusts her silky black hair.

Dr. Rodriguez likely isn't long out of college, but she's already become a role model for me. She seems so put together, but not in a way that makes her unapproachable. She's kind and warm-hearted. I hope that one day I'll be able to help others as well as she helps me.

"What are you doing to manage the increased anxiety?" she asks.

My hand continues moving, and I give myself permission not to notice whatever it's drawing.

"I've been meditating in the morning, and I've ramped up the intensity of my evening runs," I tell her.

I'm not a particularly athletic person, but once Dr. Rodriguez explained to me how physical activity can help complete the stress cycle—based on a theory about how positive stress developed evolutionarily to help humans escape danger—I tested it out and was surprised to find it actually helped me sleep better at night.

"That's very good, Echo. Do you foresee Tyler becoming part of your life again?"

I increase the pressure of the pen on the paper, glancing down at the rendering of two men facing off on a muddy lawn that's gradually coming to life.

I can't give a yes or no answer.

"I don't want him to," I say. "Or at least, I don't want to

want him to, if you know what I mean. I'm angry at him because he keeps pushing my boundaries, but every time I see him, part of me comes alive. I wish I could just hate him and be done with it. I don't want to see him, but when I do...ugh."

Dr. Rodriguez hesitates, and it's enough to make me look up from the paper again. I've learned to read her body language, and her brief hesitations usually precede a statement of question that she knows might make me uncomfortable, or that I might find triggering.

"Are you sure the reason you're so resistant to spending time with him isn't simply because he reminds you of a difficult period of your life that you'd prefer not to revisit rather than anything he specifically did?" she asks gently.

I swallow my immediate reaction because she has a valid point, and she knows it. Yes, Tyler hurt me. He broke my heart. But most people manage to see their exes without needing to book emergency appointments with their therapist.

"Maybe," I allow. "Although he did do some shitty things. But whatever my reasons, I should have a choice about who I let into my life, and he's trying to take that away from me."

She nods. "It's good to assert your boundaries, and to defend them when necessary."

It's taken me a long time for that message to sink in. For a while after The Incident, my mom spent every minute of every day with me—even sleeping in my bed—and while it was comforting, it was also overwhelming. I didn't feel like I could ask her to stop though, because I'd feel guilty for causing her any additional distress.

"Are you interested in hearing what Tyler has to say?" she asks when I don't respond.

"No." It's a lie. I'm curious, but protecting myself is more important than a little curiosity.

She tilts her head, her dark eyes seeing more than I want her to. "It might be helpful to get closure."

"Or it could set me back," I counter.

She clearly doesn't agree, but she doesn't push me on the matter. She fills her water glass from a jug on the coffee table beside her chair.

"Water?" she asks.

"No, thank you."

She takes a sip, places the glass down, and clasps her hands on her lap. "I need to ask you something that might be upsetting. Is that okay?"

My hand continues to fly across the notepad, taking on a frantic edge. "Yes."

She glances at my bag, probably wondering if I have my anxiety medication in there in case I panic. Although I'm sure she has some in one of her cupboards too.

"Is his presence bringing up memories of the assault?" Her tone is gentle. "And the trauma that followed?"

I snort. Trauma.

In some ways, it's such an inadequate word for what I went through following The Incident. The rejection. The name-calling. The way everyone turned against me the instant I accused one of their golden boys of rape.

They said I was a liar.

A slut.

An attention whore.

They spat at me, threw insults like knives, and ostracized me completely.

I had to finish my senior year listening to recorded classes in a small, isolated room near the principal's office. As if I had the mental capacity to learn without being able to ask a teacher questions when it was all my overwhelmed mind could do to get me through each day.

I was lucky the school hadn't kicked me out, but I supposed that expelling an alleged rape victim wouldn't have been a good look for them. Especially not after the jury passed a guilty verdict. Although even then, a large portion of the community seemed to believe the jury had gotten it wrong.

"Echo?" Dr. Rodriguez prompts.

I drew in a slow breath and exhaled to the count of six—long enough to ease the constriction in my chest.

"Yes," I reply. "It's brought up some old memories."

"What, specifically?"

I consider this. The memories are never buried deep. They're always right there, beneath the surface, which makes it difficult to pinpoint any changes.

"Honestly, not the parts you might expect."

She cocks her head. "Go on."

I sigh. "It just makes me think about how nice it would have been to have a support system. Someone who believed me and stood by my side. I had Mom, but that was all, and no matter how hard she tried, sometimes it wasn't enough. I was so alone."

I'd survived The Incident on my own. At first, I'd fought as hard as I could. When I'd been injured and overpowered, I'd closed my eyes and prayed for someone to save me. I'd imagined Tyler showing up at the last moment like some kind of white knight, but it hadn't happened.

No one had come. But I'd gotten through it anyway. Surely it shouldn't have been too much to ask for someone other than my own mother and our attorney to stand by me in the aftermath.

Dr. Rodriguez glances at her voice recorder, which she chooses to use rather than writing notes while we talk because she thinks it makes the conversations flow more naturally. I appreciate that. I'd feel too much like a science experiment if she was scrawling notes. As if she was weighing and judging everything I said.

"So, it's not the assault itself, or even the breakup that's on your mind?" she clarified.

I shrug. "I mean, that's there too. It always is. But it's not the main issue in my head at the moment."

"So, how can we ensure you have a support system in place now?" she asks. "How can we limit how often you feel alone and abandoned?"

I bite my lip. Dr. Rodriguez knows I haven't told my friends what happened, and she's said more than once that she thinks it would be good for me to share, but I haven't done it. Three years into a friendship feels a little too late to be dropping bombshells like, 'Oh yeah, by the way, I was raped in my senior year.'

"I have Mom," I say hesitantly.

I don't like to lean on her though. She had a difficult time with separation anxiety after The Incident and it took over two years and a lot of therapy on both our parts before she'd agree to stop calling me every morning and every evening. Now, we talk two or three times a week. That's closer to what most people would consider normal.

"And...?"

I picture each of my friends in turn. Anita has shown that she's willing to coddle me, but her overprotectiveness reminds me too much of my mom. Cassie—as much as I love her—is too self-centered to devote much time or emotional energy to anyone else.

"Ryan," I decide. "If I need support, I'll call Ryan."

"And you'll explain why?" she asks.

"If it's necessary."

She arches an eyebrow, obviously doubtful.

"I promise," I add. "I value my mental health."

"Good. We'll set a few things for you to work on before our next appointment, but before we do that, I'm giving you advance warning that next time we see each other, I'll be asking you whether there's anything you want from Tyler. Okay?"

I tear off the page I've been doodling on and scrunch it up. "Okay."

I don't want to want anything from Tyler, but I know she's right to advise me to think about it.

We agree on a few tasks for me to complete prior to our upcoming appointment and then I leave through the back exit, which opens onto the parking lot.

The sun shines overhead, but it doesn't warm me. My fingers have been cold ever since Dr. Rodriguez asked me about Tyler, and now that my nerves are scraped so raw, the chill is settling into my chest.

I scan the lot, trying to recall where I parked, and freeze.

Standing beside my battered Ford is Tyler Kinsey.

TYLER

I straighten and put my hands in my pockets when Echo appears, framed by the exit. She stares straight at me for a long moment, and I wonder whether she's thinking about running. In the end, she must decide it would be too inconvenient because she approaches warily.

As she draws nearer, I notice that her eyes are rimmed with red, and slightly puffy. Her cheeks are blotchy and the tip of her nose is pink. My heart grows heavy. She's been crying.

"What are you doing here?" she demands, holding her chin high even though her lower lip is wobbling.

If I was a better person, perhaps I'd leave. But I never claimed to be anything other than an asshole.

"Waiting for you," I admit.

She thrusts her shoulders back, but it's clearly just for show. I ache to pull her into my arms and hug the shit out of her, but stealing an embrace is a line I won't cross. Not from someone who's already had too much taken from her.

"Can you move away from my car?" she asks.

I glance at the Ford and scowl. It's a real crap heap. If I had my way, I'd drive her to the dealership and buy her a shiny new BMW right now, but she wouldn't accept that from anyone, let alone me.

"I'm glad you're getting therapy," I say.

Something haunted flickers in her gaze. She folds her arms over her chest defensively. "How do you know that's what I'm here for?"

I gesture at the sign above the clinic, which proclaims it to be a Mental Wellbeing Clinic. "Educated guess. Does it help?"

She clutches her arms tighter around herself. "What would help is if you'd stop following me."

"I can't." It's a weakness. Maybe it makes me a bad person, but I can't let her go.

Going without speaking to her for three years was hell. Sure, I kept tabs on her, but it isn't the same. I can't go back to that.

It must be the wrong thing to say because she unravels her arms and puts her hands on her hips, her puffy eyes narrowing. Suddenly, she's nothing like a cornered mouse. She has teeth and claws, and looks ready to rip my throat out.

"Yes, you fucking can." She takes a step forward and rolls her shoulders. "It's as easy as dropping a class you have no purpose for and living your goddamn life instead of trailing me around like some kind of stalker."

I press my lips together. If she knew how much I'd involved myself in her life over the past three years, she'd probably try to run me over. Death by rusty Ford.

"Don't you give me that look," she snaps, and then she does something I never saw coming. She plants her hands on my chest and shoves with all her might.

I don't budge. As someone who's spent years getting knocked around on the ice—and at home—it takes more than a ninety-pound woman to move me. She growls in the back of her throat and tries again. I fall back a step because that seems to be what she wants. My back hits the car as she advances.

"Why are you here?"

The absolute bewilderment in her voice stuns me. How can she not know?

"For you," I tell her. "I want you back. I've always wanted you, but I screwed up."

"Lies." The gold flecks in her eyes flare. "What kind of twisted game are you playing?"

"No games." I place my palms against the panel of the car door, so she knows I have no intention of pushing her back. "I missed you. I want you in my life."

The words aren't enough. They never are, but I don't know how to do better. I'm a hockey player, not a poet.

"You *are* my life," I tell her.

She shakes her head. "As if I could ever believe that. Our whole relationship was a setup. A scam."

"It wasn't." And I hate that I made her doubt us. "Just please hear me out."

Another flash of gold in her eyes. So beautiful. Far more precious than money, or the fame and recognition my father craved.

"I don't think so."

My desperation growing, I glance over her shoulder at the Mental Wellbeing Clinic.

"Would your therapist say you should listen to me?" I ask.

She exhales through her teeth, visibly fighting the urge to take a swing at me. "I don't give a shit what anyone else thinks is best for me," she growls. "It's my decision."

"But what if I could help with—"

She laughs bitterly and turns away, running her hand through her hair.

"I don't need your help," she says tiredly. "I'm managing just fine on my own. Last time you and your hockey buddies messed with me, I spent the following year self-medicating with alcohol to numb myself, and though I'm recovering, I still can't stand men touching me."

I wince, suddenly glad she's looking away. There's no way I could meet her gaze right now.

She chokes back tears. "Does it make you happy to know I haven't had sex since the rape?"

The bottom drops out of my stomach. I always thought I'd be glad to discover she hadn't created new memories with someone else, but this isn't how I wanted it to be.

She spins toward me, her eyes wild. "They all claimed I made it up, even after he was locked away. I guess I really went the whole hog, huh? It takes a lot of dedication to give up sex for years just to sell a lie."

I drop to my knees, barely noticing the pain as my kneecaps hit the pavement. Her anguish is like a stake through my heart. I drop my eyes to the ground as guilt swamps me.

Guilt for what my so-called friends did to her.

Guilt for what *I* did to her.

"I'm sorry." My voice is thick with emotion. "I believe you. I did then, and I do now."

She scoffs. "Then why didn't you do something about it?"

She pushes past me, and I let her. She unlocks the car door, gets inside, and starts the engine. I scramble out of the way as she backs out of the parking spot and drives away, leaving me to fall apart on my own.

I guess that's karma.

11

ECHO

I'm sprawled on my bed, my head propped on one hand as I work through our assigned reading for Social Psychology when there's a knock on the door. Frowning, I check the time.

Martina wouldn't be knocking, and Anita is in class right now. Cassie would breeze right inside, not even realizing she might be disturbing someone, and Ryan rarely visits my dorm. So who is it?

Perhaps one of Martina's admirers. Honestly, I'm just glad she rarely brings them back here. I don't know where they go instead, but I appreciate her thoughtfulness. I don't like having men in my space.

I get up and cautiously approach the door. I look through the peephole. It's a guy I don't recognize. I open the door, but not widely. No need to make him think he's welcome to linger.

The guy is probably a couple of years younger than me, with enormous muscles and a baby face that's at odds with the rest of him. He's carrying a cardboard box that's been sealed with thick tape.

"This is for you." He tries to hand me the box. When I don't take it, he awkwardly hovers there with his arms outstretched.

"I think you've got the wrong room," I tell him.

He draws back and glances at the number on the door. "I'm pretty sure this is the right one. Are you Echo?"

"Yes." I narrow the opening between the door and the frame, my anxiety growing. What is this about?

He looks relieved. "I thought so. He said you'd be the petite brunette, and that the curvy blonde is your roommate."

Lead lines my stomach. "Who is 'he'?"

I have a sinking feeling I know the answer.

"Oh." His cheeks turn pink. "Um. Yep. He said if you asked that, to say he was your fairy godmother. Could you just take this please?"

"No. I don't think I will."

His face falls. "I promise it's something good."

"Like what?"

He doesn't answer, leading me to believe he doesn't actually have any idea what's inside the box.

"Do me a favor, Echo?" His tone has become pleading. "If you don't take it, he won't put in a good word for me with Coach."

I'm tempted to ask why that's my problem, but I don't have the heart to upset this guy. He reminds me too much of a golden retriever. I stare at the box, as if glaring hard enough might give me x-ray vision to see what lies inside.

"Pretty, pretty please?" he begs.

"Fine," I huff. "Give it here."

If worst comes to worst, I can toss whatever is inside in the dumpster out back, or add it to the growing collection of things I need to rehome thanks to Tyler.

He passes it off quickly, no doubt in case I have second thoughts. "You're the best. I owe you."

"Uh-huh." I shut the door in his face and lock it, then I carry the box, which is heavier than I expected, to my bed. I find a pair of scissors at my desk and slice open the tape on top of the box. I pull the cardboard apart and peer inside.

All I see is bubble wrap. It's oddly disappointing.

I remove the bubble wrap. Beneath it, the box is filled with pale green packing peanuts—the biodegradable type. I'm somewhat nervous to reach inside. I'm not sure what I think is in there. The possibility of a snake hiding within crosses my mind, but even I know that's ridiculous.

I'm being paranoid. I'm sure this is another weird attempt at romancing me. Or perhaps a guilt gift. Or...I don't even know what.

Irritated with myself for delaying, I empty the box upside down onto my bed. I shriek as several colorful silicon items and two boxes land in a pile in the center, the packing peanuts scattering around them.

Oh, lord. They're sex toys.

What the ever-loving hell?

I pick up the largest one, which is inside a bright purple box. According to the label, it's a vibrating dildo made of soft silicon, with a built-in warmer to make it feel like a real cock.

I blink at it stupidly, wondering what the fuck is happening.

Moving on autopilot, I set the box aside and reach for what looks to be a tiny pink vibe. I push the button and it buzzes to life. Disturbed, I toss it on the bed, where it wriggles across the coverlet and falls onto the floor.

Why am I gazing at a collection of sex toys that would make a porn star proud? Just why?

Deciding to do a quick inventory, I clear the packing

peanuts away and study what remains. There are two small vibrators, the impressively purple dildo, and several toys I don't recognize, but the accompanying information proclaims them to be for external stimulation only.

Then, to top things off, there's a bottle of ginger-scented massage oil, a candle that smells of strawberries, and a miniature bottle of sparkling wine, along with a note to chill before drinking.

I don't understand.

That's when I spot the letter.

It's fallen off to the side, the corner of the envelope just visible beneath my pillow. I tear it open and pull out the cream card within. The letter is short, and to the point.

Echo,

From the depths of my heart, you will never know how sorry I am. There are a hundred things I could apologize for, but after the weekend, I know of one more.

It's a tragedy that you've been robbed of your ability to get pleasure from sex. I can't go back in time and protect you, or make different decisions, but I hope these might help in some way.

Tyler XO

There's a phone number scrawled beneath his name. I grab my phone and call it. He answers immediately.

"Kinsey."

"This is not okay," I tell him. "You'd already crossed a line, but now you're stomping all over it. This is way too personal. My sex life is none of your business."

He's quiet for a long moment, and then says, "Like it or not, I care about you. You don't ever have to speak to me again if you don't want to—although I hope you will, and I'm not giving up—but you should try them out. You deserve to feel good."

I gape. I honestly have no idea how to respond to that. In

a way, it's sweet. But he's also way overstepping and butting in somewhere he's not welcome.

"When was the last time you came?" he asks.

My jaw drops. "Excuse me?"

"You heard me." His tone is gentle, but he isn't backing down.

"I'm not answering that."

Years. It's been years.

To add insult to injury, the last time I orgasmed was with him inside me. After our breakup, I was too upset to be interested in sex, and then The Incident damaged something in me.

"I'm guessing way too long." He doesn't seem daunted by my refusal to cooperate.

I clench the phone, my breath growing erratic. Why can't I hang up on him? It should be easy. All I need to do is press one button and then block him. But for some reason, I can't bring myself to do it.

"Shut up," I say weakly.

"Mm. I thought so. I suggest you light the candle, get comfortable, and try out the least threatening thing in that box. Maybe the clit stimulator."

I flush. It's a good thing he can't see me because I must be ten different shades of red. How can he talk so calmly about women's sex toys?

I recall his comment about not having been with anyone since me. Yeah, right. He's way too calm and seems too familiar with these toys to have had such a long dry spell.

"Just try it, baby," he urges. "Light that candle. I know how you love strawberries."

To my absolute amazement, I'm tempted. I remember how good he used to make me feel, and based on how my body has been responding to him recently—despite my best efforts to pretend he doesn't exist—the chemistry between us is still alive and well.

But I can't, can I?

It isn't right. He *hurt* me.

Besides, I haven't orgasmed since high school, so what makes him think I'll be able to do it now?

I end the call.

I sit on the bed and stare blankly at the sex toys, my mind firing at a million miles an hour. I set my phone aside, ignoring it when it starts to ring.

I hate to admit it, but Tyler has a point.

I *deserve* to feel good.

Eric Weston stole something from me. He's serving time for his crime, but by refusing to even try to reclaim my ability to experience sexual pleasure, I'm allowing him to continue to steal from me.

The only person that hurts is me.

But I've tried before, and I wasn't able to get out of my head enough to get turned on.

I can't do it alone. But perhaps I don't have to.

Experience has taught me not to trust Tyler, but however badly he may have screwed me over, he was gentle with me when we were intimate.

Not to mention the fact that he knows what happened to me. If I can't shut my mind off properly by myself, then I need to involve someone else. The last thing I want is to have to explain to some random guy what I want and why I need to be treated with kid gloves.

Tyler gets it.

With shaking hands, I pick up my phone and redial his number. He answers immediately.

"Are you okay?" he asks. "I'm so sorry, I shouldn't have pushed you. I—"

"I'm willing to try," I whisper, interrupting him. "Tell me

what to do. But if it's too much, you have to stop as soon as I say so."

"I promise," he vowed. "You're in charge. But Echo, are you sure you want this?"

I swallowed to wet my dry throat. "I have to try. I owe myself that much."

"You don't owe anyone anything. Even yourself." His tone warms. "If it gets overwhelming, say 'stop' or 'no.'"

"I will."

"Good. Now light that candle."

I drag in a ragged breath, hoping like hell that I'm not making a terrible mistake in trusting Tyler to guide me through this.

I double check the lock on the door, take the lighter from my handbag—which is well-stocked with mace, a Swiss Army knife, an incredibly loud whistle, and several other items I've taken to carrying around.

I place the candle on the nightstand and flick the lighter above it until the flame transfers to the wick.

"Have you done it?" he asks, his voice rough.

"Yes." I speak softly, as if that somehow makes what I'm doing less real.

"Is your bed clear?"

"Not quite." The toys are still piled in the center.

"Clear it."

I move them to the desk, all except the one he called the clit stimulator, which is a wand-shaped device with a round end that almost looks like a tiny suction cup.

"Now, lie down," he orders. "Head on the pillow. Get comfortable."

I do as he says. Somehow, following his instructions makes it easier to get out of my head.

"Should I turn on the toy?" I ask.

"No. You're not ready for that yet. I just want you to

touch yourself. However it feels good. If you don't want to get naked, then just rest your hand over your pussy. You need to be reminded of how great orgasms are."

I bite my lip. It should feel strange to be doing this with him, but it's surprisingly easy to forget the pain and lies that drove us apart when I can't see his face. His voice in my ear is soft and tempting. Heartbreakingly familiar.

"Stop thinking," he says. "Just feel. Concentrate on me, okay? Don't let those whirling thoughts get the better of you."

Closing my eyes, I rest my hand lightly over my pussy. I'm wearing yoga pants, so it's easy to stroke myself through the soft fabric.

A memory flashes through my mind. Darkness as I cross the empty school parking lot, heading home from an evening tutoring session. A rough hand over my mouth. A hard body pinning me to the concrete no matter how hard I fought. Pain like nothing I'd ever known, and a bone-deep terror that has never quite faded.

I gasp and yank my hand away.

"You can do this," he murmurs. "Don't let him win, Echo."

I grit my teeth. He's right. I can't let that monster take anything else from me.

I release a shaky breath. "Okay."

"Good girl." His tone is approving, and I hate how much I like it.

"Keep talking. Stay with me?" I plead, wondering whether I should kick my own ass for essentially handing him the bloody pulp of my heart and asking him not to destroy it again.

But it's too late. I've made the decision to allow myself to be vulnerable with Tyler, and as Dr. Rodriguez always points out, there are so few people I can be real with.

"I'm not going anywhere." The somberness of his voice tells me it's the truth, and I relax a fraction.

"Tell me what to do." I need to be able to turn off my brain, otherwise this is doomed before it begins.

"I will. I've got you, baby girl."

I open my mouth to protest the term of endearment, but then close it again. I've never been someone who can dissociate sex from emotions, so perhaps it will help me feel safe.

"Is your hand still on your pussy?" he asks.

"No," I admit.

"Then put it there, and I want you to rub over it, nice and slow."

I brush myself and to my surprise, a faint sizzle of lust lights under my skin. I firm my touch slightly and repeat the movement. The sizzle builds as I continue to stroke myself, until there's no denying its existence.

"How does it feel?" he asks.

"All right."

My thighs instinctively part to make more room and I slip my hand beneath the waistband until all that prevents the touch from being skin on skin is the cotton of my panties.

"Just all right?"

"Nice."

For the first time in years, it occurs to me to consider my plain underwear as something other than safe. It's a bit boring. Silk or satin would feel so much nicer against my skin. But I made the decision three years ago not to wear anything too provocative.

Despite the fact I know victim blaming isn't right or healthy, I can't help believing that I should do everything in my power to remain safe—including covering up.

"Stay with me," Tyler says. "Let's see if we can do better than 'nice'. Did you see the lube that came with the dildo?"

My face flames. "Um, yes."

"Do you think you're ready to touch yourself with nothing in between?"

I weigh the question, refusing to answer impulsively. I don't want to spiral into a panic attack and have Martina catch me hyperventilating over a pile of sex toys.

"I think so," I reply. It will push my limits, but perhaps that isn't a bad thing.

"No pressure if you aren't," he says. "There's absolutely no rush. I can call to talk you through however much you're comfortable with every day until you do get there, if that's what you want."

His patience eases my nerves.

"No," I say more firmly. "I can do this."

He hums his understanding. "Then, if you're sure, I'd like you to squirt some lube onto your fingers and use it to get your pussy nice and slick."

I stiffen. "I'm not putting anything up there."

Not today. Honestly, I don't know if I'll ever be ready for that.

"I won't ask you to," he assures me. "Trust me."

Yeah, because that's gone so well in the past.

"I promise." Emotion is embedded in his every word. "I will not let you down this time, baby. I'd rather carve out my heart than hurt you again."

I blow out all the air that's built up in my lungs and do my best to let the tension go. I don't trust Tyler. Not completely. But I believe he means what he's saying.

I get up and find the lube, then open it and squirt a blob onto my fingers. I return to the bed, lie down, and use my free hand to shimmy my yoga pants down to my thighs. With a few deft motions, I spread the lube on my pussy, which is still dry even though I'm a little turned on.

"Are you with me?"

"Yes," I whisper.

"I want you to rub one of your fingers down the center of your pussy. Don't go further than you're comfortable with. Once you've done that, circle your clit, but don't touch it. Got it?"

"Mmhmm."

I dip one slick finger into the heat of my pussy, but stop as I draw close to my entrance. I'm not ready for anything to touch me there. Then I head back to the safer area at the top, where I trace that same finger in gentle circles around my clit. A zap of heat shoots through my lower body and I whimper.

God, it's been so long since I let myself even think about sex that I'd forgotten how addictive that slow build of desire could be.

"I bet you look so pretty." Tyler's voice is tight. "Pink cheeks, bright eyes. That perfect little pussy."

My teeth sink into my lower lip. The way he sounds, I can almost believe that he truly wants me as desperately as he claims. A thrill of power zings through me. After years of feeling powerless, it's incredible to have him in the palm of my hand—metaphorically speaking.

"You have no idea how many times I've gotten myself off to memories of you," he adds. "I know it's wrong, but nothing else feels right. I don't want to see anyone else, or even imagine a stranger. I'm yours, Echo. Every fucked-up part of me."

I don't reply. I don't know how to.

Instead, I continue the gentle circles, my hips arching in an attempt to get more. More friction, more pressure, more of the heat pooling low in my belly.

"Turn on the toy, baby," he rasps.

I reach for the clit stimulator and start it up. The device

buzzes to life. I touch the tip of one of my fingers to the end and giggle at the vibration.

"Fuck, I love your laugh. It's been too long since I heard it."

I close my eyes, wondering when I relaxed enough to let my guard down with Tyler listening. For a second, I try half-heartedly to reinforce those walls, but I don't have the motivation to do so. Not when this feels like progress.

"Do I use it now?" I ask quietly.

"If you want to. If your clit is throbbing and needs attention." He sounds wrecked.

"Tyler..."

"What, baby?"

"Nothing." My cheeks blaze hotter.

"Tell me," he orders.

"Are you...touching yourself too?" The question makes me want to vanish in a puff of smoke, I'm so embarrassed. But I need to know.

"No, my sweet shooting star." His tone has softened, but it's still ragged. "This is just for you."

"Okay." For some reason, I like that. All of his focus is on me. He's not getting off on this weird interlude. He's here for me.

I touch the wand to my pussy and jerk as pleasure zaps along every nerve in my body.

"Oh, my God," I cry, torn between pressing it closer and pulling it away.

"Beautiful. Take what you need. I'm right here."

I roll my hips, a shudder tearing through me as every-thing inside me knots tighter. "It's good."

"Yeah, it is. You're fucking perfect. Don't stop."

I roll my hips again, whimpering at the burst of sensa-tion. My head falls back and my lips part.

This is it. I'm going to come.

For the first time in more than three years, I'm going to prove to myself that I'm not broken.

"Keep it up, baby," he growls. "Don't you dare fucking stop. Fuck, I wish I could feel you clench around me."

His words send me flying into space. I stiffen, then jerk as wave after wave of pleasure crashes over me, carrying me away on a tsunami of sensation. I gasp and whimper, clinging to the orgasm for as long as I can. But as I fall apart, all I can think is...

This is the boy I fell for.

I come back to earth with a crash.

No, he's not. The boy I fell for didn't exist. He was a figment of my imagination created by a cruel person who enjoyed toying with my emotions.

"Oh, no," I whisper.

"Are you okay?"

If I didn't know better, I'd think he was legitimately concerned.

Maybe he is.

Maybe everything he's said since he reappeared in my life is true. But I can't think about that now. Not with all of the hormones coursing through my body courtesy of my first orgasm since our breakup.

I need distance. Perspective.

"Um, thank you." I sound as awkward as I feel. "I have to go. There's someone knocking on my door."

"Right." His disappointment is clear, as is the fact he knows I'm lying.

"I appreciate you, uh—"

"You're welcome," he says briskly. "I hope it helped. If you want support while you try anything else from the box, remember that I meant what I said. You can call me any time."

"Thank you," I repeat.

If I know what's good for me, I'll block his number as soon as we end the call. Somehow though, I don't see that happening.

"By the way, the dildo is the same size as my cock—or at least as close as I could find—so I know you can take it. That is, if it's something you'd like to work up to."

My jaw drops, but before I can respond, the line cuts out. He's hung up.

12

———

THE PAST

TYLER

Anticipation thrums in the enclosed cab of my Chevy. I glance toward the hotel's entrance. As soon as we pass through those doors, our relationship will change.

"Are you sure you want to do this?" I ask Echo, who's sitting beside me.

She turns toward me and smiles, her hazel eyes heartbreakingly trusting. When she looks at me this way, I'd do anything to not let her down.

"We've been dating for a while now." She reaches across the space between us and takes my hand. "I'm ready for the next step with you."

I hope she means it. I've never worried about sex before, but when it comes to her, I'm terrified of screwing up and making it so that she never wants to touch me again. Echo isn't like the other girls I've been with. Our relationship is more than the casual fun I've shared with my former hookups. I just pray she realizes that.

I squeeze her hand. "I wish I could give you my first time."

Her smile softens. "I don't need to be your first."

She nibbles her lower lip to bite back the rest of her thought, but I can read it on her face anyway. She may not be my first, but she hopes she's my last.

I want that, too.

"I don't deserve you," I whisper, and run my hand over my hair. God, I'm a mess. "I always made fun of my friends if they said they wanted to hold out for something special, but now I regret not doing the same."

"Hey." Echo leans over and kisses me. Our lips touch and linger, but the kiss remains chaste. "Tonight will be special because it's our first time. No one else matters, okay?"

I nod, not trusting myself to speak. My heart is hammering, and emotion clogs my throat.

"You're important to me," I tell her. "I feel like shit for not dating you publicly."

I want to. I'd like to announce to everyone at school that she's mine and be able to kiss her when I see her in the corridors, but the news would get back to Dad at lightning speed and his retaliation would be brutal.

If I knew for sure he'd only take his anger out on me, then perhaps I'd risk it, but I don't want to put Mom or Soraya—or even Echo herself—in the line of fire.

Her expression is kinder than I deserve. "I understand. I might get frustrated sometimes, but I know why it has to be this way."

Her tolerance only makes me feel worse. I wish she'd rail against me and tell me off for treating her like a dirty secret, but instead, she rewards my cowardly denial of our relationship with never-ending empathy.

Echo Dean is one-hundred percent a better person than me. If she'd put me in the same position, I can't be sure I wouldn't do something to force her to admit the truth.

"You're sure?" I ask again.

She rolls her eyes. "Come on, Ty. Let's go."

She gets out of the car, slings her bag over her shoulder, and I meet her beside the flatbed. We walk side by side toward the hotel, our hands brushing, but I don't wrap my arm around her the way I'd like to.

Coward.

The glass doors slide open as we approach and we step inside and stop in front of the desk, which is only a few feet from the doors. I guide Echo partially behind me, so the clerk won't get a good look at her.

"Do you have a booking?" the clerk asked, their tone bored.

I hide my smirk. He's barely paying attention. Good.

"Yes. For Johnson."

He pulls out a book, flips through the pages, and makes a note. "Got it. You prepaid so no need to worry about that." He opens a drawer and digs around, eventually emerging with a wooden keyring that had the number 102 stamped onto the side. He passed it to me. "You're room 102. Down the hall to the left."

"Thanks."

I palm the key and cross the foyer, heading to the left and keeping myself between the clerk and Echo as much as possible. Hockey is big in Charlesville, so I'm reasonably confident he probably recognized me—even if he didn't call me out on using a fake name. It's less likely he knows who Echo is, and I'd like to keep it that way.

We're silent as we walk to room 102. I stop outside and unlock the door, wondering briefly if the hotel owner knows how out-of-date it is to have actual keys rather than key cards. I reach inside and switch on the light. Echo brushes past me, smelling deliciously of strawberries, and dumps her bag beside the bed.

I look around, taking stock of the place. It's a little clinical, with white walls, a white bedspread, and gray carpet. I suppose at least the white bedspread isn't stained. The pillows and sheets are also white. If the light weren't so dim, I might feel the urge to put on sunglasses to protect my eyes from the glare.

The bedroom isn't the reason I booked this room though —although the fact the bed is king-sized doesn't hurt. No, the thing that tempted me to bring Echo here for our first time is through the door to our right.

I open the door to show Echo, and she gasps with delight. In the back corner of the bathroom is a massive spa bath with heaps of buttons and dials.

"I thought you might like that," I say.

She flies into my arms and kisses me. "I love it. We don't have a bath at home. Can we use it?"

"Absolutely." I reach into my pocket and pull out the travel-sized container of bubble bath I slipped in there earlier. "I even brought this."

She beams, the gold flecks in her eyes shining happily. "You are the best."

My chest tightens. Sometimes I wish it were more diffi-cult to please her. It makes me feel like an ass that she takes so much joy in little things when there are so many big things I'm not giving her.

I want to do more than take from her, but the situation makes it challenging to give back the way I should.

I kiss her, then step away to start the bathtub filling. It takes a few minutes, but I figure out how to start the jets and turn on the underwater lights, which flash purple and blue. I empty the bubble bath into the water bit by bit, waiting a little after each addition to make sure the bubbles don't go crazy and flood the room.

The last thing I need is to cause a scene.

Nearer to the doorway, Echo strips off her sweater to

reveal a low cut short-sleeved blouse beneath. It isn't designer, but it looks good on her, showing off the slight swell of her breasts and emphasizing the slimness of her waist.

"You're beautiful," I tell her.

She blushes. "You haven't even seen all of me yet."

"But I know you're beautiful anyway." She could be scarred from head to toe and she'd be the most stunning person I've ever laid eyes on. Her beauty is on the inside, and it shines brightly from every part of her.

I turn off the taps as the water nears the top. A floral scent fills the air, pleasant but not overwhelming.

I remove my sweater and my T-shirt in one go, baring my torso. Her quick intake of breath is gratifying. She's never seen me shirtless before. Our stolen encounters haven't been anywhere safe enough to start undressing, other than the night we watched the meteor shower, and it was too soon then. I didn't want to push her.

"Your muscles have muscles," she says. "That's not a six-pack. That's a twelve-pack."

I grin and tighten my abs, her praise going straight to my head. I know I'm good looking. Girls fall all over me, and I have to keep my body in tip-top shape for hockey. But their admiration is only surface level, whereas Echo's goes deeper. She isn't here because of who I am or how I look. She's here for me.

That said, it's still nice to know she likes what she sees.

"Your turn," I tell her.

Shyly, she grabs the hem of her blouse and pulls it over her head, revealing inch after inch of smooth, pale skin. My mouth goes dry as she tosses her blouse aside. She's wearing a black bra that barely covers her nipples and is fringed with lace. It holds her sexy little tits up as if presenting them to me.

"Fuck," I rasp out.

She trails one of her fingers across the top. "Do you like it?"

"I fucking love it, but if I touch you right now, we won't be getting into the tub."

Her smile becomes cheeky. "What a shame that would be." She gestures at my jeans. "Your turn."

I kick off my shoes and shed my jeans so fast that I almost trip over. I laugh. If I was with anyone else, I'd be embarrassed by how eager I seem, but Echo would never judge me for being myself.

Her gaze is locked on me, traveling down my legs, past my muscular hockey player thighs to my calves and my feet, then back up again. It settles on the bulge behind my underwear. I'm hard as hell, but I'm unsure if taking off my underwear without any warning might make her nervous.

With far more care than me, Echo removes her shoes and jeans. I gulp, my throat working furiously. Fuck me. Her panties are black and fringed with lace, matching her bra. I've never seen anything so goddamn sexy.

"You look like a dream." A wonderful one that I hope I never wake up from.

She smiles bashfully and pinches the sides of her underwear between her fingers.

"At the same time?" she asks.

I nod and mimic her position. Slowly, we each draw our underwear down. Her pussy is neatly shaved—or perhaps waxed—and is delicate enough I could put my mouth over her without any trouble at all. It's pink and welcoming.

I tear my gaze away just in time to see her unhook her bra and drop it to the bathroom floor. Her tits are small and perky, her nipples already peaked. I wonder if I can make them harder if I suck on them...

No, don't go there. Not until after the bath.

"Like I said: beautiful." I maintain eye contact, so she knows I'm speaking the truth. "So damn gorgeous."

Her blush deepens. "You're very sexy too."

The words are quiet, whether from embarrassment or nerves, I'm not sure. My cock doesn't care. It stands at attention, ready for whatever comes next. I ignore the demanding thing and try to keep my wits about me.

"Bath." I sling one of my legs over the edge and into the water, wincing at the heat. "Be careful. It's hot."

I climb in, gritting my teeth until my body grows accustomed to the temperature. Echo dips her finger into the water, makes a face, and props herself on the edge. I lean against the back and close my eyes. We stay that way until the water has cooled enough for Echo's liking.

She slips beneath the water and onto my lap. I wrap my arms around her waist and nuzzle the back of her neck. She reaches up and releases her hair from its tie. The tips dangle in the water and the movement wafts a soft, sweet scent toward me.

Her body is stiff, so I smooth my hands along her sides.

"Relax against me," I murmur. "Let go. I can handle your weight."

Slowly, the tension eases from her and she leans against me, her head resting on my shoulder. Her ass is pressed against my cock, so she must know exactly how she's affecting me, but neither of us mention it.

Holding her like this is so nice that it's easy to ignore my hard-on. She belongs in my arms. I never want to let her go.

I dread the day I'll have to.

13

———

THE PAST

TYLER

"This is nice," Echo says, oblivious to the dark turn my thoughts have taken. "I'm sure there's a better word for it, but I can't think what it is. I just feel so peaceful, and I love being so close to you."

"It's pretty great," I agree, trying to put my fear of losing her to the back of my mind. I can't let it encroach on our time together.

"The jets are a bit much though," she adds.

"Yeah." Fumbling around the spa controls, I turn them off. "They're a good idea, but not very relaxing in reality."

Without the buzz of the jets, the bathroom is much quieter. If I were alone, I might consider it too quiet, but with Echo here, it can't be anything other than perfect.

"Do you want to get clean?" she asks, glancing at the bar of soap just out of reach.

"I'll wash you." I longed to explore all of her, and what better way to do it? First, I'd learn her with my hands, and then I'd dry her and retrace the same path with my tongue.

I strain for the soap, but Echo straightens for a moment

to grab it and hand it to me. Fortunately, she seems content to return to her position against my chest, and I soak in the sensation briefly before lathering the soap.

I soap her chest, cupping each of her breasts and thumbing her nipples, then I clean her arms before journeying down to her belly and hips. I skirt around her pussy, and she helps me wash her slim thighs and calves.

I massage the suds into her back, using my thumbs to dig into the small knots on the inside of her shoulder blades. She groans and becomes boneless against me.

My cock throbs, and I want nothing more than to slide it between the globes of her ass, but I resist the urge. Instead, I slip my fingers over her pussy and stroke. She lets out a stuttered breath and rocks into my touch.

"No." Her eyes are unfocused as she pushes my hand away. "It's my turn to wash you."

She shimmies around in the tub, splashing water over the rim, until she's straddling my thighs. I grit my teeth, doing my best to pretend the heat of her pussy isn't nestled over my eager cock.

She takes the soap from me, rubs it between her palms, and follows the same path I did, washing my chest, then my arms, before venturing lower. Her fingertips brush my cock as they pass it by, and I groan at the feather-light tease. Her eyes widen and then turn sly.

Taking far more time than necessary, she cleans my thighs, my calves, shins, and even my feet, ignoring me when I squirm. I've always been ticklish, but thankfully, very few people know it.

Finally, after what seems like an eon, she works back up my body and pauses beside my cock. Her hesitation reminds me that this is her first time, and I immediately kick myself for not doing or saying something to put her at ease.

"You can touch it," I assure her huskily. "Or not. Whatever you want. We don't have to go all the way tonight. I'm just happy you're here with me."

"I want to touch you," she says, and wraps her hand around me.

I'm on a hair trigger when it comes to her, and her gentle grip is almost enough to send me over the edge. I grab her hips, struggling to get myself under control, but she doesn't seem to give a shit about that. She slides her hand to the end of my cock and runs the pad of her thumb over the weeping slit.

"Feels too good," I warn.

She glances up at me, her eyes twinkling with mischief and desire. "I don't think there's such a thing as *too good*."

"Trust me, there is."

She strokes me again, this time a little more firmly. My hips jerk instinctively, aching to thrust my cock into her hand again and again until I come all over her. But I manage to stop them from moving. I don't want to come in her hand. I want to come inside her.

"It's silky," she murmurs, her lower lip caught between her teeth. "I didn't think it would be."

Oh, fuck. Does she realize how much of a fantasy she sounds like right now? So innocent, but so curious. And she's all mine.

For as long as I can hold onto her.

Fear shimmers in the back of mind, an unwelcome guest. Echo won't put up with me hiding our relationship forever. When she gets tired of pretending, will she leave me?

"I think we should take this to bed," she says, and I force myself back to the present.

"You sure?"

She rolls her eyes. "Yes, Ty. I'm sure."

I chuckle. "All right, all right. Just asking."

She gets out first, since she's on top of me, and then extends her hand to help pull me out. I take her slender hand in mine just for the joy of holding it. I don't actually need her help.

We both dry off but stay naked. Our gazes meet, and she smiles shyly.

In the bedroom, she sits on the bed, her feet on the floor, waiting for me to take the lead.

"Lie back," I tell her. "In the middle of the bed."

She does as I ask, her eyes soft and trusting. There's no way I deserve this girl, but I'm not a good enough person to let that stop me from taking her.

I straddle her waist and press a chaste kiss to her lips. "Lie still and enjoy."

Her expression is curious, but she nods.

I bury my face in the side of her neck and breathe her in. The aroma of strawberries and a hint of the floral scent from the bubble bath lingers on her skin.

I kiss her neck, then rub my stubbled cheek against her. She shivers. I pepper kisses down the stretch of soft skin below her ear and across her shoulders, then tease her collarbone with my tongue.

Her breathing becomes shallow, and her hands flex toward me a couple of times, as if she wants to touch me but isn't sure if it's allowed.

I find her gaze. "You can have anything you want."

Her eyes darken with liquid heat, and she runs her fingers through my hair. Unfortunately, it's too short for her to grip properly. Perhaps I should grow it out a little.

I kiss down her abdomen, which is flat but untoned. I rub my face against her there, reveling in the smoothness.

She giggles and pushes me away. "That tickles."

"What about this?" I ask and settle my mouth over her pussy. I consider going easy, but I want to hear her scream, so I use every tool in my arsenal, licking, sucking, and nuzzling until she's a panting mess, barely able to string two words together.

"Does that tickle?" I ask, raising my head. I blow a soft gust of air over her pussy, and she shudders.

"Ty, please."

"Please what?" I ask, determined to drive her crazy.

Her glazed eyes narrow. "Please, more."

Oh, yeah.

I slip my arms beneath her thighs and use them to tilt her toward me, opening her up more as I get back to work. I close my eyes, absorbing each whimper and sigh that falls from her lips. She rocks back and forth, seeking more friction.

That's it, baby. Take what you need.

Her thighs tighten around my head, and I ease off. Much as I'd love to get her off with my mouth, I want our first orgasm together to be with my cock inside her. I pull back and stroke myself a couple of times to ease the ache.

Echo watches my movements, enraptured. "Should I...?"

"Next time." If she puts her mouth on me now, it's all over.

I suck my finger into my mouth, wetting it, and then press it against her entrance. She stiffens for a second.

"Relax, baby girl."

She releases an audible sigh, and her muscles loosen. I slip inside her hot channel, keeping my eyes on her face so I'll know if she needs me to stop.

"Okay?" I ask, losing the battle not to imagine how amazing she'll feel around me.

"Yeah." Her tits move with her breaths, which she's making a visible effort to slow.

Using my thumb, I toy with her clit.

"Oh," she gasps, swaying closer.

I slide another finger inside her and cup my palm around her pussy. She rides it until I'm sure she's ready for me, and then I withdraw my fingers, roll on a condom, and line up my cock.

I push in, inch by inch, giving her time to adjust. Her eyes are locked on mine, the black of her pupils almost swallowing her irises. When I bottom out, her eyelashes flutter and she bites her lip.

"So damn sexy," I growl.

This girl will be the death of me.

"You feel good," she whispers, her tongue darting out to touch her lips. "But I'd really appreciate it if you'd move."

Despite the intensity of the moment, I laugh. "You think you're funny, do you?" I ask.

She grins. "Not funny. Just really turned on."

"Good." I thrust into her with small, gentle motions, gradually increasing the tempo once I'm sure she's comfortable.

I wrap my hands under her hips and angle her so that my pelvis bumps her clit each time we come together. Her head drops back, and she whimpers. Her pussy tightens around me. She isn't coming, but she's close.

Fuck, I'm close too. This first time might not take long. It's a good thing we have all night. My parents think I'm camping with friends, and Echo told her mom she's staying with one of our classmates, so no one is expecting us back.

She spasms around me again, the clench of her body almost making me lose it. I glance away from her for a moment because drinking in the visual of her heaving chest, flushed cheeks, and pouty lips is just too much. I grit my teeth and give her everything I have. She cries out, muttering things like:

"Don't stop."

"Oh, my God."

"It's so good."

"Oh, God. I'm gonna come."

Then, thankfully, she does. Her pussy contracts around me and I snap my gaze back to hers as she moans her release. The rippling silken walls around my cock drag me with her, and I spill into the condom, gasping her name.

After I've caught my breath, I nuzzle her cheek and kiss her forehead.

"That was really fucking good," I say. "How do you feel?"

There's a sleepy, sated smile on her lips.

"As if I want to do it again as soon as I can," she replies.

I wink. "Your wish is my command. Just give me a few minutes to recover."

She smothers a laugh. Being careful not to crush her, I get off her and deal with the condom, then return and flop onto the bed beside her. I wrap my arm around her shoulders, draw her close, and kiss her temple.

"Was it okay?" I huff as soon as I ask the question. I'm not usually needy, but I have to know that I did right by her.

"It was wonderful." She sighs contentedly. "A-plus."

"Thank God." I don't know what I'd do if she answered in the negative.

"By the way." She sits up, and her hair falls around her shoulders in a tangled mess. "I have a gift for you."

My heart leaps. "You do? It's not my birthday."

"I know." She shrugs. "I just saw it and thought of you. Wait here."

She goes to her bag and opens the front pocket, drawing out a small black box. She leans over the bed and passes it to me, then snuggles up to my side.

I take it, choked up. Other than on my birthday, no one ever gives me anything. On the contrary, most people expect something from me since I come from a wealthy family. Echo has so little money, and she wasted some of it on me. How does she believe for even a moment that I'm worthy of her?

"Open it," she urges.

As gently as I can with my rough hands, I open the little box. A pendant is nestled inside. It's made of some kind of black stone and is surprisingly masculine. With trembling fingers, I pick it up and examine the design. It's a stylized moon.

"Why a moon?" I ask.

She leans her head against my shoulder. "You said I'm bright like a shooting star, but you shine too, even if you don't believe it. I wanted something that would remind you of that."

My vision blurs with tears, and I quickly blink them back. I turn and kiss her, my chest so full of emotion, it feels like I might explode. Echo is incredible. Am I really going to risk losing her by being a coward who's afraid to deal with his dad and asshole friends?

"I love it," I tell her, and then, impulsively, I add, "Will you go to prom with me?"

She blinks her big doe eyes at me. "Are you sure you're ready for that? There's no rush."

Yes, there is. If I drag this out too long, she'll get sick of waiting for me, and I wouldn't blame her for it.

"I am," I say firmly, even though my stomach has plummeted to my feet. "And then, afterward, I want to meet your mom—if you're okay with that."

The smile that transforms her face is breathtaking. It makes me feel like a dickhead for not offering her any type of recognition earlier.

She kisses my cheek and slots her hand into my unoccupied one. "I'd like that."

Maybe I can keep my father from finding out. There's no way to avoid my friends discovering the truth, but as long as Dad doesn't, perhaps everything will be all right.

If he does... I'm screwed.

14

———

ECHO

On Monday, we have another group project session, and I arrive at the study room we booked just as Tyler arrives from the opposite direction. The instant I see him, my cheeks burn. It's the first time I've laid eyes on him since he talked me through an orgasm, and I'm not mentally or emotionally prepared to come face to face with him.

My grip tightens on my skinny caramel mocha and I glance at the door to the study room, noting that Jin and Elle are already inside. Hopefully, they won't question my blush. I steal a peek at Tyler, and his devilish grin says he knows exactly where my mind has gone.

But really, how am I supposed to think of anything other than the husky tone of his voice in my ear and the pleasure that zapped through every cell in my body because of him?

I haven't had much interest in sex since The Incident. Or even before that, if I'm honest. Not since Tyler and I broke up. But, somehow, he must have shattered the barrier around my sex drive because I got myself off twice more over the weekend after our phone call.

I don't think I'd be comfortable with another person

131

touching me yet, but I've come much further than I imagined possible.

"Good weekend?" Tyler asks, cocking one of his eyebrows.

"All right," I say weakly. No way am I acknowledging what happened between us or what I did afterward.

Before he can speak again, I push the door open and enter the room. Jin and Elle have claimed seats on the far side of the large desk, leaving us the two seats that are easier to access—and also beside each other. Based on the dirty look she sends me, Elle isn't thrilled about that, but Jin must have talked her into it.

"Hey," I say in greeting.

"Morning, Echo," Jin replies, then glances at Tyler. "Hi."

I hesitate for a couple of seconds before sitting, wondering briefly if I could persuade Elle to swap places with me, but doing so would only make things more awkward. I can handle being beside Tyler for an hour without making a fool of myself by crawling onto his lap.

I pull the chair out and sit, breathing in the mouthwatering aroma of coffee. There's a thermos in front of Jin, and Elle has her hand wrapped around a takeout cup. Tyler is the only one who hasn't brought caffeinated support.

"Great game over the weekend," Elle says to Tyler as he slides into the chair beside me, taking up more space than necessary. He spreads his legs and his knee brushes mine. To my astonishment, he immediately jerks it away.

"Thanks," he replies, barely glancing at her. "We're still in pre-season, but it was a good chance to see how we work together on the ice."

Elle leans forward, her low-cut top slipping further down her chest. "I think you're going to lead the team to the trophy."

I meet Jin's gaze and roll my eyes, refusing to allow

myself to look at Tyler. Jin is about as much of a sports enthusiast as I am—which is to say, not at all, unless the right incentive is there. Honestly, I don't think Elle loves hockey either. She just wants a hockey-playing boyfriend she might be able to latch onto all the way to the NHL.

"I'm not the captain," Tyler says. "I'm not leading the team anywhere."

Elle laughs, as if he's joking, but I know Tyler's various tones well. He's completely serious.

Perhaps I'm judging her too harshly. I hardly know her, and it's not her fault she reminds me of Whitney.

No. Don't go there.

I adjust my position on the uncomfortably hard seat. "Let's go over everything we've already done."

We each report back on our work so far. Surprisingly, everyone seems to be on top of their part of the project, even Elle, who seems more interested in making cow eyes at Tyler than completing our assignment.

Don't be so judgmental, Echo. She doesn't deserve it.

After we're all up to speed, we compile a list of reference books we might need. The room is overly warm from all four of us being crammed into it, and the stuffiness is getting to my head, so I volunteer to track them down.

"I'll help," Tyler says, pushing his chair back and jumping to his feet.

I barely resist the urge to look up at the ceiling and groan. Of course he can't let me have a little time and space to clear my thoughts.

"Would you?" Jin asks. "It saves us having to squeeze out around the desk."

"Yeah, no problem," Tyler replies.

Jin sends the list of books to us in a group message, and we leave the study room. I know the library well after several years here, so I know where to start looking, but I doubt Tyler does. He follows behind me but keeps a respectful distance.

"I'll look for the first one," I tell him.

"Then I'll take the second."

I turn into an aisle and begin skimming the titles. They're not on the first side, so I pivot to check the other and find Tyler much closer than I expect. I jolt in surprise, and he jumps out of the way.

Literally.

The man is beside me one second and three feet away the next.

Strange.

I reach for the book and out of the corner of my eye, I see him lift another down from a shelf and check the front cover. I tuck the reference book under my arm and refer to the list. The next one is back the way we came, so I brush past Tyler, but as I draw level with him, he jerks away, knocking into the shelf beside him.

"What is with you?" I demand, stopping and crossing my arms over my chest. "In our last meeting, you were going out of your way to touch me, and now you can't seem to get away fast enough."

"I'm trying to respect your physical boundaries," he replies, not meeting my eyes.

I almost laugh. 'Respectful' is the last thing he's been toward my boundaries until now. A thought pops into my mind.

"Is this because of what I told you after therapy the other day—and what happened after?" I ask.

He scowls, but it isn't aimed at me. It's more like he's annoyed with himself. "Look, I knew you had some hang-ups because of the way you panicked when that asshole grabbed you at the sorority party, but I didn't realize how deep they go. I don't want to upset you."

My stomach sinks, and I have no idea why. I shouldn't be disappointed by the fact he's finally trying to behave like a decent person. It's exactly what I've been asking for.

But something doesn't add up.

"If you're so worried about triggering me, then why send the sex toys and do...what we did...on the phone?"

He clutches the textbook to his chest, and I can't help but notice the way his thick bicep flexes with the movement.

"That was different," he says. "It was all about making you feel good, and I knew you could stop any time you wanted. You were in control. If I start touching you or getting into your space, then I'm taking that control away from you, and I don't want to do that."

I stare at him, taken aback by his perceptiveness and the genuine concern reflected in his ice blue eyes.

"I appreciate your thoughtfulness," I say slowly. "But you're being weird, and it's making me self-conscious. Just be yourself, and I'll tell you if I don't like something."

He looks doubtful. "Will you?"

"Yes."

Tyler may make me nervous, but he's never physically harmed me, and I don't expect him to start now. Off the ice, his mode of warfare is of a more psychological nature. He's a black belt in manipulation.

"You know what I think?" he asks.

The twinkle in his eye tells me the answer to that.

"No," I say.

"I think you secretly like it when I'm in your space." His smirk is a little too smug. I don't like it, but I'm more familiar with this teasing, egotistical version of him, so I don't cut him down.

He moves closer, until only an inch separates us. "Maybe you like my touch more than you want to admit."

I don't say anything, and a taut silence stretches between us. Gradually, his face falls, and he begins to back away.

"Fine," I say, part of me still weak for him no matter how many years have passed. "Maybe I don't entirely mind the touching."

The corners of his mouth lift and he places the book on a shelf. With single-minded focus, he reaches for me slowly, giving me time to change my mind. Then his hands—those strong, rough hockey player hands—skim down my sides, tracing the contours of my body.

His touch is fleeting. Barely there. But it consumes my entire awareness.

My breath hitches, and he stops.

"We have all the time in the world," he says, picking the book back up. "There's no rush."

He leans forward and his lips ghost over my forehead.

I shiver as he pulls away. I want to tell him that nothing is going to happen between us, but that's beginning to feel like a lie. I've already let him cross too many lines.

TYLER

My heart is light as I stride toward the squat brick and glass building that houses the ice hockey rink.

She let me touch her.

I've been terrified I'd never know how it felt to put my hands on her again, and even if the caresses were innocent, I know how monumental they were for her. Perhaps she doesn't trust me, but she no longer loathes me the way she did when I first arrived on campus.

I'm making progress.

I push one of the massive wooden doors open and step inside, inhaling the familiar odor of damp sweat combined with the spicy tang of liniment. I turn toward the corridor that leads to the changing rooms and frown. Echo's friend, Ryan, is leaning against the wall, his arms crossed over his chest.

He straightens and saunters toward me. Ryan isn't as big as me, but he's a college baseball player so his arms are muscular and he's only an inch or two shorter than me. His strength is part of the reason I chose him.

"What are you doing here?" I demand as he stops in front of me.

"Echo has been different since you arrived," Ryan replies, his dark eyes studying me carefully. "Not in a good way. I need to know what your game is."

"I told you; I want her back." I glance at my watch. Practice starts soon, and I don't have time for this. "That's all there is to it."

"Uh-huh." A skeptical line forms between his eyebrows. "And you think giving her expensive gifts and stalking her are the way to do that?"

I shift from one foot to the other. How does he know what I've been doing? I haven't discussed it with him. Has Echo talked to him? Or is he playing his own angle here?

"How did you—?"

"Not important." He cuts me off. "If you know anything about Echo, you should know that you can't buy her forgiveness for whatever happened between you before."

I huff. "Maybe not, but it's the only way I know how to try." I hate admitting that to him. "She won't hear me out, so what else am I supposed to do?"

He snorts with a wry sort of amusement. "You hurt her. I don't know how, and I don't know why, but of course she isn't going to be open to hearing what she probably believes will be excuses. She's protecting herself."

"I don't want her to have to protect herself from me." I

want to be the person she goes to when she needs protection. The man she leans on. The person she'd use her one phone call to contact if she were ever arrested. But I surrendered the right to be that person a long time ago.

"Yeah, well, if wanting something made it true then I'd already have a contract with a major league team and a million dollars in my bank account."

I narrow my eyes, silently warning him to get to the point.

"Maybe you should try something more subtle," he suggests.

I scowl. Subtle isn't really my thing. "Like what?"

He shrugs. "It's not my job to sort this shit out for you. I'm just doing my best to keep Echo safe—emotionally, as well as physically." He scratches his stubbled jaw. "Do you have any mutual friends who could ease her into the idea of talking to you?"

"No," I say instinctively, but then stop and think. I can't afford to dismiss any idea without at least considering it. Not when I have so much ground to make up. Sure, I'm moving forward with her, but there's a long way to go before she might be willing to give me a second chance.

We didn't share any friends in high school because we were from different worlds. My friends were rich, privileged, and for the most part, on the hockey team. Other than that, the only people I spent time with were the girls I hooked up with.

The few students who didn't shun Echo for being there on a scholarship—and therefore beneath them—were more academically inclined. To them, her brilliant mind made her their equal. But those same people weren't interested in my average grades and didn't understand my love of hockey.

Or my occasional hatred of it.

Even if we had gone to school with someone who fit the bill, I'm not in touch with anyone from high school anymore, and that's the way I like it.

Well, except for my sister.

Of course. Soraya.

Echo never got to know her other than in passing, but surely, she'll be more open to listening to another woman. Especially a younger, non-threatening one.

"Ryan, you're a genius," I exclaim.

He eyeballs me. "I'm not sure I like your expression, but I won't ask. Just remember that if you blow it, I know how to wield a bat and I'm not afraid to use one to crush your ball sack."

I wince. Maybe he's not as nice as I always thought he was. "I won't. There's no need to threaten my nuts."

He mimes smacking a bat against his palm as he walks past me and out the exit. I glance at my watch and swear. Better get a move on.

Someone slaps my shoulder.

"Come on, Kinsey. Move it." It's Matthews. He yanks me along beside him, heading for the locker room.

"Let go, you dick," I growl, jerking my shoulder free of his grip.

He just laughs. "God, you're so uptight. Who was that guy?"

I debate staying quiet, but the whole damn team knows I'm hung up on Echo, so there's no reason to hide it. "One of Echo's friends."

He turns toward me, his eyebrows inching toward his hairline. "Just a friend?"

"Yes."

"So, how's that going?" He pushes open the locker room door and a cacophony of voices greets us. "Can we expect to see her wearing your number in the stands during our next game?"

I grimace. "It might be a while before that happens."

If ever.

Matthews shakes his head. "And here I thought you're the kind of guy who has game with the ladies."

"There's only one lady I want."

"We know," Ruiz cries, obviously eavesdropping. "You're whipped, man. But you've gotta keep us updated. We need details."

A grin steals over my face. "You're all idiots."

They drop the topic after that, and we all get our gear on and head out for practice. It's a brutal one. Coach is in a bad mood, and he works us hard. But despite my teammates' bitching, I don't have any complaints. I'm too busy plotting what I'm going to say to Soraya when I call her.

As soon as practice ends, I shower and leave the stadium. I sit in my Audi in the parking lot and find my sister's number.

"Hey," I say when she answers.

"Is everything okay?" she asks.

I frown. "Fine. Why?"

"You don't usually call for no reason. Especially not when we live so near to each other that you could just drop by." I can practically hear the shrug in her voice.

"Sorry for worrying you. I just had an idea that I'm hoping you'll help me with."

"Oh?" She sounds interested but not upset, which is a relief. "What?"

"I need a favor."

15

ECHO

As I jot down the article's details in the notebook I keep for my social psychology class, I hear someone speak behind me.

"Excuse me?"

I ignore the voice, certain the person isn't addressing me. It's quiet in Full of Beans this afternoon, so it's easy for me to pick up on pieces of other people's conversations. I reach for my skinny caramel mocha and my lips curve down when I realize the mug is empty. I'm on a tight budget, so I'd better not have another.

"Excuse me," the voice repeats, and this time, there's a tap on my shoulder.

I jolt, my heart racing as I spin to face them. "Don't do that," I squeak. "You scared me."

The young blonde toys with a charm on the bracelet around her wrist, her expression anxious. "I'm sorry. I didn't mean to. Are you okay?"

"I'll be fine." I take a slow breath to get my pulse under control. "Can I help you?"

"Um." Her eyes flick away and then back to me. "Are you Echo?"

"Yes." Something about the way she asks makes me suspicious. I study her more closely. Flawless golden complexion, eyes the color of a summer sky, and a build not unlike my own, although she's a little taller. She's familiar, but I can't put my finger on where from.

"I thought so." She rests her hand on the back of the seat beside me. "Can I join you?"

She doesn't wait for an answer. I can't help feeling as if I'm supposed to know who she is.

"I'm sorry, but I don't recognize you," I tell her apologetically. "Have we met?"

She angles her chair toward me and sets an espresso cup on the table. "I'm Soraya Kinsey. Tyler's sister."

A sudden coldness permeates me. I should have realized. Her coloring is so similar to his, except that her eyes are bright where his are cool, and she has more of a tan— presumably from spending time outside. He likely spends all of his spare hours indoors at the rink.

"I didn't realize," I say.

I've seen Soraya Kinsey in the past, but she was a freshman when I was a senior, so we rarely crossed paths. And because Tyler wanted to keep me away from his friends and family, we never said more than a hello to each other in the school corridors.

"Can we talk?" she asks, her fingers finding their way back to her charm bracelet again, in what must be a nervous habit.

I quickly catalog what I know about her, and what can easily be seen. She must only be in her first year of college, making her eighteen or nineteen. Her body language says she's anxious, and nothing about it is aggressive, but I still worry she intends on harassing me the way so many others did before I left Charlesville.

"Why?" I ask. "Tyler and I aren't friends, and if you're here to rehash the past, then I'm not interested."

Soraya's hand stills, and she stiffens. "The past? Are you talking about the charges against Eric Weston?"

I stack my hands one on top of the other, hoping she won't notice that they're trembling. My insides are turbulent, and suddenly, I'm glad I only had one mug of coffee. It's less to throw up.

I make an effort to relax my tight jaw. "I haven't heard that name said out loud in a long time."

She claps her hand to her mouth, her eyes horrified. "I'm so sorry. I shouldn't have—"

"It's fine," I assure her. I need to be able to get through life without being triggered anytime someone mentions the name 'Eric'.

"No, it's not." She presses her lips together, her eyes shining with emotions I can't pinpoint. "I should have been more careful."

"It is what it is."

She nods and blows out a breath. "For what it's worth, I believe that the jury was right to convict him. He did what you said, and I would never try to make life harder for you because you were brave enough to stand up and expect a monster to face the consequences of his actions."

I stare at her with my lips parted as tears fill my eyes. With effort, I force myself to swallow a lump of emotion.

Very few people ever believed me, or at least were willing to say so to my face, and I'm unprepared for the wave of emotion that crashes over me. My throat tightens and I raise a hand to my chest, feeling the pounding of my heart beneath the skin.

"You believe me?" I whisper.

"Yes." Her tone is fierce, and she reaches for my hand but then stops. "Tyler does, too."

I reel back, her words striking me like a slap to my face. "He certainly didn't give that impression at the time."

Maybe he believes me now. Based on his actions over the past few days, I'd even venture to guess that he does. But if he believed me back then, why wouldn't he have called off his friends, or even just taken a minute to ask if I was all right?

I wasn't.

It took a long time for me to be anywhere near all right.

Soraya twists her hands together. "He was in a difficult place."

I scoff. "I'm pretty sure I was in a worse place."

She nods, her eyes flitting around like a wary bird as she considers her next words carefully. "I can't imagine what you were going through. It's most girls' worst nightmare, and for you to be so alone... It must have been awful."

"It was," I confirm.

She stops twisting her hands and wraps one of them around the small espresso cup instead. "There's nothing that can justify my brother's behavior, but I swear he did believe you." She pauses. "Did you ever ask where your mom got the money to hire such a good attorney?"

Whatever I'd thought she might say, it wasn't that. I frown, wondering what she's getting at, but as I think about it, I realize it's a good question. I was too overwhelmed at the time to wonder how Mom managed to hire a top criminal law attorney to act as her advisor during the trial.

"Are you implying the money came from your family?" I ask, refusing to beat around the bush.

Another thought occurs to me, and my frown deepens. I got lucky with the prosecutor, too. The district attorney personally handled my case, and he'd been a staunch source of support from day one.

I hadn't questioned it at the time, but he had plenty of underlings who could have done the job. After all, I was the daughter of a working-class single mother. Nobody special.

"Or did they pull strings?"

Mr. Kinsey loves doing that, but why would he help me?

Soraya shrugs and tosses back the espresso. "No comment."

I pick up my pen because I need something to occupy my hands or else I might grab her and demand answers. Does she have any idea how frustrating it is for her to drop sly little questions like that and then not follow them up with something tangible?

"What are you doing here?" I ask because the longer we spend together, the more this feels like a set-up. Once again, Tyler and his family are trying to pull strings, but I'm not some puppet for them to manipulate.

Soraya places the espresso cup back on the table and pushes it away from herself. "I go to school at Newbury. I'm studying sociology, but I'm pre-law. I intend to specialize in domestic violence cases."

A hint of darkness passes through her eyes, reminding me that no matter how wealthy and privileged the Kinseys are, all isn't well in their world. Or at least, it wasn't in the past. It wasn't uncommon for me to find bruises on Tyler, and he explained most of them away as hockey injuries, but I never forgot what I saw in his driveway that day.

"That's an admirable goal," I reply, treading just as cautiously as she has been with me. "I'm surprised your father allowed you to attend a second-rate college like this one. Surely, he wanted you to go to Harvard or Yale."

And, surely, he'd insist on a different area of specialization. One that wouldn't make anyone wonder why she'd chosen it.

Soraya laughs, and for the first time since she sat down, her face lights up. "Dad is dead."

"Dead?" I stare at her, uncomprehending. Mr. Kinsey couldn't be much older than fifty. Surely, I must have misheard.

But she nods. "Completely and totally. He had a heart attack six months ago."

"I'm sorry for your loss." I don't know what else to say. I didn't like Mr. Kinsey, but he was still her father.

"Don't be," she replies. "The world is a better place without him."

My eyebrows fly up. "You don't miss him?"

She purses her lips. "I miss the father I could have had, but not who he actually was." She cocks her head, appraising me. "I'm not sure if you know this, but he was abusive."

"I suspected as much," I admit.

"He controlled all of us," she goes on. "Our choices. Who our friends were. Who we dated. What classes we took. And on and on and on. Even if he'd never raised a hand to us, he'd still have been a horrible man."

I glance away to hide my surprise at her sharing all of this so candidly.

"He didn't even have the decency to die without hurting us." Her tone is full of venom. "Tyler was with him when it happened. He couldn't save him, and it messed with his head."

I shut down the voice in my mind urging me to find Tyler and hug him. This happened months ago, and even if it had been more recent, he isn't mine to comfort. He never really was.

"That must have been difficult," I say, for lack of anything better to offer.

"Yeah." Her nostrils flare, and I can't help but wonder how deep her anger at her dead father goes. "As soon as he was buried, Tyler started planning to transfer to Newbury, and I wanted to be near him, so I enrolled here, too."

A faint ringing begins in my ears and builds gradually until it's a piercing drone that can't be ignored. I shake my head, but it doesn't dispel the noise.

"What?" My lips form the word, but I don't hear myself say it.

It feels like the world is tipping upside down, throwing everything I thought I knew off balance.

"But why would he do that?" I ask, hoping she can't make out what I'm saying.

She gives me a knowing look. "Because of you." She rests her hands on the table and leans toward me. "Despite his dumbass behavior in the past—which you should make him grovel for, by the way—you've been the only girl for him since you started tutoring him in high school."

"That can't be right." I shove back my chair and get shakily to my feet.

Soraya bolts upright, as if to give chase.

"I'm not running away," I tell her. "Just...give me a moment."

I go to the counter and request a glass of water. I drink it quickly and wait while the barista refills it, then I carry the glass back to the table. I sit and close my eyes. It takes a few meditative breaths before the drone in my ears fades to a whine.

"You can't be serious," I say, opening my eyes and blinking as they adjust to the light. "Maybe Tyler has woven a good story, but I saw him with Whitney at prom, and then again the following week."

"He wasn't—"

"Besides, girls always throw themselves at college athletes," I interrupt, unwilling to listen to her defend the man who shattered my heart. "I refuse to believe that he's never been with any of them."

Soraya sighs. "All I can say is that, as far as I know, he's never touched anyone else since you were together."

That can't be right.

The wheels of my mind turn, trying to make sense of the information Soraya has unloaded on me.

Is there a chance—even if it's a slight one—that Tyler is telling the truth?

Or has he put Soraya up to this, knowing that I'm more likely to hear her out than I am to listen to whatever useless excuses he's come up with over the past three years?

Even if a portion of what Soraya has told me is the truth, I can't forget that Tyler hurt me. He broke my trust and utterly humiliated me. Then, when my world crashed down, he didn't stand by me.

Soraya stands and twists a lone silver charm between her fingers. "It was nice to meet you. I hope you'll give Tyler a chance. He's an idiot, but he's made himself sick over what he did to you—and what happened after. He really does care for you."

I can't force myself to nod, so I just meet her eyes. She reaches into the pocket of her designer jeans and withdraws a folded piece of notepaper, then holds it out to me. I take it with some trepidation.

"My phone number," she explains, confirming that this was a set-up from the beginning. Why else would she have her number ready to hand over? "Don't be a stranger."

She leaves.

I watch her go, then turn toward my laptop screen, which has gone black while I was distracted. I massage my jaw with one of my thumbs. There's no way I'm going to be able to focus on my essay now. There's no point even bothering.

I pack up my laptop, put my notebook in the laptop bag, and carry it outside, where I walk toward my dorm. Thankfully, I don't run into anyone I know because I'm not in a good headspace to talk. Even more luckily, Martina isn't in our room.

I ditch my laptop bag on the desk and flop onto the bed. I pull my phone out of my pocket and call Mom. She answers on the fourth ring, which is progress. For a while there, she'd always picked up after one ring, which made me wonder if she was living with her phone fused to her palm just in case I needed her.

"Hey, Mom," I say.

"It's so good to finally hear from you," she exclaims, making it sound as though it's been weeks rather than two days.

"It's nice to talk to you, too." I know better than to call attention to her clinginess when she's making progress, even if it is slow. At least she hasn't moved to Newbury to be with me all the time. She wanted to, at first.

"What have you been doing today?" she asks, the sound of rushing water in the background, as if she's running a tap. Washing the dishes, maybe? Or she could be at work.

"Just finding references for an essay," I tell her. "Otherwise, things have been quiet."

"I'm glad to hear you're taking some down time."

I hesitate for a beat too long, uncertain of how to broach a subject that will upset her.

"What is it?" she asks, noticing immediately.

I jump into the deep end. "Mom, after I was...you know...where did the money for our attorney come from?"

There's an intake of breath. "Why do you ask?"

"Please." I can't bear to explain everything right now. "I need to know."

"Actually, the attorney approached me," she says. "He said that an anonymous benefactor believed in your case and had arranged to pay his fees so he could ensure everything was being done properly."

The bottom dropped out of my stomach.

An anonymous benefactor.

Could it have been one of the Kinseys?

Could it have been Tyler?

But where would he have gotten his hands on the money? His father was generous with them but liked to know where every cent was going.

"Do you have any idea who?" I ask, needing to know the truth even as I fear the answer.

"What's this about?" Mom sounds disturbed.

"Please."

"Okay, honey. No, I don't know. I never did. To be honest, I never questioned it much. I was just so grateful."

I bite the inside of my cheek. "So, there were no clues?"

I'm not sure I can handle not knowing.

She pauses for long enough that I realize she's thought of something.

"What?" I prompt.

"The attorney passed along a message. It was strange, and that's why I remember. He said that the benefactor wanted to get justice for a shooting star."

I drop the phone, the room spinning around me.

It's true. It must be.

Somehow, Tyler paid for my attorney.

He didn't totally abandon me. And if I was wrong about that, then what else might I be wrong about?

16

TYLER

My phone rings as I add a scoop of protein powder to the blender, screw the lid on, and start it up. It's the ringtone I assigned to Echo. The ingredients whizz together, forming a thick brownish liquid. I glance at the phone, but my smoothie will only take a couple more seconds, so I leave it.

Once the drink is at the right consistency, I turn the blender off and reach for my phone. Unfortunately, by the time I pick it up, the call has gone to voicemail. I try to call her back but get the busy dial tone.

I set the phone down, pour the smoothie into a tall glass, and take both the phone and the smoothie to the breakfast bar. The phone rings again, so I answer.

"Hey, beautiful."

"Why did you send me a hockey shirt with your name and number on it?" she demands.

I can't help grinning. She sounds so indignant. I wish I could see her expression. I bet her face is all pinched up and cute.

"I'm flattered you know my number," I tease.

"I assumed," she snaps. "It's not like you'd put your name and someone else's number on the shirt."

"I've always loved that big brain of yours," I tell her, amused when she huffs in response. I like her like this. Fiery. Not afraid to fight back.

When we first reunited, she had two modes: scared, and cornered animal. Now, she seems comfortable being snarky with me without fearing that the fate of her world hinges on our every interaction.

"You liked my big brain when I helped you get good grades," she retorts.

I wave my hand dismissively, forgetting she can't see. "That was just a side benefit."

"So," she prompts. "The shirt?"

I eye the smoothie, which looks about as appealing as a raw egg. "I'd like you to wear it to the game today."

She sputters, clearly outraged by my audacity. My grin widens.

"No," she says. "Absolutely not."

I wrap my hand around the glass, raise it to my lips and sniff. I should probably have drunk it before speaking to Echo. The bitter aroma isn't doing much for my appetite. I take a sip. It's tart and the texture is disturbingly grainy.

"I bet I can persuade you."

She snorts. "I'd like to see you try."

Bracing myself, I gulp down the smoothie, swallowing mouthful after mouthful until it's gone. I go to the sink, fill a clean glass with water, and rinse my mouth out as I evaluate her tone.

Is it just me, or is there a little less heat in her words than there used to be? Perhaps her conversation with Soraya went well. I couldn't get any of the details out of my sister, who claimed to be willing to talk to Echo but not prepared to report back.

"Have you come since our last phone call?" I ask.

A weighty silence follows. She makes a noise, as if she's about to answer, but then doesn't.

"I'm going to assume that's a yes." I pack both glasses into the dishwasher. "Because you'd have immediately said no if you could have. Was it as good as when you had me on the phone, telling you what to do?"

The silence continues. I stroll over to the window and look out. My apartment is on the third floor, and the windows in the living area are angled to catch the morning sun.

When it's clear that Echo doesn't intend to reply, I go on.

"If you wear that shirt to the game today, I'll call you as soon as I'm home and we can do it again."

She hangs up.

Great job, Kinsey. You just had to go and push her too far.

HOURS LATER, I'M WARMING UP ON THE ICE, STILL KICKING myself for how I handled Echo's call. She's fragile. It's so easy to forget that, but I can't afford to if I want her permanently in my life. I sent her a text message to apologize for pushing her, but she never responded.

In this case, her silence spoke as loudly as words. Music plays through the loudspeakers—a combination of pop and classic rock—and my teammates zip around me. It's our first official game of the season, against our neighbors from Benton, the next town over.

The stands are almost full, and even though I doubt Echo will show, I can't help scanning each new arrival in case she does.

"Kinsey."

I glance up just in time to stop a puck flying across the

ice toward me from Anaheim. I glide toward the goal and fire it at Jackson, our goalie. He whacks it away with his gloved hand and Anaheim sweeps in, collecting the puck. He passes to me, I feign a shot at goal, then pass it back, and Anaheim flicks it past Jackson's left foot and into the net.

Anaheim claps me on the back as he skates past, then gestures toward his helmet. "Head in the game."

"Got it, Cap." He's right to call me on my distraction.

Anaheim summons the other first-line forward, Welch, and we run drills together, taking turns shooting at Jackson, until a whistle indicates that it's time for us to wrap it up.

As we skate over to meet Coach Danvers, a ruddy-faced man in his fifties or sixties with thinning gray hair, a flash of movement near the entrance catches my attention. It's Echo, wearing a shirt with the Newbury logo on the front. On the back, out of sight, is the number 21 and my last name.

I can't see it, but I know it's there, and my chest inflates with pride.

She came.

She's here.

I don't even care that she's brought Ryan with her. She isn't wearing a shirt with his name on it. He isn't the one who promised her an orgasm later.

Matthews jostles me. "Dude, what are you staring at?" He follows my gaze and a grin spreads across his face, mirroring my own. "How did you manage that?"

"I don't know," I say honestly.

Coach Danvers calls our names and I force myself to look away from Echo and focus on the game. It's hard, though. This would have been a dream come true when I was in high school. I knew at the time there was no chance I could have Echo in the crowd, wearing my number, but I wanted it.

Badly.

Now, here she is.

She's making a statement with her presence. I'm not quite sure what it is yet, but I'll figure it out. The most important thing is, I know that this is monumental for her, and I won't let her down ever again.

Coach gives his pep talk and sends us out. I'm starting, and I've never been more determined to win a game—not even the year we took the championship at my former college.

The air is thick with anticipation. We've shaken off the summer slowness over the course of our exhibition games and we're beginning to be able to communicate wordlessly on the ice. There's plenty of room for improvement, but we'll win today. I can taste victory already.

The chill chaps my cheeks, but the rest of me is warm as the referee indicates for us to faceoff. I stare down my opponent, and the second the puck drops, I'm on it. Sticks clack, but I get it past their front line and flick the puck to Anaheim, who skates toward the goal, evades one of the defensemen, and passes back to me.

My eyes dart up to the stands, searching for Echo, but don't linger long because I have to focus. I hit the puck toward the corner of the goal, but the goalie stops it with his stick. Welch is there almost immediately, and a moment later, the puck crosses the goal line.

One up, less than two minutes in.

I congratulate Welch and we skate back to our end. This time, I allow myself more time to scan the stands, and eventually I spot Echo, standing near the front on my left. Her hair is tied back and tucked under a cute, knitted hat. She's wearing matching mittens, and she's the best thing I've ever seen.

I return my focus to the game, and seconds later, we roar into action. I earn another assist—this time with Anaheim

—and I score twice. Both times, I meet Echo's eyes, hoping she can read the silent message that they're all for her.

Late in the third period, I'm racing up the ice, the puck on my stick, when the other team's left defenseman barrels into me out of nowhere. I go down hard, the impact jarring my bones. The puck is snatched away and my hip throbs as I get to my feet. That's going to bruise.

I rip off my gloves and helmet and square off against the defenseman. He does the same. He's a big, stocky guy, with the beginnings of a beard and a smirk that says he's loving every second of this.

I throw the first punch, bloodying his lip. He strikes back, but his blow glances off the side of my face as I dodge. Little does he know, I have more experience escaping hits than he can possibly imagine. I ready my fists to go again, but then others swarm us, and I'm pulled away.

The referee calls a penalty against Benton, I don my gloves and helmet, and we're off again. Unfortunately, Benton turns the play around quickly and scores over Jackson.

I grit my teeth. Despite my aching hip and a faint throbbing in the back of my skull, I'm determined to get a hat trick. I can't let Echo's last impression of me be as the guy who took a face dive.

Together, Anaheim and I work the puck up the ice, drawing the defenders to us before Anaheim sends it back to Welch. His first attempt on net ricochets off, but I catch it on the rebound and send the puck past the goalie's ear.

A few minutes later, when the buzzer sounds, the final score is 5-1.

We skate a victory lap while the home crowd cheers and then retreat to the locker room. Coach Danvers gruffly congratulates us, then warns us not to get too big for our britches. He warns us that we'll be practicing some of our weaker plays on Monday, and then he and the assistant coach leave.

I get out of my gear as quickly as possible and rush through the shower. I pull on a pair of jeans and a team hoodie, and I'm checking my phone when Ruiz nudges me.

"There's a party at Jackson's place," he says. "Beers and pizza. You in?"

"Nah." I grimace, aware that I should be making a better effort to integrate into the team. "I have something else to do."

He cocks his head, his dark eyes gleaming. "Your girl? I saw her in the stands."

My chest puffs out. "Damn right."

He holds his fist out and I reluctantly bump it. "Good luck, man. Don't screw it up."

"I won't." Hopefully.

I sneak out one of the side doors and manage to avoid some of the girls who hang around in the hopes of catching the players as we leave. I beeline to my Audi and drive home as fast as I can without risking being pulled over by the cops.

When I'm holed up in my apartment, sprawled on the big gray sofa in the living room and gazing at the massive painting of the night sky hung on the wall, I call Echo. I don't really expect her to answer despite showing up at the rink earlier, so I'm surprised when the call connects.

"You came," I say, at a loss for words. Apparently, I didn't take the time to think through what I'd actually say to her if I got the chance.

"I did." Amusement laces her voice.

"You have no idea how much that means to me."

She clears her throat, and I get the feeling I went too far. "You played well. I was worried when you took that hit though. Are you okay?"

My insides warm. She was worried about me. That must mean she cares, right? At least on some level.

"I'm fine," I tell her.

I'll have the mother of all bruises, and I'll be achy for a couple of days, but that's just how hockey is. There's no point worrying her more.

A silence descends between us. I'm tempted to let it linger and find out what she might say to fill the void, but she's too skittish for that. It's more likely she'd hang up and refuse to answer the next time I call. It's better to keep her comfortable. Or at least comfortable-ish. I wouldn't be me if I didn't push things a little.

"Since you held up your end of the deal, it's time for your reward." I lower my voice. "Have you tried any of the other toys?"

"Just one," she admits.

"Which one?"

"The mini vibe."

That makes sense. It's non-threatening and she didn't have to put it inside her. I could be wrong, but I get the feeling that the idea of penetrating herself—even with a sex toy that's completely under her control—intimidates her.

That's all right. We can work up to it—if she lets me help her. As much as I'd love to listen to her fucking herself with a dildo that I can imagine is my cock, it isn't in the cards today.

"Are you ready to use it again?" I ask.

"Yes," she whispers. "But I need you to...take control like you did last time. Tell me what to do."

"I can do that, baby." In fact, it would be my pleasure. "Are you alone?"

"Martina is out with her friends. She shouldn't be back for hours."

"Good." We'd have plenty of time then. "Get the vibe,

the lube, and light that candle. Maybe put on some soft music. Do you still like to listen to classical music?”

“Sometimes.”

“Find something gentle, so it won’t distract you.”

She’s silent for a couple of minutes, and I assume she’s doing as I asked. Faint sounds come through the line, rustling and muffled bumps.

“Done,” she says.

“Are you comfortable on the bed?”

She laughs nervously. “As much as I can be.”

Closing my eyes, I allow myself to picture her. I can perfectly recall how her cheeks flush a delicate shade of pink when she’s turned on, and her eyes darken with need. I imagine her lying on white sheets, twisted around her legs, that satiny underwear I used to like so much barely covering her.

“Let’s warm you up first. Put a bit of lube on your fingers and slide them through your pussy, then rub that pretty clit of yours.”

There’s a click—presumably as she uncaps the lube—and then more rustling as she shifts around on the bed.

“Is that okay?” Just because she enjoyed this last time doesn’t necessarily mean she’ll have the same response this time. I don’t want her to feel pressured.

“Yeah,” she murmurs. “Just takes a bit of getting used to. It’s been so long...”

My chest constricts. Damn, I hate what happened to her. What I allowed to happen. If I hadn’t ruined our relationship, or if I’d seen the warning signs, maybe she wouldn’t have been assaulted. We could be blissfully happy, after having spent more than three years together.

But stewing in self-recrimination won’t fix anything.

“Ty...”

My heart leaps. It's the first time she's called me that since I came back into her life. "Yeah, baby?"

She hesitates for a long moment. "Last time, we only focused on me, and I was relieved about that, but this time, I'd really like it if you could join in."

My mind short circuits. "What do you mean?"

"I want you to get off too."

My eyes snap open. Surely, I didn't just hear her say that. "Are you sure? I'm happy for it to be all about you."

In fact, if I participate, I can't guarantee I won't be wracked with guilt about it later.

"Please, Ty."

If she feels any doubt, it isn't present in her tone. My subconscious screams that this is a terrible idea, but Echo asked for it and there's very little I'd deny her, so I strip off my jeans and underwear, freeing my cock.

"Do you want me to tell you what I'm doing?" I ask, needing to know the boundaries.

"I... I think so."

Some of her certainty has dissipated, which means I need to tread carefully.

"Are you ready for the vibe?"

"Yes." This time, she's sure.

"Then switch it on and put it against your pussy. Just nice and gentle. Leave your clit alone."

I grit my teeth as the buzz begins. It was torture last time, knowing what she was doing without being able to see or touch her, but after everything, I deserve a little pain. I wrap my hand around my cock, putting pressure on it, but I don't stroke yet.

Instead, I focus on the small tattoo on my hip. One I put there on my 19th birthday, in a place I knew my dad wouldn't see.

A shooting star.

It's for her. Everything I do—and am—is for her.

"Feels good," she breathes.

Relief floods me. The last thing I want to do is trigger her, but it's an ever-present possibility.

"Rock your hips for me," I order. "Tease yourself."

"Mm."

The moan cuts off, but my cock flexes in response. Slowly, I guide my hand along the length. After so long without sex, Echo's gasps are enough to make me come with hardly any stimulation.

"I'm stroking myself," I tell her. "Slow and steady."

She whimpers, and I squeeze the base of my cock to stop it getting over-excited.

"Can I use it on my clit now?" she asks.

I stifle a groan. I want to make her beg. To instruct her to hold off until she's desperate, but that isn't what she needs right now. Making sure she finds pleasure in sex is the most important thing.

"Do it." I pump my cock more quickly as her breaths grow increasingly ragged.

She keens. "Oh, my God."

Pleasure zaps up my spine and a spurt of precum dribbles out the head of my cock.

"Touch your entrance," I tell her. "Lube your finger and tease yourself."

"Ty." Her voice is strained.

"You can do it," I croon. "Just the tip. You can stop whenever you want. Just try, baby girl."

A shaky breath. "O-okay."

Another click. The buzzing continues. And then she sucks in a breath.

"Relax," I urge. "Breathe out and let all your muscles go."

She exhales softly.

"Keep circling your clit with the vibe." If she's distracted by pleasure, perhaps her mind won't travel down any dark rabbit holes.

"I am." She definitely isn't as relaxed as she was earlier. "The tip is in, but I can't relax."

"Close your eyes. Keep breathing in and out. In for four, and then let it all out at once and soften your muscles. Ready? One, two, three, four…"

Her breath gusts out. "It worked."

I chuckle. "No need to be so surprised. I have some good ideas."

"Are you still…?"

"Touching myself?" I ask gruffly. "Yeah."

"I want to hear you come."

I clench my jaw. "Only if you come with me."

"Do I have to keep the finger inside?"

"Of course not, baby girl. Take it out if you don't like it there."

"Thanks." Some of her tension seems to dissolve. "I don't think I'm ready for that."

"Thank you for telling me." I won't take it for granted that she's willing to be honest.

I spit in my hand and stroke myself, picturing her flushed cheeks, and the rapid rise and fall of her chest. I remember how pretty her tits were, and how much I loved having her slender thighs wrapped around my head.

"Turn up the vibrator," I rasp. "Put it right on your clit and don't even think about pulling it away."

She cries out. "Oh, God. It's too much."

"You can take it." This much, I'm sure of. Her voice is thick with pleasure, not strain.

Her next cry is muffled, as if her hand is over her mouth.

"Let me hear you," I growl. "Don't try to hide."

"It's too much, it's too much," she whispers over and over again. "I'm gonna... Oh, God."

She moans as she comes, and the sound shoots right to my balls. Pleasure licks at my nerves and I empty all over my stomach.

"Fuuuck," I pant. "Echo. Baby. Fuck, you're so perfect."

She doesn't respond, and we're both quiet as we catch our breath. Just as I'm beginning to wonder if she has regrets, she finally speaks.

"I hope you know what it takes for me to be vulnerable with you," she says. "If you do or say anything to make me think I shouldn't have taken the risk, you'll never hear from me again."

17

THE PAST

TYLER

I get comfortable on my bed and add a heart emoji to the end of the text message I've typed to Echo. Footsteps bang up the hall and I bolt upright. The only person in this house who would make that much noise is Dad, and it sounds like he's coming toward me.

An instant later, the bedroom door flies open and crashes against the wall. He glares at me as if it's my fault he's probably just dented the wall.

I stiffen. I don't know what I did, but whatever it was, it can't be good.

He stops halfway into the room and puts his hands on his hips. His expression is darker than the rainclouds outside, and I shiver involuntarily.

"Why did you rent a room at a hotel?" he demands, practically bristling with fury.

My stomach clenches, any trace of hunger vanishing. I've only booked a hotel room once—when I took Echo there. If he knows about the room, it's possible he's figured out what I was doing, but on the off chance he's just fishing, there's no way I'm going to cause problems for her.

I swing my legs off the bed and sit up. "It's none of your business."

He gestures for me to stand. When I don't, he grabs my shirt and yanks me roughly to my feet.

"Want to rephrase that?" he asks, dangerously low.

I raise my chin. "No."

Whatever happens, I'm in trouble, but I can protect my girl.

My beautiful shooting star.

Dad backhands me. I'm expecting it, so I don't stumble. Instead, I press my palm to my cheek as blood fills my mouth. My instincts are driving me to spit it out, but if I do that, he'll only get angrier because of the mess on the carpet. Disgust turning my gut, I swallow.

"I spoke to the hotel's staff." He drops his hands to his sides but comes closer, getting right in my face. "They confirmed you were there. You used a fake name and you were with a girl. Who is she?"

"No one," I lie.

He scowls. "Try again."

Feeling nauseous, I mutter, "Just a cheerleader I fucked a couple of times."

Even the thought of being with someone other than Echo sickens me, but him believing that is better than him knowing the truth.

"Tyler." He shakes his head. "I'm disappointed in you. I know how you work. If you want to fuck girls, you do it at their houses or in the back of your Chevy. This was more. Stop lying to me."

My heart stutters. "What makes you so certain I'm lying?"

He folds his arms, his lips twisting smugly. "I have connections."

Unconsciously, I step back, then force myself to stand

firm. I can't let him get the best of me this time. Not when the stakes are so high.

"So, I thought it might be nice to try something fancy," I say. "You're always reminding us to hold ourselves to a higher standard."

"That's not what I meant," he grinds out, then he runs a hand through his hair and sighs. "Look, Tyler. You can't have a girlfriend when you're aiming for the NHL. We've discussed this. You need to focus on hockey, not some slut who's hoping you're her ticket out of here. She'll distract you."

Ah, so now he's trying the 'voice of reason' approach. I wonder what will be next? More violence? Or the subtle psychological manipulation that he thrives on?

"She's not a slut," I snap, my fists balling at my sides. I won't be thrown off by his change of tactic.

His eyes sharpen. "So, she does mean something to you."

Damn it.

"I love her." I may as well admit it. He's going to assume I have feelings for her anyway. "She's not a distraction, either. She's actually making me better."

We've been studying together, so my grades are up, and she has a more level head than me, so I've been getting her opinion on my games—things I can improve, and things I kick ass at. She isn't really interested in sports, but she's been coming to my games and sitting alone in the stands to support me—even if I don't acknowledge her so as not to draw Dad's attention to her.

That will all change soon.

Prom is tomorrow, and I'm taking her as my date. Soon, everyone will know how gone I am for her. I just have to survive this first.

"You stupid asshole," Dad says, shaking his head. "You really think you're in love with some puck chaser who's willing to let you up her skirt? You're pussy-whipped. That's all. Tell me who she is, and I'll fix it. I would've fixed it already, but the damn hotel clerk gave me a terrible description."

If he doesn't know, and has no way of finding out, then I'm not going to come clean. At least, not yet. He's bound to hear about her soon enough, but I want a chance to warn her before he does.

"Fuck off," I snarl.

It's the wrong response.

He grabs my shoulders and shoves me against the wall. The impact jars my spine, and my phone falls from my grasp.

I expect him to lay into me, but instead he ducks and snatches my phone off the floor. My stomach bottoms out. It's open on my message chain with Echo. His eyes flick from side to side as he scans the most recent messages. I try to get it off him, but he angles himself away, evading me.

Second by second, his scowl deepens. I lunge again, and he shoves me. When I recover my balance, his eyes are burning into me with undisguised fury.

"It's even worse than I thought." His tone is soft but deadly. "Kinseys do not fuck around with little working-class whores. Especially not when they're smart enough to get more out of you than just sex."

When his lips form the word "whore", my lizard brain takes over. I plant my hands on his chest and shove him back.

"Don't you fucking talk about her like that. I don't care if her mom is a fucking cleaner. She's better than you'll ever be. They both are."

Dad smashes my phone against the wall. The screen splinters. "I'll do whatever I goddamn want, you ungrateful bastard."

ECHO

I wince as the comb snags on a knot in my hair. Mom carefully works it out, twists the lock of hair, and pins it into the elaborate knot on the back of my head. I can't afford to get my hair and makeup done at the salon, but fortunately Mom has plenty of experience doing hair and makeup for her three younger sisters.

I gaze at my reflection, admiring her work. I don't look much different overall, but my best features have been emphasized. Thanks to some crafty use of eyeliner and eyeshadow, my eyes look bigger than usual, and the gold flecks are brighter. My lips are pinker, and my complexion is dewy.

"I can't believe you're so good at this," I say.

Behind me, Mom grins. She meets my eyes in the mirror. "It's just practice."

"No, it's talent. You have serious skill." She never lets me talk down about my accomplishments, and I refuse to allow her to do so either. Especially when all I can do, if left to my own devices, is mascara and the most basic eyeshadow, with a smear of lip gloss.

"If you say so, sweetheart." She pins back another strand of hair and grabs the canister of hairspray. "Close your eyes."

I shut them while she sprays the knot until I'm certain it's set as hard as cement. She puts the spray aside and messes with my bangs, sweeping them to one side and pinning them so they won't hang in my eyes. Then she covers my eyes with her hand and sprays the front too.

"What do you think?" she asks, far more nervously than is warranted.

"I think you should go back to school to become a hair-dresser or a beautician," I tell her.

She smiles, but it's wistful. "You flatterer."

My heart squeezes. Mom had me young, and my father didn't stick around. Because of that, she never had much opportunity to study. She had to make ends meet however she could, and cleaning was a job that didn't require much training and for which there was almost always work available.

It would be fine if she enjoyed it, but she doesn't. As I've grown older, it's become more and more obvious how much she's sacrificed for me, and I want to change that. I'm bound to get a scholarship to college, and once I do, she won't have to provide for me anymore. She'll be able to put herself first —if she's willing to.

"Can you help me into my dress?" I ask.

"Of course."

I grab the dress from the hanger. It's the most expensive clothing item I've ever owned. Tyler insisted on paying for it using cash he'd squirreled away. He couldn't risk putting it on his credit card in case his dad noticed.

I strip off everything other than my flesh-toned bra and a pair of skimpy panties that I'm hoping Tyler will get an eyeful of later. Mom doesn't comment. We've already talked about safe sex and making sure I use protection—high priority topics for her since she had her own teen pregnancy.

She lifts the dress up and I duck underneath, sliding my arms through the armholes. The skirt swishes into place around me and I smooth down the bodice. It's a stunning silvery blue dress, with beautiful floral details on the bodice and spotted down the tulle skirt. The neckline is lower than I'd usually wear, but not so low that I feel exposed.

"Beautiful," Mom murmurs. "I hope that boy appreciates what he's got."

"He does, Mom."

Nerves fizz in my gut. When Tyler comes to pick me up, it will be the first time he and Mom meet. I've told Mom a bit about him, but not everything. For instance, she doesn't know we've used the "L" word already. Not that she'd be upset about it; it just seems like something special that should be private between us.

While Mom zips my dress, I check the time. It's nearly eight. Tyler should be here soon. Prom starts at eight-thirty, and he promised to arrive early, so he'll have time to talk to Mom and pose for a few photos.

"Remember to be home by midnight, or I'll send out the search party," Mom warns good-naturedly.

"I will." Briefly. After that, Tyler and I have plans to return to his spot by the lake.

Being careful not to wrinkle my skirt, I sit on the sofa. Mom joins me.

"You really like Tyler, huh?" she asks.

"I do." Even thinking of him makes my heart feel too big for my chest.

"Then I'm excited to meet him."

I hope she likes him. Mom means a lot to me, and I value her opinion. I won't dump Tyler if she doesn't like him, but it would give me reason to pause and evaluate him more closely.

Mom snaps a photograph of me on her phone. I bounce in place, hardly able to contain myself. I'm about to be the subject of more attention than I've ever experienced in my life. All eyes will be on me and Tyler. It's scary, but also thrilling. I'm pleased that everyone will know we're together. I'll be proud to say he's mine.

Fifteen minutes pass, and I frown. I should have heard

from Tyler by now. I check my phone, but he hasn't messaged. I sent him a text, but he doesn't reply. Another ten minutes later, I call him, worried he might have been delayed or forgotten the address. The call goes straight to voicemail.

"Let's take some more photos while we wait," Mom suggests. "Go stand in front of the curtains."

I pose for a few photos, doing my best to smile, but I'm worried. When it's closer to nine than eight, Mom sighs.

"Is it possible he's standing you up?" she asks.

"What?" My heart hammers. Despite the situation, that thought hadn't occurred to me. "No. He wouldn't do that."

She shrugs helplessly. "Then maybe there's been a miscommunication and he thought you were going to meet him there."

I doubt it. We were quite clear about him coming here and meeting Mom, but perhaps he panicked and went straight to prom because the idea of talking to Mom freaked him out. I can't forget that I'm the first proper relationship he's had. Meeting my mother might be too much for him right now.

"You're right," I say. "I'll drive there and see if he's around."

She smiles, but anxiety is etched in the lines of her face. "Want me to come?"

"No, I'll be fine. Can I borrow your car?"

"Of course." She hands me the keys. "Don't drink and drive."

"I would never."

She kisses my cheek. "I know, sweetheart. You're a good girl."

I message Tyler to let him know what I'm doing and then tuck my phone into my purse and slip it into a hidden pocket on the side of my dress.

"I'll be home before midnight," I promise.

"Have fun."

I put on the strappy black shoes I chose to go with the dress and make my way out the front door to where the car is parked on the side of the street. The drive is short, so I soon arrive outside the school gymnasium, where the prom is already underway.

There's no line to enter—presumably because most people are already here—so I show my ticket to the teacher standing by the door and walk right in. As I enter, a Dua Lipa song is playing. Silver and blue balloons hang from the ceiling, and the walls have been covered.

Rochelle, one of the popular girls, glances up from the mocktail she's drinking and flashes a predatory grin.

"Are you all by yourself, you little loser?" She bats her eyelashes, and the guy with her laughs as if she's a comedian.

I roll my eyes. Just wait until she sees who I'm with tonight.

I scan the throng, searching for Tyler. Hopefully he's received my message and knows to be on the lookout for me.

I spot him almost immediately, standing with a group of guys from the hockey team. The way he's swaying slightly from one foot to the other makes it obvious he's had a bit to drink. Does he really need that much liquid courage to get through our big reveal?

Dread unfurls in my gut as my gaze shifts to the girl under his arm. She's slightly taller than me, but much curvier, and every single one of her curves is on display in a figure-hugging black dress.

Whitney Lewis.

A cheerleader I know he's hooked up with in the past. Why is his arm around her?

At that instant, he looks up and meets my gaze. For a moment, something flickers through his eyes that might be regret but then he lowers his head and kisses Whitney. She clings to his chest and kisses him back.

A stabbing pain lances through my chest, and I'm suddenly hot all over.

I blink rapidly, my mind struggling to process what I'm seeing, even though, on one level, it's blatantly obvious.

Tyler didn't pick me up tonight because he didn't want to. Not because he was too nervous. Maybe he never intended to take me to prom in the first place. I don't know. All I know is that he's lip-locked with someone else and doesn't seem to care if I see.

Perhaps he even relishes it.

As I watch, something cracks inside me. I can't stay for this.

I look around frantically, hoping to find an easy escape, but Rochelle and a couple of her friends are now between me and the door. They aren't paying me any attention—why would they when no one knows Tyler and I are together? They don't understand that a betrayal is playing out right in front of them.

I glance back at Tyler, as if, somehow, I might discover that the past two minutes have been a trick of my mind, but he's still with Whitney. They've stopped kissing, but he's talking to her quietly.

Intimately.

Raising my chin high, I turn and push past Rochelle, ignoring her cry of protest. I walk faster and faster, and by the time I'm outside, I'm running.

"Miss Dean?" The teacher at the door calls after me, but I ignore her.

My heart is breaking, and no one knows it but me.

TYLER

Just as I reach into my school locker to find the books I need for my next two classes, an achingly familiar voice calls my name.

"Tyler!"

I close my eyes, bile rising up the back of my throat. My stomach is knotted, and I've barely been able to eat all weekend, yet I still feel like throwing up.

Forcing a cocky smirk to my lips, I turn toward Echo.

"What's she want?" Lee, one of my hockey teammates, asks.

"Dude, it's the charity case," another of them says loudly enough for Echo to hear.

She flushes, but her eyes shine with determination as she comes to a halt in front of me. I cringe on her behalf, knowing how much she hates being called that, and her sharp gaze tracks the movement.

Damn. I can't afford for her to think I'm soft on her. I need her to hate me, or she'll ask too many questions. I thought I'd accomplished that with my display with Whitney, but maybe Echo is an even better person that I gave her credit for.

I have to admit, if the shoe had been on the other foot, and I'd seen her kissing someone else, either their face would have been smashed in or I'd have already had a revenge hookup.

My gut sours. I don't think Echo is the kind of person who would fuck someone for revenge, but she didn't believe I'd ever betray her and look where we are. I wouldn't blame her if she spent the rest of the weekend with someone else, even if the thought of it makes me want to cry for the first time in fucking years.

Echo tips her chin back. God, she's incredible. She's like a medieval warrior woman striding into battle. Fearless and utterly captivating.

"Why did you stand me up for prom?" she asks.

To anyone else, her voice might sound level, but I know her well enough to see through her facade. This confrontation is taking a lot out of her.

My insides crawl. I'm not good enough for her in any way, shape, or form. Not after what I've done. And honestly, not before then either. It's just that now, she finally sees the truth.

"I was never going to go to prom with you," I tell her flatly.

Beside me, Lee snorts with laughter. Several bystanders have stopped to watch. I silently beg Echo to drop the subject. To turn around and walk away before I'm forced to do something else unforgivable.

Leave, baby girl. Walk away. You deserve better.

But she stays.

She inhales deeply, her face a mask of calm, even though she's surely simmering with hurt and rage.

"Yes, you were," she says. "We had plans, and then you broke them and went with Whitney instead. Why?"

My gut plummets. Seriously. How is she so brave?

Lee steps up beside me. "Listen, charity case. Ty would never go to prom with a poor little nobody like you."

My fists clench subconsciously. I want to smash one into Lee's face and break his nose for daring to speak to her that way, but I don't have the right to. Not after the shit I've pulled. Besides, in a way, he's helping me.

I laugh. It's strained and false, but no one seems to notice. At least, no one other than Echo.

"He's right," I say. "You're nothing to me. I don't know

where you've got this crazy idea from, but maybe you need to get your head checked."

Someone whistles, and murmurs, "Ouch."

Echo flinches but still doesn't leave. My insides wrench, desperate to throw up the coffee I managed to drink at breakfast, but I swallow it back down. The bitterness burns my throat, and I draw comfort from the pain. It's what I deserve.

Echo holds my gaze. "I don't know why you're doing this, but there must be a reason."

I fight the urge to glance away. There is a reason, but I can't admit as much to her or she'll try to fix it, and there's no fixing this. I'm doing what I can to protect her. But in order for it to work, I can't give her any reason to doubt what an asshole I am.

I steel myself against the pleading in the depths of her hazel eyes. Now is not the time to be weak.

"I fucked you," I tell her loudly. "That's it. We were never together. We fucked, and now it's over. No prom, no great love story, and no cutesy happily ever after. I got what I wanted from you. Get that through your head."

Her expression shatters.

My heart does, too.

She sobs, then claps her hand to her mouth in an attempt to hide it. She turns away and runs down the corridor, but not before the absolute desolation in her eyes makes me wish I'd jumped off a goddamn bridge.

People jeer as she goes, and self-loathing settles deep into my soul. This is all on me. She trusted me, and I hurt her. I knew her insecurities, and I used them against her. Then I humiliated her in front of the people who've always treated her like trash.

She'll never forgive me for this.

It's exactly what I was aiming for, and yet, I want to get on my knees, crawl after her, and beg for another chance.

I open my locker again and roughly yank out the books, then slam it shut.

"Can you believe—"

"Fuck off," I snap at Lee, unable to listen to a second more of his bullshit.

"Whoa. What the fuck?" He backs away, his hands raised.

Ignoring him, I click the combination lock into place and stride toward the men's bathroom. I need a moment of privacy to get a hold of myself. But before I reach them, a slim hand lands on my upper arm.

I spin around, ready to unleash the full force of my temper on whoever has dared to interrupt my getaway, but I bite my tongue as Soraya's disappointed eyes meet mine.

"What did you just do?" she asks, disgust curling her lip.

I stiffen. "What I had to."

She tilts her head to the side. "You shouldn't have. Without even seeing you together, I can tell there's something special between you. The way you talk about her...it's like you can't really bring yourself to believe she's yours."

"Well, she's not anymore," I grit out, desperate for her to stop speaking because I just want to scream, and Soraya gets enough abuse from Dad without me piling it on too. Besides, she's right to call me out on my shitty behavior.

"Uh-huh." She crosses her arms. "Whose fault is that?"

I shift from one foot to the other, uncomfortable beneath her scrutiny. How much of that conversation did she hear? Does she know I kissed another girl?

The memory makes me gag, and I cough to hide it.

Maybe there was another way I could have done it, but I panicked and went for the first option I could think of to push Echo away.

"Dad found out," I tell her.

Her eyes soften, and sympathy flickers in them. "How bad was it?"

I swallow. "Bad."

So bad I felt trapped into a corner. I did what little I could to fight my way out, and now I have to live with the consequences.

Soraya rubs my arm and then lowers her hand to her side. "It must have been, because you just ruined something that could have made you happy."

18

———

ECHO

My nerves jangle as I let myself into the building Tyler lives in and head for the stairs. Soraya gave me his address and told me he occupies the third floor. When I woke this morning, I felt like I needed to see him in person, but now that I'm here, I can't help wondering what drove me to come.

I don't have a plan—or at least, not much of one. I just want to know why he did what he did when he broke us, and I think I'm finally ready to listen. Perhaps learning the reason for his actions won't change anything, but it might provide a sense of closure I've never had.

I take the steps up quickly, so I won't have time to over-think my decision. When I reach the third floor, I stop at the door and knock. I don't hear anything on the other side. Maybe Tyler isn't home. Or maybe he has good soundproof-ing. I sigh and scrub my hand down my face. At this point, I'm just looking for an excuse to escape.

The door swings open, and Tyler is standing on the other side, wearing soft gray sweatpants that mold to his thick thighs and a faded T-shirt with the Princeton logo printed on the front.

His eyebrows knit together. "Echo, what are you doing here?"

"I came to talk." I resist the urge to wrap my arms around myself. I'm not going to self-comfort in a visible way. It's important that he not view me as a victim right now.

"Okay." He opens the door wider and steps aside. As he does so, the collar of his shirt shifts, revealing a small moon on the end of the necklace he's wearing.

My heart stutters. It's the necklace I gave him all those years ago. He's still wearing it, even though the metal has darkened slightly with age. I step past him, ignoring the thundering in my chest and the way my mind is whirling, trying to figure out what it means that he's wearing my necklace.

The living area is open, and the scent of rice and cooking onions hangs in the air. I breathe it in and my head swims. I haven't eaten yet today because I've been so nervous about this visit.

"How did you find me?" he asks, closing the door behind us. When he doesn't lock it, a little of the tension releases from my shoulders. "Soraya."

I nod, although it doesn't seem like he needs the answer. Perhaps there are so few people who know where he lives that it's obvious who spilled the beans.

"I'm cooking lunch," he explains as he heads toward the adjoining kitchen. "It won't take much longer."

I glance at the clock. It's late morning. Early for lunch, but not by much.

"Sorry, I should have thought about that before I turned up." If I'd been brave enough to come when I first had the idea, rather than wasting the morning building up the courage to face him, I'd have had his undivided attention.

Although, come to think of it, perhaps it's best not to have his focus all on me.

"It's fine." His smile is almost shy. "Can I get you a drink while I finish this?"

"Just water, please."

While he fills a glass, I take the opportunity to look around his apartment. It's clear that his furniture is top-of-the-line, but it isn't showy. The large gray sofa is made for comfort, and the color scheme is peaceful—all soft neutrals.

That said, the living area is by no means bland. That would be impossible when one of the walls is dominated by a massive painting of a night sky, featuring the faint gold arcs of shooting stars splashed across it. In the corner of the painting, a crescent moon overlooks it all.

"Do you like it?" Tyler asks.

I jolt, surprised by his voice. I was so taken in by the painting that I hadn't realized he'd approached me.

"It's beautiful," I admit.

"I think so, too."

There's a weightiness to his tone that I'm not ready to address yet, so I turn away from the painting and instead check out the photographs on the cabinets. There's one of him with Soraya at her high school graduation, and another of her in the stands at one of his games, wearing a shirt with the same name and number as the one he sent to me.

Frowning, I scan the other photographs. There are another couple of him and Soraya, but none of his parents. Behind me, the pan sizzles, and the aroma of chicken joins the others.

"Would you like some chicken and rice once it's done?" Tyler asks.

I stroll to the kitchen, moving slowly because it's so

strange seeing him prepare a meal. I didn't even know he could cook.

"Only if there's enough," I say. "I'm not very hungry."

I'm too anxious for that.

"There will be plenty," he assures me. "Just let me add some vegetables."

My eyebrows rise as he grabs a pepper, a stalk of broccoli, and a green leafy vegetable from the refrigerator. He rinses them and begins to dice the pepper, adding it bit by bit to the chicken, which is frying with the onion.

"That looks healthy," I remark.

He nods. "Rice, chicken, and vegetables is a great combination for my lean protein intake and getting good carbs into my system. I try to have it, along with a protein shake or a smoothie, after most of my practices and games."

"Makes sense." What doesn't make sense is this inane conversation. Why can't I get to the point?

"How come you're here?" he asks.

I bite my lip, pleased he's too focused on chopping broccoli to notice my nerves. "I want to know why you did what you did back in our senior year."

His head snaps up and his eyes lock on mine. His hand stops instantly. "You're ready to listen?"

"I am."

"Okay." His nostrils flare as he draws in a long breath. "I'll tell you, but only once lunch is finished. I don't want to do this while I'm distracted."

I'm almost disappointed by that. Hearing him out might be easier while he has a task to distract him, but I understand his reasoning. He's worked hard to get me to this point, so he won't want to ruin it by giving the conversation less than his complete concentration.

"Can I help?" I ask, hoping to speed him up. Being in his private space, with the necklace and the painting to remind me of our shared past, is messing with me. The sooner I can leave, the better.

"Could you shred the spinach?" he asks, gesturing to the leafy vegetable on the counter beside the chopping board.

"Sure."

"Great. Just put it straight into the pan."

I shred one leaf of spinach quickly, making sure to remove any gross bits. It wilts as I add it to the pan. "All of it?"

He glances over. "Maybe a third."

I separate out a third and put the rest back in the refrigerator, then make quick work of tearing it into small pieces and mixing it into the chicken, onion, and bell peppers. When Tyler adds the broccoli, he places a lid over the pan, and it fills with steam.

We stand in awkward silence, neither of us quite sure what to say. Eventually, he mixes a protein shake and I watch while he drinks it, sipping from my glass of water just to have something to do.

When the chicken and vegetables are done, he portions them out onto plates, creating two huge servings. One is bigger than the other, but he's definitely forgotten how much normal people eat because the amount he's dished up could cover my lunch and dinner. Once he adds a scoop of rice, there's really no chance of me finishing the meal.

"Thanks," I say, following him as he carries his plate to the sofa. There aren't any chairs, so I sit as far from him on the sofa as I'm able to. With the coffee table in front of us, the setup reminds me of the room where I used to tutor him.

Tyler sets his cutlery on his plate, and the plate on the table. He turns to face me.

"Let me start by saying that I'm sorry for what I did to you. I know that an apology isn't worth much, especially not this many years too late, but I wish more than anything that I hadn't hurt you."

"Why did you?" I ask, wrapping my hand around the fork to ground myself in the present. I couldn't risk my mind slipping into the past.

His pale gaze holds mine, burning with a passion I remember well, but the level of intensity is more than I ever witnessed from him in the past. We were crazy about each other, but our relationship wasn't the only thing that mattered. I get the feeling that for Tyler, that's changed.

"I was trying to protect you," he replies.

I look down at the fork, unable to bear the intensity of his gaze for any longer. A lump forms in my throat. He was trying to protect me?

On what planet does crushing my heart and publicly humiliating me somehow protect me?

"You—" I cut myself off before I finish snapping at him. It won't achieve anything. I came here to listen, so listen I will. "Go on."

He inclines his head, the slant of his mouth showing that he recognizes my restraint. "My father was abusive."

"I suspected as much," I admit.

"I know you did."

"He's dead?" I haven't yet acknowledged this to him.

"Yeah, and good riddance."

My eyes widen at his vehemence. But then, I don't have an abusive parent. My mom is wonderful, so I can't understand what he went through growing up.

He touches the moon hanging from the chain around his neck and rubs it between his fingers. "The day before prom, he found out about us."

My breath catches. "How?"

And what had he done to Tyler to punish him for disobeying one of his edicts by dating someone?

"Somehow, he made the connection that we'd been at the hotel. He, uh, got his hands on my phone and the messages made it obvious who I'd been there with."

My hand twitches, oddly eager to reach for his. "He must have been furious."

He makes a weary sound. "That's an understatement."

I try to put the pieces together, but I still don't see how they fit. "So, because of that, you stood me up?"

He shakes his head, his lips pressed into a firm line. "Dad knew you were at school on a scholarship, and that you were hoping to get a full scholarship for college. He threatened to have your scholarship revoked if I didn't end things with you. He was on the school board, so he could have made it happen."

My mouth falls open. "What?"

I'd wondered what might happen if Mr. Kinsey found out about us. I'd have been a fool not to. But I always feared more for Tyler than myself. I'd never thought he'd find a way to punish *me* for our relationship.

His jaw tightens. "He said he could get your mom fired as the school cleaner too, and if he spread the word to his friends, she wouldn't have been able to find work anywhere."

Even though dozens of questions sit on the end of my tongue, I remain silent, digesting everything he's said. I believe him. I can imagine Mr. Kinsey making exactly that kind of threat. Whether he had the pull to follow through on it, I'm less sure of, but Tyler clearly believed he did.

"He also..." He reaches across and touches my knee. I flinch, taken by surprise, and his face falls. "Sorry. I just wanted you looking at me, so you'd know I'm being honest."

"I didn't mean to—"

"It's fine. I get it." But he looks devastated. "Dad also told me he could make it impossible for you to get a college scholarship. I don't know what he would have done, but if he'd come up with some bogus charge against you, no college would have looked at you twice."

I'm beginning to understand the situation he was in. Even if I can see potential flaws in Mr. Kinsey's threats, he'd mentally, emotionally, and physically abused Tyler for years. Of course, Tyler wouldn't doubt his ability to follow through.

"Or..." He nibbles his lip. "He said he could make sure you'd have a full scholarship that would get you through your undergraduate degree. Housing, course fees, everything. All I had to do was end it."

"So you did," I say quietly.

"Yeah." He glances at his meal, which is steadily growing cold. "It wasn't just that though. I was afraid of what he might do to Mom or Soraya if I refused. Or to you. He might not have stopped at sabotaging your schooling."

"Why didn't you tell me?" I ask, keeping the accusation out of my voice. I'm still trying to get my head around this, but if he's telling the complete truth—or at least, his understanding of it—then so much of what I believed about the past is a lie.

He scoffs. "I was a dumb kid. I panicked. I didn't have the emotional maturity to deal with the situation."

I grimace. "I understand that. I'm still working on my emotional maturity. Some days, I just want to hide from the world."

Lines of relief groove his face. "It wasn't just that though. I... I didn't trust myself to stay away from you. I was worried I'd change my mind and that my selfishness would cost you everything, so I needed you to make the decision. I had to be sure you'd want to stay away from me, so I did the worst thing I could think of."

Tears fill his eyes.

"I'm sorry, baby. I'm so fucking sorry. Not a day goes by that I don't regret what I did. I can't forget your expression that morning beside the lockers. You were so brave, and I hurt you unforgivably just because I was too weak to be a better person."

His voice is muffled, as if he's speaking through a wall of water.

I shake my head.

All this time, I thought he treated me abominably because he's a terrible person who enjoyed breaking me down in front of his elitist friends. He still did wrong by me —nothing can erase the pain he caused or the damage he did to my self-confidence—but the reason behind his actions makes a difference.

The *why* matters.

But he still ended our relationship by kissing another girl in front of me. I'm haunted by that image the same way he's haunted by our encounter at the lockers.

He humiliated me, but he was trying to protect me, in his own misguided way.

"I need some time to process this," I tell him, because honestly, a lot of what he's said in the past few minutes has gone right over my head.

His shoulders slump, and he tugs his hand over the short ends of his hair. "Yeah. That's fair. Take as long as you need."

Unenthusiastically, he reclaims his plate and begins picking at his lunch. I do the same, and once again, a strained silence falls between us. This time, I have to acknowledge that I don't actually hate Tyler anymore. I just don't know how to feel about the choices he made.

When we're done eating, I offer to help clean up, but he turns me down.

"It'll take me two minutes," he says.

Honestly, I'm surprised he's not looking for a way to keep me around for longer. A couple of weeks ago, he would have been. But perhaps he's as off-kilter as I am.

He walks me to the door but pauses before opening it. "Are you okay?"

I consider the emotional shitshow unraveling inside me, and nod. "I think so."

I'm a mess, but it's cathartic. Perhaps Dr. Rodriguez was onto something with her talk of closure. Even if the truth hurts, it's still good to have answers.

"Can I call you?" he asks hesitantly.

I purse my lips. "Maybe in a couple of days. Let me have some time first."

Then I stretch onto my tiptoes and brush a chaste kiss across his lips. My own lips tingle, the sensation unfamiliar. I haven't kissed anyone on the mouth since him.

"Goodbye, Tyler."

I leave while he stands frozen with shock.

19

TYLER

The lecture hall is buzzing on the day of our group presentations. Students are packed in tightly, and every now and then, I inhale a whiff of B.O. from someone nearby. I barely notice, too eager to see Echo.

This will be our first time face-to-face since she came to my apartment, and I hardly slept last night because I was twisting myself in knots about how she might react to me.

I've been on my best behavior. I haven't called or texted, even though the anticipation is driving me crazy.

I need to know how she is.

Ryan tells me she's fine, but he can't read her the way I can. What if she's upset and is hiding it from him?

I'm staring at the door so intently that I don't notice someone approaching from the other side until they're sliding onto the chair.

I spin around. "That seat is—oh, Echo."

She smiles and tucks an invisible piece of hair behind her ear. The force of that smile whacks me in the gut, driving the air from my lungs.

Damn, she's beautiful. The light that shines inside her

never stops glowing—not even when people have done their best to extinguish it.

"I came in the other entrance today," she explains, opening her backpack and pulling out a notebook.

My pulse leaps. She came in when I wasn't looking and willingly sat beside me. That's significant. She could have easily taken a seat somewhere else, and I might not have noticed until the presentations had begun.

I grin at her like the smitten idiot I am.

"You ready?" she asks, setting her phone on the pull-out desk and scrolling through to find what look to be notes for her portion of our presentation.

"I think so." Usually, public speaking wouldn't bother me, but the fact that it's in front of Echo—and that my performance will contribute to her grade—has ramped up my nerves. I want to impress her, and I don't want to let her down. We may have handed in our essay, but the presentation is worth a significant percentage of the grade.

"You will be." Her smile is softer than I've seen it in more than three years, and my tummy flips over in response. This is good, right?

The professor calls the class to order, and we focus our attention on the first group to present their findings. We know what order we're going in because we were assigned a random number ahead of time.

The first presentation is so good that I rethink everything, but the second group clearly has only one person who put in much work, with the others hoping to ride on their coattails. Based on the professor's expression, I can't see that happening.

Most of the presentations are decent. A couple are snooze-worthy but still thorough. By the time we're up, some of my nerves have dissipated. At least our entire group put an equal amount of work into our project. Because of that, we're already head and shoulders above half of the groups we've seen so far.

Jin starts, outlining the methods portion of our topic. He's a good speaker. Relaxed and confident. Elle follows next with the pros. She speaks a little too fast and laughs a bit too often, but all the content is there.

I come next, and my mouth automatically forms the words I've practiced so many times. I know the topic well. A lot of what we've covered reminds me of my dad. He basically spent years trying to condition us into behaving as he wanted. That's why I chose to speak about the cons. I'm perfectly positioned to know what they are.

Echo brings the presentation home, and it could just be me, but I think she's phenomenal. Afterward, we answer a few questions and return to our seats.

I'm buzzing. I'm pretty sure we knocked it out of the park, and the others seem to agree.

We sit through the remainder of the presentations, then walk together to Full of Beans to debrief. For once, Elle doesn't make a pass at me and, as we order, it becomes clear that Jin is more interested in the tattooed male barista than he is in Echo, so I'm more relaxed than I've ever been around them.

We chat for a while, and then Elle says she has a class to get to. Jin leaves shortly after, citing an assignment that's due later, but his eyes twinkle and he winks as he leaves me alone with Echo.

I like him, I decide. He's an okay guy.

"So," I say when Jin is out of earshot. "We did good, right?"

"Yes," she agrees. "I'd say we've got at least an A minus."

"Awesome." I get decent grades—I have to, to stay on the team—but an A of any form is still better than my usual.

The tattooed barista delivers a caramel-shot decaf

mocha, and Echo accepts it with a smile. After seeing how much she enjoyed her first coffee, I couldn't resist ordering her another, but she insisted on decaf since she limits how much caffeine she has each day. Apparently, being too wired is bad for her anxiety.

"Thanks again for this," she says, gesturing at the coffee.

"No problem." I'll buy them every day of her life if they make her happy. "Echo, you've had some time to think now. Where's your head at when it comes to me?"

She purses her lips, and her expression grows serious. "You shared a lot with me, and it changed my perspective in someways, but you still really hurt me. I'm having difficulty deciding whether I should trust you."

My stomach clenches. "I understand."

But where does that leave us? I can't just give up on her.

"I'm not saying I'll never trust you," she adds gently. "Just that it will take time and effort to get to know each other again, and to build trust between us."

My heart is somehow heavy and light at the same time. The sorrow of knowing how badly I damaged her weighs on me. But hope bubbles inside me too. Hope that we can get past this. That one day, it will be a blip on our radar. A stumble on our path to happily ever after.

"Take as long as you need," I tell her. "I'm not going anywhere, and I won't let you down again."

I couldn't bear it if I did.

"Are you keeping any other secrets from me?" she asks.

I open my mouth to tell her no, but then close it again. The truth is, I do have secrets. Many, many secrets. I'm willing to share them with her, but I'm not mentally prepared to do that right now, and honestly, I don't think she's ready to hear them either.

"You are," she says, reading me like a book.

"I'll tell you. Just...not today."

She sighs, and it stirs a few strands of her hair. "If you can give me time, then I suppose I can do the same for you."

Relief settles my gut.

"It won't be forever though," she warns. "I need to know everything, so I can make an informed decision. I can't do that if you hold back."

"That's fair." Probably more so than I deserve. "Thank you."

She sips her coffee, her brain working overtime, by the looks of it.

"Can I begin to make a new impression now?" I ask. "I'll tell you everything. I promise. But I want to connect with you as the person I've become while we were apart."

She cocks her head. "What do you have in mind?"

I hesitate, but only briefly. "Will you come to Slice of Heaven with me?"

Her eyes widen. "A dessert place? I'm sure that doesn't fit within your approved training diet."

"I can make an exception. I'll just have to burn it off at training later." Putting in a bit more time, or pushing harder, is worth it to spend time with her.

To my delight, she grins.

"Okay, then. Let's go. But you're buying."

I laugh. "Done."

With Dad gone, I have access to more money than I could ever need. Technically, he left it all to Mom, but she split it in three and gave a third each to Soraya and me, as if a bunch of zeros at the end of my bank statement make up for the years she stayed silent as we suffered Dad's abuse.

While Echo drinks her coffee, I ruminate over the issue of my mother. Soraya has always been more understanding of her than I have. They're trying to establish a stronger mother-daughter relationship, but I haven't jumped on board.

Mom has made a couple of overtures toward me, but I'm more hesitant than my sister. I know Mom was a victim as much as we were, but it's still hard to reconcile that she was willing to let us be hit and emotionally manipulated.

Moms are supposed to be protectors. Echo's always was for her. I never met the woman, but I saw how staunchly she supported Echo after the rape, and how fiercely she fought for justice. That's how a mom should be. Not the wispy shadow of a woman who raised me.

When Echo pushes her cup aside, I stand and reach for her hand, but then think better of it. She surprises me, interlacing our fingers together as we leave the coffee shop. Her palm is much smaller than mine, but it's warm from the heat of the coffee and I wish I could raise it to my lips for a kiss.

We don't talk much during the walk, but it isn't an uncomfortable silence. It's freeing to be with someone and know I don't have to fill the space between us. I wasn't sure if I could get to this place with her again, and it makes me optimistic for the future.

Slice of Heaven is located in a small, brightly lit shop fronting onto one of the roads near campus. It's in a great spot to attract drunk college students on their way home, and it stays open late several days a week for exactly that purpose.

I order a raw vegan Snickers slice, figuring that the dates and nuts are surely better for me than the pure sugar of the other options. Echo, on the other hand, orders a decadent piece of chocolate cake, warmed so that the frosting oozes everywhere, and served with cream and ice cream.

We sit at a small table by a window while we eat. My slice is okay, but nothing to write home about. Hers, on the other hand, must be the stuff of dreams based on the way she moans with every mouthful. My cock is rock hard beneath the table, and I just hope I'll be able to get it together before we leave.

"So, Soraya is in Newbury too," Echo notes between mouthfuls. "What about your mom?"

I stiffen. "Mom didn't leave Charlesville."

She still lives in that too-big house with my father's ghost. One of Soraya's goals is to convince her to move into a smaller, cozier home, but she has her work cut out for her. Mom spent even more years being conditioned by our father than we did.

She nods, her sharp eyes no doubt noticing every micro-expression that flickers across my face, cataloging them to revisit in the future.

"Soraya told me she wants to be an attorney specializing in domestic violence cases," she says. "That's pretty impressive."

My posture loosens. "Yeah, I'm proud of her."

"She seems like a smart girl."

I stab my fork into the last piece of Snickers slice. "She's like you, in a lot of ways."

Echo looks intrigued. "How so?"

I shrug and raise the bite of cake to my mouth. "You've both been through a lot, but, somehow, you're still strong."

"Did she..." She trails off, rubbing her lips together as if she's unsure how to go on.

"What?" I prompt. "You can ask me anything."

Her teeth sink into her lip, and then she busies herself portioning off another bit of cake. "Your dad abused her too?"

"Physically, she had it worse than me." I drop my fork, no longer hungry. "He'd threaten her as a way to control me."

"I'm so sorry. That must have been awful." She puts her

fork down too. At least we finished most of our dessert before we lost our appetites.

"It wasn't great." I glance at her plate. "You done?"

She nods.

"Let's get you home then."

We both stand, and I leave a tip on the table. As we stroll down the pavement, our arms brush every now and then. I'm tempted to grab her and refuse to let go. Having her so close, it's like the thing I most want is within reach, but I'm not allowed to touch it.

Realistically, I know she probably wouldn't mind a little physical affection, but our new bond is weak, and I won't do anything to jeopardize it.

When we arrive outside her building, I come to a stop.

"Can I see you again?" I ask, knowing my feelings for her are plastered all over my face.

She holds my gaze for a long moment. "Okay, but anywhere we go has to be public."

A flash of movement to our left catches my attention, and I glance over. It's Ryan, and he's coming straight toward us. I try to meet his eyes, and shake my head silently, but I'm not sure if he notices.

Damn, I'm going to have to come clean about at least one of my secrets soon, or there's every chance that Ryan will do it for me.

20

A little after 11 am on Saturday morning, I pull up outside the dorm where Ryan lives, along with the other members of the baseball team. He's waiting outside, and he raises his hand as I park on the side of the road.

He opens the passenger door and gets in. "What brought this on?"

"My way of saying thank you," I reply.

I'd messaged him a couple of days ago and invited him to join me at a Seahawks game. Even though we haven't shared many personal details with each other throughout the years, I know he's an NFL fan. He'd have played football rather than baseball if he had any talent for the sport.

"For?" he asks.

I glance over as he closes the door. "Taking such good care of Echo since she started college."

I rejoin the quiet stream of traffic and head toward Soldier Field stadium.

He tenses. I understand why. Our arrangement has never sat well with him. Honestly, there have been times when I didn't like it either, but it's been necessary.

"I don't need your thanks," he says. "I was paid to do it, and I was glad to. I know this started off as a job, but she's important to me."

"Good." I'd hoped he'd come to care for her over time, and based on his defensiveness toward her, I'd assumed as much, but it's nice to have it confirmed.

I stop at a traffic light and neither of us speaks. When the light changes color, Ryan sighs.

"Are you going to tell her the truth?" he asks, resting his hands on his thighs and then shifting them as if he can't decide what to do with them.

"I will soon." When I figure out how to break the news. With this, and the other things she needs to know, there's a chance I'll overwhelm her, so it's best if I don't dump it all on her at once.

"Could you give me a heads up before you do?" He hesitates, then adds, "She might be upset, and I want to be prepared for that."

"I'll make it clear that I only paid you to keep her safe," I assure him. "So she knows your friendship is genuine."

He snorts, his expression cynical. "With you manipulating things behind the scenes, is anything in Echo's life truly genuine?"

"Fuck you."

He grimaces. "Sorry, man. I know you mean well. I just feel for her, and I'm not sure she'll care about the technicality."

"I'll make sure she isn't hurt again," I promise. "So, do you intend to stick around her?"

With me at Newbury, there's no need for him to continue working on my behalf. He's been my eyes and ears when it comes to Echo for the past three years. He's watched over her, scared off men who weren't worthy, and ensured her safety. But now I can do that myself—if she'll let me.

Ryan nods. "I'll graduate at the end of this year, but until then, I'll be around…if she doesn't send me packing."

"I'm glad to hear it." In the past, I might have been jealous of her having another man in her life. Honestly, I'm still a possessive bastard, but I have nothing to fear from Ryan.

The stadium looms up ahead. I pull into a parking garage and find a spot on the second level. We get out and take the stairs down. It's a short walk to the stadium, and we join the shorter, more quickly moving line for premium ticket holders.

The sky is gray overhead, but it's warm. The scent of fried food is the best possible advertising for the carts selling hot dog and fries speckling the area.

"We're VIPs today, are we?" Ryan asks as we're ushered through.

I guide him to the elevator that will take us to the upper floor. "We have a suite."

His eyes widen, and he grins boyishly. "Really?"

The doors glide shut.

I shrug. "Go big or go home."

He shakes his head. "You are something. I'm still trying to figure out if it's a good something though."

"Let me know when you work it out."

He rolls his eyes.

When we reach the top, the elevator opens onto a luxuriously appointed viewing room positioned above the rows of seats circling the stadium. The wall facing the stadium is entirely made of glass, providing a great view of the action on the field.

A bar is set into the other wall, and a bartender stands quietly behind it, ready to leap into action if we have any requests.

"Over here." I gesture to our seats, which are black

leather, comfortably padded, and adjacent to a round table upon which sits a platter of delicate hors d'oeuvres.

Ryan whistles. "This is insane." He stands in front of the glass wall and peers out. "Wow. I thought it would be hard to see from here, but it's not."

I lower myself onto one of the seats. "Because we don't have to fight to watch over everyone else's heads."

"But that's part of the experience," he protests.

"Heathen," I tease.

"Trust fund baby," he shoots back.

"Speaking of," I say. "Order whatever you like from the bar. I'll pick up the tab at the end."

He grins for a moment, but then it fades. "Are you sure? I don't mind paying for a drink or two."

I suspect he'll think differently once he sees the price tags.

"Just do it," I tell him.

The grin returns. "If you insist."

The strangest warm sensation fills my chest. Is this how it feels to do something nice for someone who doesn't expect it? Damn. Perhaps I should have been a better person sooner.

We chat idly until the game begins. At that point, any chill Ryan had goes out the window. He shouts, waves his arms, and lectures the players as if they can hear him. I chuckle to myself as he goes off on the ref, attracting more than a few sideward glances.

I yell once or twice, just so he doesn't feel out of place. Football isn't really my thing, but I can appreciate the athleticism of it. An athlete is an athlete, whatever they play.

At half time, I get a beer for Ryan and a Coke for myself and start picking at some kind of vegetable curry wrapped in leaves that's been placed in front of us in bite-sized portions.

"What is that?" Ryan asks, his nose wrinkling.

I shrug. "I dunno, but it tastes okay."

He lifts a piece to his face, sniffs, and sets it down again. "I think I'll stick with things I can identify."

The elevator opens and a pair of middle-aged men enter. One of them is going on about draft picks. They pass behind us and move on.

Ryan turns to me. "Do you plan to enter the NHL draft?"

"Yeah." Hockey is the only thing I know how to do. It's the most straightforward option for me. "What about you? You're aiming for the majors?"

He nods and drinks from his glass of beer. "I am. I have a couple of prospects, but if they don't pan out, I'm confident I'll at least be able to hit the minors and work my way up from there."

"True." I suppose he has that option in the same way I could enter the AHL. I have no intention of doing so though. I may not be the NHL's number one draft pick, but I'll be surprised if I'm not in the top ten.

My hatred of Dad fueled me the past few years, turning me into a machine on the ice—as did my desire to set up the best possible life I could for Echo. It was always clear to me that my best chance to be with her was to enter into an NHL contract with a large enough salary that I could afford to protect my family from Dad.

Not that he's an issue anymore.

Perhaps I should feel bad about his death, but the miserable bastard got what he deserved. My occasional pangs of guilt are misplaced, and I do my best to ignore them.

"So..." Ryan says as the silence drags on between us. "What will you do if you and Echo get back together and then you're drafted somewhere hundreds of miles away?"

"First, I'll ask if she'll consider changing universities. If not, then I'll turn it down."

He looks skeptical. "Just like that? You'd turn down the NHL for a girl?"

I gaze out over the stadium, where half time is soon to end. "Yeah. I'd like to join the NHL. Hockey is all I know. But I don't need the money, and hockey isn't more important to me than she is. I'm sure I could work as a coach or an agent somewhere nearby to keep myself busy."

I've considered doing that anyway. I'm particularly interested in coaching for one of the charities that works with lower income families, but I'd be disappointed not to get to play at least a few years with the NHL first. There will be decades after I retire from professional sports that I can dedicate to the cause.

"I'm impressed," Ryan says. "I don't know if I'd do the same if someone offered me the choice between a major league contract and love."

I chuckle. "Everyone is different. Maybe if you met the girl first, you'd make that choice, or maybe if you knew you wouldn't have to worry about finances then you would. My position and yours aren't the same."

"Don't I know it. I appreciate what you've done for me though. Taking care of Echo hasn't felt like work, but the fact you've paid me well for it means I've been able to focus on my grades and my game rather than having to run around with part-time jobs like some of my teammates do."

"I'm just glad you were willing to do it."

Play resumes, and he focuses on the action while I surreptitiously study him.

It was difficult to find someone for this role. It had to be someone who needed money, was in some of the same classes as Echo, was physically capable of protecting her, and whose personality I thought would be well-matched to hers but who wouldn't fall in love with her.

Ryan has been a lifesaver. I'd have paid him as much as he asked for, provided I was able to get it out of Dad. Although Dad loosened the purse strings a little after I broke up with Echo.

Perhaps it was his way of rewarding me——I don't know —but I appreciated him being freer with money and fulfilling his part of our deal by setting Echo up to have a college experience relatively free of financial limitations.

Not that the scholarship she was awarded could be in any way linked back to him, but I knew it was his doing. It was one of the only good things he ever did, even though it came on the back of one of the worst.

I grab another curry leaf thing and bite into it, enjoying the spicy flavors. Most of my cooking at home is bland. On the field, the Seahawks score a field goal. Ryan pumps his fist. I just smile and return to my musings.

I always wondered if Dad felt a little guilty about what happened to Echo. After all, if I'd been with her, she might have been safe. I was surprised when he allowed me to set up ongoing legal advice for her following the assault— although I did have to threaten to get caught with drugs before he signed the paperwork.

I knew he'd be furious if I ruined my chances at getting onto a good college hockey team and continuing to the NHL. For the first time in my life, I'd had leverage over him because I no longer cared about what happened to me.

Players run back and forth, a blur of black and blue. Ryan hollers again, and it takes me a moment to figure out what's going on. After that, I try to keep my mind on the game, but it's hard not to dwell on how Echo might react when she learns how I've been interfering with her life.

By the time the game ends, Ryan is hoarse from

shouting and my temples are beginning to throb. He's a good guy, but fucking hell, no one warned me how loud he can be when he gets worked up.

On the way out, we're heading away from the stadium when a familiar voice calls my name. I spin around. Soraya is with a group of girls walking in the same direction as us, but twenty yards back.

I stop, and Ryan does the same. As his gaze lands on the girls, his eyes narrow and he shoots me a sidelong look, perhaps wondering if I've been sneaking around behind Echo's back.

"Hey, Ty. I didn't expect to see you here," Soraya says, stealing a peek at Ryan from beneath her lashes. "Who's this?"

Ryan folds his arms across his chest, his posture stiff, and his arched eyebrow asks how I'm going to explain away the fact a group of eighteen- and nineteen-year-old girls are on friendly terms with me.

"This is Ryan," I tell her. "Ryan, this is my baby sister, Soraya."

"Oh." He unwinds his arms and runs one hand through his hair. "Nice to meet you."

"You too." She raises her eyebrow at me. "I didn't know Ty had any friends here."

"I met him through Echo," I say, which is only a lie in some lights.

"And now you're bonding." A smile spreads across her face. "How cute."

I scowl, and Ryan shuffles from foot to foot, obviously as uncomfortable with being called 'cute' as I am.

"Do you study at Newbury?" Ryan asks, glancing at the other girls, who are absorbed by something on the redhead's phone, before focusing on Soraya. There's a gleam of interest in his eye that I don't like.

Soraya nods. "Sociology. Then, once I graduate, I'll go on to law school."

His eyes warm with approval. "Nice. You must be smart."

She blushes. "I do all right."

Oh, no.

Hell, no. The way they're looking at each other is not acceptable.

"We need to go," I say abruptly, grabbing Ryan's arm and yanking him away from her. "Bye, Soraya. Study hard."

Ryan raises one hand in a wave. "See you around."

"No, you will not," I hiss as I drag him into the parking building. "She's too young for you."

He shrugs. "A couple of years isn't a big deal."

I level my finger at him. "My sister is off limits."

"Fine," he grumbles. "But when I'm a bigshot baseball player, you'll regret warning me off."

I just laugh. "Sorry, buddy. Soraya doesn't need a guy with money. She has plenty of her own."

He drops the subject, and we chat about our respective sports during the drive back. I drop him off outside his place, but before he gets out of the car, he turns to me.

"Don't break Echo," he says. "She's vulnerable."

My gut rolls. "I'll do my best not to."

But some of the secrets I'm keeping are heavy enough that I'm not sure our fragile new relationship will hold up underneath their weight.

21

ECHO

Tyler's apartment door opens almost immediately after I knock. He must have been waiting on the other side. As soon as I lay eyes on him, my breath catches. He's devastatingly handsome in dark jeans and a blue button-up shirt that makes his eyes appear even more piercing than usual.

He's shaved, and when he leans forward—slowly, carefully—to kiss my cheek, the scent of menthol lingers on his skin.

"Are you ready to go?" I ask.

He steps past me and locks his door. "I've been looking forward to tonight."

"Me too." Well, that and fearing it in equal measure.

I've spent several days weighing my options, and after an appointment with Dr. Rodriguez yesterday, I'm more confident in my decision. Now, I just have to tell him, and hope that I'm not blindsided by one of his secrets in the future.

I haven't taken a risk in years. Not really. But now, I'm ready to take the leap. I just have to hope he's going to catch me.

We walk down the stairs together and out to my car.

He'd offered to drive, but if our relationship is going to be at all equal, then I need to be comfortable having him in my space. I also need to stop being so self-conscious about the difference in the value of our possessions. My car may not be fancy, but I have nothing to be ashamed of.

"Where are we going?" Tyler asks as he gets into the passenger side.

I slide onto the driver's seat, shut the door, and start the engine. "A little Italian restaurant a couple of miles from here. Francesca's. Have you been before?"

"No, but I love Italian."

I pull out onto the road. "Who wouldn't? They make pasta and pizza."

He groans. "I'm going to have to skate extra hard tomorrow. Worth it, though."

"I hope so." I squeeze the steering wheel as nerves crowd my stomach. He's been telling me since our first encounter that he wants me back, and I'm finally ready to give him that chance.

Please don't mess it up.

I navigate to Francesca's. There are no parking spots outside, but I find one on the next block, and we walk back to the restaurant. My hand brushes his as we move side by side, and I'm tempted to thread our fingers together, but my palms are sweaty, and I don't want to give away how nervous I am.

When we reach the entrance, I push the door open and step inside. My mouth waters from the rich aroma of tomatoes and pasta. I glance at Tyler, who is studying our surroundings. I wonder what he sees. I've been here several times, so I've stopped noticing the yellow walls and the chips and scuff marks on the red vinyl floor.

"Table for two?" a waitress asks.

"Yes." I smile at her. "I have a reservation for Echo Dean."

She returns my smile. "You're over here."

She leads us to a table in the corner nearest the kitchen. Before I have time to sit, Tyler rushes around and pulls my chair out for me. My heart flutters.

I'm making the right decision with him. I know I am.

He sits opposite and rests his massive hands on the red-and-white checkered tablecloth.

"Here are your menus." The waitress hands us each a laminated sheet. "Can I take your drink order?"

"I'll have a sparkling grape juice, please," I say.

Tyler requests a Diet Coke.

"I'll be back in five minutes to take your order." The waitress leaves.

Tyler looks around once again. "This seems like a nice place. Have you been before?"

"A few times." I try to scan the menu, but the words all blur together. I'm too anxious to focus properly. Across from me, Tyler is having more success. "See anything you like?"

"It all looks good. What will you get?"

"Margherita, probably." Considering I know I like it and I can't concentrate on the menu enough to choose anything else.

"Classic."

The waitress returns with our drinks and we both order. I get the margherita and Tyler asks for mushroom risotto, presumably because it's the option that fits most closely into his meal plan.

"So..." I sip my sparkling grape juice, knowing it's time to get to the point. "I've been thinking, and I've decided that I want to try a relationship between us again—if you're still interested."

His face lights up and he reaches across the table and

takes my hand. "Interested isn't the right word. I need you, Echo."

I shoot him a look. It's sweet, but he doesn't need me, and we both know it. He just really, really wants me, and that's flattering.

"We have to go slow," I warn. "Like, very slow, and you have to share any secrets you're keeping that are relevant to our relationship with me sooner rather than later. I'm not saying right this second, but soon. Can you do that?"

He squeezes my hand. "I'll be a truthful tortoise. Promise."

I giggle, his humor breaking the tension. "Thanks."

"You deserve the best."

I wet my lips, remembering the other thing I need to tell him. "Um, you'll need to be patient with me about the physical stuff too. I know we've kinda crossed some lines there already, but I don't know when I'll be ready to go all the way. Or if I ever will."

His expression creases with understanding, and I'm grateful for it. I couldn't have handled pity.

"Baby, I've been waiting for you for years. I can wait a while longer. Even if there are some things you're never ready for, I'll be happy just to have you."

A warm glow suffuses me. He knows just what to say to make me feel better. God, I hope he's being honest.

Our dinner arrives, and we dig in. I offer him a slice of pizza, and he swaps me a little of his risotto.

"It's good," I admit. "But it's not pizza."

He folds up the last bite of his slice of pizza and stuffs it in his mouth. "S'great pizza."

I can't help being charmed by him. He never completely lost the shadows beneath his eyes when we were together years ago. He wouldn't have let go enough to act like a goof. But now, he doesn't seem to be wound as tightly. I wonder if it's the loss of his dad that has made it possible, or something else.

When our meal is done, we order a tiramisu with two spoons. Tyler shifts around the table, sitting beside me so we can share the dessert more easily. I eat most of it, but he has a few mouthfuls, and the noises of appreciation he makes are sinful. His body heat radiates toward me and it's all I can do not to lean into him.

"I got you something," he says as he pushes the empty dessert plate away.

"You didn't have to do that. You know you don't actually have to buy my affection, right?" That may have been his experience with others, but I hope he knows that isn't necessary with me.

He raises himself off the chair and reaches into his back pocket to withdraw a folded sheet of paper. "I wanted to."

He passes it to me, and I promptly unfold it and scan the text.

The star at the coordinates...

Raising my eyes to his, I frown. "What is this?"

He glances at the tabletop, his cheeks coloring. "I named a star after you, since you've always been my shooting star, lighting up the darkness."

Emotions riot in my chest, tumbling over each other so rapidly, I can't recognize them all. Wonder, shock, confusion, and something else I can't put my finger on. This is an over-the-top gesture, but it's so him. My eyes prickle, and I squeeze them shut.

"Go big or go home?" I joke, opening my eyes again, unable to think of anything appropriate to say.

He shrugs awkwardly. "It's probably a scam, but it's the thought that counts, right? Maybe one day we could use the astronomy department's telescope to check it out."

"That would be amazing." I clutch the paper to my chest. "Thank you, Ty. I can't believe you did this."

He named a star after me.

A literal heavenly body.

I read the certificate again. Even if it is a scam, it's a romantic one, and it reminds me of how things used to be between us. Of how he used to look at me and make me feel like the only person in the world.

His star.

"I love it." Another swell of emotion clogs my throat and I do my best not to tear up.

He clears his own throat, perhaps also choked up. "Good."

At that moment, the waitress interrupts to ask if we'd like coffee. We both turn her down.

"That must be our cue to sort out the bill," Tyler says.

"I'll get it," I tell him.

He stiffens, and I can see he doesn't like the idea, but if we're going to have an equal relationship, he needs to let me play my part. For a moment, it looks as if he might protest, but then he sighs.

"Only if I pay the tip."

I beam. "Deal."

We pay, and I drive him home. When I park outside, I leave the engine going, assuming he'll jump out and head back in, but he doesn't move.

"Will you come in?" he asks. "I can make you a nightcap."

I narrow my eyes at him. Does he mean an actual nightcap or is that code for something else?

"How about a hot chocolate?" he suggests.

I hesitate, torn between accepting and keeping up another barrier between us. But when I allow myself to think about what I actually want, I know I'm not ready to say goodnight yet.

"Okay," I say.

His answering smile is beautiful. "You won't regret it."

I hope he's right.

I stop the car, and we both get out and take the stairs to his apartment. He hurries ahead, while I puff along behind him, too full of good food to be bouncing up stairs.

He unlocks the door and goes straight to the kitchen. I watch as he starts up his coffee maker and prepares two hot chocolates.

"Marshmallows?" he asks.

"Of course."

We sit side by side on his sofa while we drink. The hot chocolate is frothy and rich, and the company is even better, though we don't speak much. When my mug is empty, I rest my head on his shoulder and close my eyes. I'm so warm and comfortable that it would be easy to fall asleep here.

He puts his arm around me and shifts me so that I'm lying against his chest, while he rests his head on the arm of the sofa. I tilt my face up and kiss his cheek. Contentedness settles into my bones.

I must doze off because a while later, Tyler gently shakes me awake.

"Echo," he murmurs.

Reluctantly, I blink against the brightness of the overhead lights. "What?"

"It's time to get you home," he says. "Or would you rather sleep on the sofa?"

I would've been happy sleeping exactly where I was, but for some reason, he felt the need to disturb me.

I sit up, hoping to clear my sleep-addled mind. "I'll go home."

He shimmies around until he's sitting beside me with his feet on the floor. "You're welcome to stay here if you'd like. I just don't want to take advantage of the fact you're worn out."

"That's sweet of you." I appreciate that he's being straightforward with me rather than pressing his advantage while he can. Honestly, I didn't expect that. Perhaps I should stop judging him so harshly and stop expecting the worst. The fact is, Tyler isn't the person I thought I hated. That guy was never real.

I lean over and kiss him chastely. He returns the pressure but doesn't take the kiss further. It's reassuring, but a pulse of want beats in my core.

I gasp. I haven't experienced physical desire for a person since...well, since I was with him.

Even though Tyler and I have proved I can bring myself pleasure, I fear that being with an actual person would be different. I press closer to him and dip my tongue between his lips. His hand slides around my waist, leaving a trail of shivering, needy skin behind it.

I can't get enough of this feeling.

I deepen the kiss, tasting the chocolate on his tongue, along with a hint of coffee from our dessert earlier in the evening. He cups my face with his free hand, and I lean into his touch.

But then he pulls away. Blue eyes with blown-out pupils gaze down at me, and his chest heaves. His thumb brushes across my lower lip, and I bite the tip of it softly.

"We should stop." His voice is ragged. "We're taking it slow, remember?"

Frustration zaps through me. Why did I say that? I can't even remember now.

"But I want..." I trail off. "It feels so good, Ty. Just a little more. Please."

He groans, his eyelashes fluttering as he looks at the ceiling. "Fuck. How am I supposed to say no to you?"

"You don't?" My tone is hopeful.

He moves his face closer to mine, crushing the tips of our noses together. "Stop me the second something doesn't feel good to you anymore."

I grin, satisfaction racing through me. "I will."

He kisses me again, but then eases off, letting me control the rhythm of our kiss. I push him back onto the sofa and straddle him, but keep my lower body apart from his. No matter how lost in desire I am, I don't think I could handle feeling his erection against my pussy.

We take our time, rediscovering each other with our mouths. I learn what makes him groan, and he breathes me in as if I'm oxygen.

I grab the hem of his shirt. "Can I take this off?"

He nods, and I undo his buttons, my fingers fumbling. He doesn't rush me, just lies there and waits for me to finish. I push his shirt aside and run my hands down his muscular chest. There's a tattoo just beneath his collarbone on one side and I trace it with my fingers. An eagle.

He lifts himself up and we slide his shirt off, revealing the tattooed left arm that I'd noticed but never been brave enough to study up close. He must have had the work done after he left home, because I can't imagine his father would have been pleased about it.

Among the art, which is intricately designed and spans from his shoulder to his wrist, I make out another bird with feathers falling from its wings.

"I love this," I breathe, but then something else catches my attention. There, on his hip, is a small tattoo of a shooting star. "Oh, Tyler. Is that...?"

22

———

ECHO

"This way, you're always with me," he whispers, pink highlighting his cheeks, as if he knows he sounds like a sap and is embarrassed but can't seem to help it.

Adorable.

I follow the trail of the shooting star with the tip of my pointer finger and then, in an effort to distract him from his embarrassment, begin to lift my own shirt.

He stills me with one hand. "You don't have to."

"I know. I want to." It scares me, but in a good way. So far, I've had none of the symptoms of an oncoming panic attack, just anticipation and the usual nerves of having someone see you naked for what feels like the first time.

Technically. I've been naked with him before, but so much has happened since then that I feel like a different person. Even if there are no scars on my body, they're in my mind, and they make me see myself differently.

Drawing in my breath, I pull off the shirt and position it over the back of the sofa, giving myself a chance to gather my thoughts before turning back to Tyler. His eyes are darker than usual, and completely focused on my face.

There isn't even a flicker to indicate he'd rather be looking at my chest or anywhere else.

"Beautiful," he says.

A smile tugs at the corners of my mouth. "You are."

His skin is smooth over hard muscles, with a dusting of blonde hair arrowing down to his waistband. His nipples are dark, and I toy with one and then the other. Somehow, even in this vulnerable position, I trust him not to push me too far. After all, he's already tried to stop. It's my choice to keep going.

I bite my lower lip, considering what to do next. I take a moment to appreciate that I had enough forethought to wear the nicest bra I own, although it's nothing fancy. For some reason, even though I know I'm physically safe, I don't want to take the bra off yet. It's a layer of protection.

"How far do you want to go?" he asks.

"I want to come." The words are out of my mouth before I have time for second thoughts.

His eyebrows climb up his face. "Are you sure?"

"Yes." It may be impulsive, but I'm not backing out.

He cocks his head. "I have an idea."

"Tell me."

He scans my body, his gaze hot but not lingering anywhere for too long. "Why don't I move down and you can ride my tongue?"

My face goes up in flames. "Excuse me?"

He smirks. "If you're on top, you have control. You can stop whenever you want. Also, I've been dying to get my mouth on your pussy again."

Wetness forms at the V between my legs, soaking my panties. Why is that so hot?

"I don't want to suffocate you." I can't even imagine how embarrassing it would be to have to explain that to the police.

He rolls his eyes. "You won't. I'm strong enough to lift you if I need to, but even if you did, it's a damn good way to go. You in?"

I nibble on my lip, pressing my thighs together. I'm still turned on, and I want to take this as far as I can, both to prove I'm capable of it and so I know what my limits are.

"Okay." I moisten my lips. "Yes, please."

"So polite," he teases.

I widen my stance and he slides down the sofa until my knees are tucked beneath his armpits.

"You'll need to put your legs on the other side of my shoulders," he says.

Awkwardly, I get off him and remove my jeans. I hesitate before finally pulling my panties down too. The soft catch of his breath is rewarding in ways I didn't know I needed. I climb over him, my knees on either side of his head, a little self-conscious of the close up view he must be getting.

"Fuck, you're hot." He grabs my hips and gently but insistently tugs me lower, until I'm hovering right above his face. "I never thought I'd get to taste this little bit of heaven again."

He licks down my center, and I jolt in response, partially from pleasure, but also because the touch shocks me. No one other than me has had their hands or mouth on me there in a long time.

No. Don't think of the last time.

"Okay?" he asks, his lips moving against me, slightly ticklish.

"Yes." Exhaling slowly, I make a conscious effort to relax my muscles.

He blows on me, and a shiver ripples up my back. Then he presses the softest kiss to my pussy. Then again. At first, they're close mouthed, just getting me used to his touch. He must have realized I was overwhelmed.

For several minutes, he brushes his lips over me, almost reverentially. Eventually, his tongue gets involved. It's all very tender and considerate, and as my body loosens, it's no longer enough.

I need more. More firmness, a stronger touch.

"More, Ty." I arch into him. "Stop treating me like I'm breakable."

Thankfully, he doesn't ask if I'm sure. He just moans and buries his face deeper between my legs, lathing open-mouthed kisses over me. His nose bumps my clit and I whimper and grab onto the arm of the sofa. He moans again, and the delicious vibrations make me quiver.

I glance down and find him staring back at me, his eyes burning with blue fire. His hair is mussed, and he looks absolutely debauched.

"Oh, God."

I bite my lip as his gaze intensifies and he shifts one of his hands around to rub my clit, the other splaying across my hip to hold me in place.

He murmurs something, but it's lost against my flesh.

All of the emotions he's ever felt for me—and all the ones he claims to feel—are right there for me to see in the vibrant depths of his eyes. He's hiding nothing.

Everything he's said about his reasons for pursuing me is true.

All he wants is me.

His rough fingertips circle around my clit over and over again, and I can't take my eyes off him as I wind tighter and tighter, my hips shifting slightly against his mouth as I search desperately for that last little bit I need to push me over the edge. He stops moving his fingers and just presses them against me.

I cry out, and the earth seems to shake around me. Pleasure rolls through me, robbing me of my ability to think of anything other than the slick heat of Tyler's mouth and the things his skillful tongue is doing to me.

I tremble as the band of tension snaps, and I gasp his name. Everything turns hazy. When my mind clears, I'm snuggled against Tyler's chest. He kisses the top of my head, and his arms tighten around me.

I reach down. His erection hasn't deflated at all. I cup my hand over it, but then he brushes me away.

"No," he says. "This was just for you."

"But..." I don't feel right without reciprocating.

"Nothing else is happening tonight." His firm tone tells me there's no changing his mind, so I relax against him.

As our skin is beginning to cool, Tyler's phone vibrates.

"Ignore it," he says.

It buzzes again.

I sit up. "It could be important. Where's your phone?"

He waves his hand toward the coffee table, and I lean over and grab it, then frown at the name that crosses the screen.

"Why is Ryan messaging you?"

<hr>

TYLER

Fucking hell.

I'm in so much trouble.

My chest is tight as I try to come up with a way to explain Ryan's message that she'll actually listen to. Based on the stiffness of her expression, she's already fortifying her walls, just in case she's about to be slammed by another betrayal.

I hate that I've put her in a position to get hurt. Again.

I should have told her about Ryan earlier. I was enjoying our date and didn't want to end on a sour note, but I should have just sucked it up and done it. Then we wouldn't be here. I might not have gotten to taste her either, but then, I never expected to tonight, so it was a delightful bonus. I didn't think she'd be willing to be so vulnerable with me yet.

And look what happened.

"Tyler?" She passes me the phone, even though it's obvious she wants to read the message. She's too good to encroach on my privacy like that though.

That makes one of us.

Is there a way I can gloss over it? Make my arrangement with Ryan sound less significant than it was?

No. I need to be completely honest with her if this is going to work.

"There's something you need to know."

She scrambles off me and snatches her shirt off the back of the sofa. "What?"

I swing my legs around so I'm seated properly and pat the cushion beside me. She narrows her eyes but sits and dons the shirt.

"What is it?" she repeats. "You're worrying me."

To my relief, she lets me take her hand.

"When you went to college, I was worried about you— especially after what Eric did to you." I choke on my former friend's name, and guilt spikes through me, hot and cold at the same time.

"So...?"

I swallow. "So I found a guy who was in some of your classes and who was on a sports scholarship and needed financial help, and I paid him to keep an eye on you."

Her eyes are flat. "Ryan."

"Yeah."

I search her face, looking for a trace of the sparkle from before, but it's gone. Instead, she seems weary to her bones.

"I'm sorry." I squeeze her hand, but she pulls it away. "I wanted to make sure you were safe."

Saying I was worried is an understatement. I was frantic when I realized that Echo would be attending university on a different coast than me—thanks, Dad—and without any friends or even her mother around for in-person support.

I guess she wanted a fresh start, but she was so vulnerable.

"Was our whole friendship fake then?" she asks dully. "Was it all an act to get close to me so you'd keep sending him money?"

I wish I could take her into my arms, but the way she's holding herself screams to keep my distance.

You're breaking my heart, baby.

"It wasn't fake." Although I doubt she'll believe me. "I didn't ask Ryan to be your friend. He did that himself because he liked you. It wasn't part of our arrangement."

She sniffs. "I bet it was convenient though."

Well, yeah. But I'm not stupid enough to admit that.

"And how flattering to know that Ryan genuinely wanted to be friends with the pathetic girl who needed someone to be paid to take care of her." She turns toward me and raises one shaking hand to her mouth. "How much does he know?"

"Nothing. Only what you've told him." Or what he may have guessed. He's an observant guy. I'd be willing to bet he's put some of the pieces together.

She stands up, her gaze fixed on the door.

"Wait." I lurch upright and block her path. "Please, let's just take a few minutes to talk it through."

She crosses her arms and scowls. "A lack of talking seems to be one of our problems. Or at least, a lack of you sharing things I really ought to know."

"I did it out of fear." I hook my thumbs into the pockets

of my jeans because, otherwise, I'll reach for her, and that would only be courting rejection. "I planned to tell you. I've already spoken to Ryan and let him know that I meant to come clean. I just..."

I hang my head. There's really no explanation. I should have told her already. I was just enjoying the fragile new connection between us too much to risk breaking it, and that was selfish of me.

Echo purses her lips. "Whatever your reasons were, I can't help feeling like you've been manipulating every part of my life."

"I—" Was. I totally was.

"You made the decision to end our relationship without my input, you apparently hired me an attorney after the rape, you made a deal with your dad that landed me a scholarship at a university far from yours, and then you kept influencing my life through Ryan even though our relationship was over."

I slump. "That's all true." There's no denying it. "Maybe it's messed up, but I didn't know what else to do. I didn't have good role models for what love or a healthy relationship looks like, but I've been doing my best to protect you and give you what you want."

She arches her eyebrows. "Did you, or did you not, *buy me a friend*?"

"I didn't." Hoping she doesn't take the opportunity to push past me, I swipe my phone screen and hit the Call icon beside Ryan's name.

He answers almost immediately. "Hey."

"Ryan, I have Echo on speakerphone. She knows about our arrangement. Can you please tell her the truth about what you think of her?"

"Echo?" he asks cautiously.

"Yes," she snaps.

"You're a great person. I consider you to be one of my best friends, and I hope you feel the same about me."

"How many of your best friends do you get paid to spend time with?" she asks tartly.

He sighs. "You fucked up the explanation, didn't you?" He doesn't wait for a reply. "Echo, I didn't get paid for spending time with you. I received a flat rate for watching over you regardless of whether that was from a distance or up close."

Echo narrows her eyes at me, but an ounce of hostility drains from her. "So why didn't you do it from a distance?"

Ryan huffs a strained laugh. "Because I liked what I saw. You're kind and clever, and I needed a friend whose world didn't revolve around baseball. The first time we talked, I was just scoping you out, but I felt good after spending time with you, so I made a point to do it again."

Echo's pinched expression eases a fraction more. "You aren't a pity friend?"

"You know me better than that." He sounds exasperated. "I'm the same person. Our friendship just wasn't quite as organic or accidental as you thought."

"Hmm." She's clearly reluctant to fully believe us, but she's softening.

"I care about you, Echo. But if you don't want to see me again, I'll understand."

"No," she says slowly. "Just...give me a chance to get my head around this. I can tell that both of you were coming from a good place when you made this plan, but I still feel like so much of the past three years have been based on a lie. It'll take me a while to come to terms with that."

My heart is heavy. Once again, I messed up. Perhaps she would have been better off if I never transferred to Newbury.

"I have to go."

This time, I don't stop her as she passes me. The door clicks shut behind her, and only then do I turn. The living room is empty now, except for me.

She's gone.

"Catch you later." I end the call and hurry after her. Not to talk, but to make sure she gets home safely. I get into my Audi, which is parked just off the street, and follow her beat-up Ford all the way back to her dorm.

She parks around the side, and I wait until she comes back around the front and enters. Only once the door is firmly shut behind her do I depart. Whatever happens, I won't leave her vulnerable to being hurt again. I made that mistake once, and I won't repeat it.

As I pull away, it feels like I'm back where I started. Except now, I've had another taste of her. Just enough to remind me of what I'm missing out on.

Somehow, that makes being without her so much worse.

23

—————

ECHO

Someone drops down beside me, but I don't look over, even though I can feel them staring at me. Instead, I keep my eyes trained on the textbook on my lap. The sun is warm on my shoulders, but the breeze in the university courtyard is just enough to keep me from napping.

"Echo?"

Damn. I should have known better than to think she would take a hint.

I turn toward my new companion. "Hi, Soraya. Did Tyler send you?"

Soraya arches her eyebrows. "As a matter of fact, no. But I did hear that he messed up again."

My stomach churns. I'm so sick of everyone knowing my business. "I suppose you knew about Ryan before me?"

"Ryan?" For a moment, she seems taken aback, but then her expression smoothes over. "I knew that he had someone keeping an eye on you. I didn't know who that person was."

Every goddamn person around me knows more about my own life than I do. I can't decide whether I'd prefer to bury my face or scream. It's embarrassing that others know one of my most trusted friends is nothing more than a liar who was using me as a way to make money.

"How many people know?" I ask quietly.

"About Ryan?" She shrugs. "You, me, and those two idiots, if I had to guess."

I snort. "They are idiots."

She picks at her cuticles. "What are you more upset about? Tyler keeping things from you, the fact he's been trying to manage your life, or Ryan befriending you under false pretenses?"

I shake my head. "I don't know. All of it."

"If it helps, I'm sure they both genuinely care about you."

I level her with a gaze. "How would you know that? Do you even know Ryan?"

"We met recently." She focuses even more intently on her nails, her cheeks a pretty shade of pink. "He seemed like a good person. Loyal to you. He had no reason to fake anything around me, and that's the impression I got. He seemed ready to tear Tyler's head off before he realized I was his sister and not a random hookup."

Somehow, that makes me feel better—or at least, more willing to accept Ryan's claim that he honestly considers me a friend.

"Thanks for telling me."

Her gaze flits around the courtyard. Once again, I'm struck by how similar her features are to Tyler's. Except that on him, they're broader and more masculine, whereas hers are delicate. She's very All American.

"No problem." Her eyes settle on me again, a little brighter than Tyler's. "Just so you know, Tyler would worship the ground you walked on, if you let him. He may not always come across well, and sometimes he makes stupid decisions, but Dad was fucked up, and none of us got out of that house without scars."

"You don't have to tell me—"

"Tyler's scars are mostly psychological," she continues, ignoring my interruption. "Mine are more physical. Although I didn't escape the psychological warfare either."

"I'm sorry."

She shrugs again, looking away. I get the feeling she doesn't like talking about this, and I don't blame her. It must bring back a lot of bad memories.

"Tyler regrets the choices he made back then. After Eric Weston got sent away like the criminal he is, Tyler just wanted to make sure you were safe, and he was prepared to do whatever it took. He might not have gone about it the right way, but his intentions were good."

"That's the problem." I sigh. "He always has good intentions, but how many other secrets is he keeping?"

"He was emotionally damaged, and he's doing the best he can. He's trying."

"I know." Perhaps I'm not being entirely fair to him. It's just hard to continually have the rug pulled out from beneath my feet. "Still, you grew up in the same household and you seem to understand what's okay and what isn't."

She grimaces. "You can thank several months of intense therapy for that. Tyler and I have both been seeing professionals since Dad died."

"Oh." I frown. "He never mentioned it."

"He probably didn't want you to worry about him."

I wince, experiencing a pang of guilt. Sure, I have my own issues, but I care enough about Tyler that I should have at least taken the time to find out something like whether he sees a therapist. I've had plenty of opportunities to ask, but I never did. What does that say about me?

"I'll do better." Provided we continue to see each other.

Soraya chips away at the paint on one of her nails, dislodging flecks of pink. "I wouldn't take it too personally. It can be hard to get things out of him sometimes, especially if he doesn't want you to know. He had to learn to keep a lid on his emotions. I may have borne the worst of Dad's physical abuse, but Tyler was never allowed to show weakness."

My chest squeezes. "If your dad were still alive, I think I'd like to kick him in the balls."

A laugh bursts from her, and her eyes widen as if she's surprised by it. "Get in line."

Something softens in the air between us. A sense of understanding.

"Hey, would you like to get an ice cream?" Soraya suggests. "It's a nice day for it, and we can keep talking for a while longer."

I snap my textbook shut. "Let's do it. Honestly, I was just staring at the page anyway. None of it is going into my head."

She pulls a face. "I get that. My mind goes down a rabbit hole sometimes if I start thinking of the past or letting myself dwell on negatives."

Sympathy wells up within me. Somehow, despite our different backgrounds, I'm beginning to believe we might be kindred spirits.

I pack my textbook into my backpack, stand, and sling the bag over my shoulder. "The ice cream place a block over?"

"Perfect." She grins. "I'm craving their salted caramel swirl."

We walk side by side in companionable silence. After a few minutes, Soraya glances at me out of the corner of her eye.

"Would you like to hear more about Dad?" she asks.

"Only if you're willing to talk about him. I know how triggering it can be."

"It's fine. He can't hurt me now."

Does it make me a bad person that, for a second, I wish I was in the same situation, with Eric Weston dead rather than in prison?

We pause at a crossing and wait for the walking light to turn green.

"As far as I know, Dad was always violent toward Mom," she says. "When I was young, I didn't realize that most dads didn't shout and hit people when things didn't go their way. I don't know when it started. Mom doesn't talk about it, although I've been working on getting her into therapy, so hopefully she will soon."

"Whose idea was it for you all to go to therapy?" I ask, curious.

She flashes me a small smile. "Tyler's."

For some reason, that doesn't surprise me. Ahead, the light changes, and we hurry across the street.

"Dad hit me for the first time when I was maybe five or six. At least, that's the first time I can remember. It's strange, but I was so shocked that he'd hurt me, even though I'd seen him do the same to Mom."

Nausea rolls in my gut. "You felt safe with him. He was your father."

"I guess. Anyway, he was never as physically violent with Tyler as he was with us. At first, I thought he loved me less, or that perhaps it was a man/woman thing, but eventually I grew to understand that he just didn't want to jeopardize his chances of having an NHL player son. Injuring Tyler was too risky."

"He sounds like a real piece of work."

She nods. "He was. He put so much pressure on Tyler as soon as he realized he had potential. He monitored his food intake and insisted he spend hours training every day—to the extent that his peewee coach banned Ty from extra ice time because he was worried about him. That didn't stop Dad though. He just came up with backyard drills instead."

"That must have been hard for Tyler." And Soraya too. She'd been abused or ignored, while Tyler had been controlled and pushed to his limits.

"It only got worse over time." Her arm brushes mine and she seems to instinctively put more space between us. Is that an ingrained self-protective habit? I know I tend to do the same.

"How so?"

"He wouldn't let Ty go out with his friends, and he wouldn't let up about his grades. Ty did pretty well, considering, but how was he supposed to find the time to study when Dad was constantly hounding him to train?"

"He put him in an impossible position." I know I'm academically gifted, but even my grades would suffer if I didn't have any time to do my assignments or prepare for tests.

"It didn't stop there though. He refused to have any treats in the house. No chocolate or chips. If a game went poorly, he'd break down every single thing he thought Tyler had done wrong and then work him until he puked. He wouldn't even let him choose what college to go to. He'd already decided that Princeton was the only acceptable option."

"He told me that. About Princeton, I mean. He didn't want to go there."

At the time, I'd had no idea what I could do or say to help. He'd insisted that I not talk to his dad as I'd proposed, and in hindsight, I understood why he'd been so adamant about it.

Someone coming the other way bumps into me, and I shift closer to Soraya.

"What doesn't make sense to me is why I was such a threat in your father's eyes that he had to force us apart."

She glances over. "My guess is that he was worried you'd interfere with the plan he'd set out for Tyler. None of the other girls he'd been with mattered to him, but Dad knew that you did, and he might have thought Tyler would begin pushing back against his orders."

"I suppose that makes sense." Oddly, it pleases me to be told that I meant more to Tyler than the others—especially coming from someone other than him.

The ice cream parlor is on our left, and I push the glass door open and hold it for Soraya. There's a long line in front of the counter, so we cross the black-and-white checkered floor to join it. A collection of bubblegum-pink bar stools are positioned in front of the counter, but no one is sitting at them.

I scan the selection of ice creams, but I can't see far enough to tell what flavors are at the other end of the cabinet.

"Echo." Soraya's fingertips brush my upper arm.

I turn to her. "Yes?"

She lowers her voice. "What Dad did to Tyler fucked with his head so badly that he hardly slept for months. Sometimes, he was in such a bad frame of mind that I thought he might just decide to end it all."

"No," I gasp, pain burning in my chest.

The world shouldn't exist without Tyler Kinsey in it. I refuse to even imagine it.

"I'm completely serious."

I know she is, and tears fill my eyes. "I'm so grateful he didn't."

"Me too. I'm not trying to make you feel bad. I just want you to understand that, sometimes, the only thing that got him through those dark times was counting down to the day he'd sign a contract with the NHL and Dad wouldn't be able to hold our safety or your education over his head anymore."

My brain goes blank. Is she implying that Tyler would have come for me eventually, even if his father hadn't died? That he was biding time until he could financially support us all? What kind of person even does that?

A selfless one.

One who's much better than I've given him credit for.

Certainly a better person than me.

"Excuse me, Miss?"

I jolt around. Somehow, I'm now at the front of the line.

"What would you like?" the girl behind the counter asks.

Barely able to think straight, I ask for a salted caramel swirl because Soraya mentioned it earlier and it's the first thing to pop into my head. She orders the same, and once we have our ice creams, we slide into a pink-and-white vinyl booth near the door.

"Are you okay?" Soraya asks, her face creased with concern.

"Yeah." I rub my temple. "Just having a hard time accepting that Tyler spent years planning for a future with me. After what happened at the prom, I assumed that none of our relationship had been real and that he wouldn't think of me again."

The edges of her mouth twitch. "Don't you hate it when people make you rethink things you thought you knew?"

"Yes." The frustration in my tone is obvious. "Because now I doubt everything that I think happened, and I can't help wondering if I'm to blame for not seeing what was going on and helping him. You were both stuck in a nightmare situation, and I didn't do anything about it."

Soraya swirls a wooden teaspoon in her ice cream. She

had opted for a cup, while I took a cone. "You offered to help though, didn't you?"

"At the beginning, yes. But I shouldn't have let him put me off." I lick a trickle of ice cream that's melting down the side of the cone and savor the salty sweetness.

"Then he might have pushed you away before anything between you went further," she pointed out. "And what could you have done, really? Dad had friends in the police, at our school, and plenty of clout. I doubt you would have made a difference."

"But we'll never know."

She seems unbothered. "We all have our burdens to bear. I guess that 'what if' is one of yours."

"How are you so calm about this?" I ask.

"For me, it's just the facts of life. None of it is a surprise, or new information. I've had time to process." She licks ice cream off her spoon and murmurs her appreciation. "So good. I needed this."

I nod and get to work on the ice cream before it melts all over my hands. As I eat, the anger simmers within me. Instead of going away, it builds. When I've had enough, I toss the rest of the cone in the bin and wipe my hands on a napkin.

"I hate your dad," I say calmly. "I wish I could bring him back just to make him pay for everything he did to you all."

Soraya tilts her head to the side. "I hate him, too. So does Tyler. But neither of us want him back. Not even for punishment. Not even to ease Tyler's guilt."

"What do you mean? What does he feel guilty about?"

She pushes her cardboard cup away, the spoon sticking out of what remains of her salted caramel swirl. "I told you before that he was with Dad when he died. When I found out, for about two minutes, I wondered if he had something to do with it."

I stare at her for a long moment. Tyler twisted himself into knots for everyone around him, and his own sister could still believe him capable of that?

"How could you think that? He's a good person."

"Even good people hit their breaking point sometimes." She's so calm. So measured. It isn't right.

"He wouldn't—"

"She's right to wonder." The voice comes from my left, and I spin to face the intruder.

It's Tyler.

His expression is impossible to read, but it's obvious he overheard at least some of our conversation.

"Ty..."

"It's okay." He drops onto the bench beside me. "She wasn't wrong to ask the question. The truth is, when Dad started having chest pains, I hesitated before calling the ambulance. If I hadn't, he might still be alive."

24

———

"We should talk outside," I say, as if my heart isn't pummeling the inside of my chest.

I glance at Echo, waiting for her reaction. Will she be disgusted?

I deserve it.

So far, all I see in her wide eyes and parted lips is shock.

"Yeah, let's go outside," Soraya agrees, exiting the booth and hovering beside it.

I join her.

"Okay." Echo seems distant as she stands and follows us out the door and onto the sidewalk. Hopefully, this isn't the start of her inevitable brush-off.

Maybe I shouldn't have approached them. I could have avoided this conversation, or at least put it off, but I had to make sure Soraya wasn't pressuring Echo to give me another chance. I want her, but not like that.

"Are you stalking me?" Echo asks, turning to face me.

I wince. "No." Not today, at least. "I was walking past and saw you both. I was worried Soraya might be pushing you into talking to me before you're ready, so I stopped to check on you."

That seems to soften her a bit.

"What were you saying about your father's death?" she asks.

I look around, noticing a group of girls watching us with interest. "Walk with me."

I start off along the sidewalk, purposefully slowing my pace so they can keep up.

"Tyler, you don't have to—" Soraya begins.

"It needs to be said," I interject. "Putting stuff off hasn't gotten me anywhere. Echo, what I meant is that I was with Dad when he had the heart attack that killed him. He was yelling at me about one of my grades when he suddenly sat down and clutched his chest. I..."

I sneak a look at her to see if she's figured out where my story is going, but she's just watching me levelly, waiting for me to say my piece. There's no judgment in her expression. How long will that last?

"I hesitated before I called the ambulance." The confession pours from me on an exhale. "I don't know how long. Maybe thirty seconds. Maybe a couple of minutes. It felt like fucking forever. I couldn't help thinking that it seemed like the universe was handing me a solution to all my problems. If he was gone, everything would be better."

"But you did call for help," she says softly, with every confidence in my ability to be a good person. Misguided, but sweet.

"Yeah, but they couldn't save him. If I'd been faster, he might still be alive."

Soraya huffs. "It's only a 'might'. No one has ever actually said he'd definitely have survived if help arrived sooner. With a massive heart attack, it's pretty much impossible to know for sure."

"But he would have had more of a chance," I say stubbornly.

"Or maybe if the ambulance driver had gone faster, or if the paramedics weren't near the end of a long shift, he'd have survived, too. We can't know."

I pretend not to hear her. We've had this argument before, and no doubt we'll have it again.

"You feel guilty anyway," Echo says, and it's only then that I realize she's looking at me. Those hazel eyes can read me like a book.

I swallow past the lump lodged in my throat. "I was relieved when I heard he was dead. What kind of person does that make me?"

I wait for her to tell me to get lost, but the words don't come.

"Human." To my surprise, she takes my hand. "You had a very complicated relationship with him. I have no idea what that was like because I didn't live it, but he hurt you and manipulated you, and it's only human for you to think about how much easier your life might be without him."

"She's right," Soraya says firmly.

Echo flashes her a look of gratitude. "Soraya, do you mind if Tyler and I go somewhere more private so we can give this conversation the attention it deserves?"

"Sure. No worries." She fidgets with the hem of her top. "See you next time."

"Bye." Echo smiles at her and keeps her fingers intertwined with mine as Soraya strides away. "The gardens?"

"Sounds good."

The botanical gardens are near campus, but with the trees and thick rosebushes, they're surprisingly private. We walk together, but with each step, the relief in my gut eases and the dread increases.

Echo is still standing beside me, even after finding out

that I could have played a part in my father's death. Because of that, I owe her one last truth. It might break us. The guilt over my last secret has festered like a contaminated wound in the back of my mind for years.

Only a handful of people know. One is my therapist. One is dead. One is in prison, and I doubt the others would talk, but I can't hold this in for any longer. If she decides she doesn't want to see me again, I'll accept that. I'll leave her alone, no matter how difficult it may be.

I'm an asshole, not a monster.

As we stroll between the opening in the hedge and into the gardens, my pulse picks up and sweat slides down the back of my neck. I lead Echo to a garden bench that's tucked away beneath a pergola that's buried beneath an overgrown white rosebush, and we sit.

I release her hand. She might not want me touching her in another few seconds.

"So, about your dad…" She trails off, frowning. "Are you okay? You've gone pale."

"There's something else I need to tell you." I look down at my hands. Big, calloused palms. Great for hockey. Bad for handling someone as delicate as Echo. "After this, I can't think of any other secrets I'm keeping. I'm an open book. You can ask me anything."

"What is it?" she whispers, nerves threading through her voice.

My jaw clenches involuntarily. "First, I just want to say I'm damn sorry for hiding this from you for so long. You should have known from the beginning."

"Hiding what?"

Finally, I dare to look at her. She's watching me steadily. I can't bear to imagine how she'll look at me once she's heard my confession.

"You know how I was trying to push you away, to make it

seem like I didn't care about you, so my dad would get off my back?"

"Yes." She's clearly uncertain where this is going.

"One night, the guys from the team were over at my place after a game. We'd done well, so Dad had eased up on his rules about having people over. He stayed with us though. Didn't trust us to be alone."

I never knew exactly what he was afraid I'd do. Tell a bunch of teenage guys that my Dad hit me?

Not going to happen.

Even if I admitted that he hurt Mom and Soraya, they'd just want to know why I didn't do something about it, and I had no way to make them understand.

"The guys all knew we'd had sex."

My stomach curdles at the memory of how I'd announced that in the school corridor, calling it meaningless. It's amazing she's with me now. That she was generous enough to hear me out.

"Eric asked if you were done with me, and whether he could move in."

Her face blanches.

"I said yes." Shame threatens to swallow me whole. "Dad was listening, and so were the other guys, and I didn't know what else to say."

She looks at me as if she doesn't know me at all. I clamber off the garden bench and drop to my knees, moisture from the grass soaking my jeans.

"I'm so sorry." I reach for her hands, but she tucks them beneath herself. "I swear, I had no idea that he'd... That he'd rape you. I just thought he'd start coming onto you again, the way he used to, and that you'd shoot him down, like you always did."

She lets out a forceful breath and kneads at her chest. "It doesn't matter what you thought would happen. Even if we pretend Eric never laid a finger on me, it was still a crappy thing to do. You knew how much I hated his attention, and you promised me you'd put a stop to it, even before anything happened between us."

"I…" I have no defense.

"You promised me, Tyler." Her voice breaks, and the fragile trust between us snaps entirely.

I hang my head. "I was scared, and I reacted badly. I've regretted that every minute of every day since."

But especially after I learned what she'd accused my former friend of. Not that most of our classmates believed her.

I had, though, and it had gutted me.

Echo draws in a ragged breath, and exhales sharply. She breathes in again, and I can tell she's struggling for air. A chill races over my skin. Is she having a panic attack?

I wrack my mind for the advice my therapist gave me about helping someone through a panic attack. I asked after the last time I'd failed spectacularly at getting her through one.

"Breathe in with me," I say, inhaling for the count of four. She can't match me, and exhales part way through. "Try again."

Eventually, her breathing is under control, but her pupils are pinpricks and it's impossible to know how grounded she is in the present.

"Tell me three things you can see," I tell her.

"You. Roses." Her voice shakes. "Grass."

"Good. Now, three things you can feel."

"The bench beneath me." Her eyelids flutter as she hesitates. "The warmth of the sun on the top of my head. The soles of my shoes against my feet."

"Three things you can hear."

"Your voice. Birds. A lawn mower."

"Perfect. How are you?"

She focuses on me, her pupils back to a more normal size. "Better, thank you. But that doesn't mean I forgive you."

"I don't expect you to." My actions have been unforgivable. I hesitate, then add, "Would it bring you any comfort to know that Eric got the shit beaten out of him on his first day in prison, and that he was told it would be ten times worse if he ever tried to contact you?"

She shakes her head, although there's something satisfied about the twist of her mouth. "This is too much at once. I can't concentrate now. My mind is still spinning. I need to think."

"Okay. Let me get you back to your dorm."

But she shakes her head again. "Not you."

Fuck. That shouldn't hurt as much as it does.

I reach for her, then stop myself and curl my hands into fists.

Don't touch. She doesn't want that.

"If you never want to see me again, I get it, and I'll disappear. That's something I can do for you. But I want you to know that I don't have any secrets from you now. I love you, and for me, there will never be anyone else."

I'm hers, until I take my last breath.

She nods, the movement jerky. "I just...Do you want to know something I've never admitted to anyone?"

"Yes," I say, although something in my tone warns me I might not like what I hear.

"The night it happened." She draws in a deep breath. "The night Eric raped me. I'd been tutoring a junior in the school library after hours."

"I know," I whisper.

I forced myself to listen to her testimony in court. She doesn't know I was there, but I had to hear it all for myself. I had to know how badly I'd failed her.

"I was crossing the car park when he attacked me from behind. I tried to fight back."

I nod, my throat tight. I've seen the photographs of the cuts and bruises he gave her. The ring of finger-shaped smudges around her neck.

"I had no chance against him; especially after he knocked me unconscious. When I came to, he was already..."

A sob escapes her, and my fingernails embed themselves in my palms. I want so badly to reach for her.

"There was nothing I could do. But even as I lay there, I dreamed that you might turn up out of nowhere and save me. Now, to find out you egged him on—even if it wasn't intentional... I don't know how to deal with that."

My heart is breaking for her, and I don't even try to stop the tears that leak from the corners of my eyes. I hate to think of her so alone and scared, hoping for a hero when all I've ever been is her downfall.

"I'm sorry, Echo. So damn sorry." It will never be enough.

She blinks rapidly. "I want to go home."

"I'll call Ryan and ask him to come and get you." Since it's clear she doesn't want me taking her anywhere, and I don't blame her.

"No." She stiffens. "I'll call Anita. But you don't need to wait. I'll be fine here."

"Echo..."

"Go."

With a heart weighed down by sorrow and regret, I stride away—but not far. I round a corner and duck behind a bush, shifting around until she's back in view. She's too vulnerable to be alone right now.

I wait in the shadows until her redheaded friend appears. She slings her arm around Echo's shoulder and escorts her from the gardens. I watch her go, painfully aware that this might be the last time she walks away from me.

What will I do if she tells me to leave her alone for good?

Can I really do it? Can I sit back while she makes a family with someone else?

The future without her stretches before me, long and bleak. An eternity with no light to chase away the darkness. Maybe it will finally consume me.

25

———

I approach the batting cages warily. Ryan is the only one here. He swings and makes contact with a cracking sound. The ball flies away. Almost immediately, the machine lobs another one at him.

I stop behind the cage. It only takes him a moment to notice me. He presses a button and the balls stop coming, then he leans the bat against the wire and faces me.

"Hey." His smile is awkward. Hesitant. "Thanks for coming. I know you probably didn't want to."

He's right. When he messaged me the invitation, I almost ignored him, but my need to know what he has to say outweighed my caution.

"I'm here, aren't I?" I wince, irritated by how prickly I sound. I promised myself I wouldn't come in with all guns blazing, but the past few days have been overwhelming and my nerves are rubbed raw.

"You are." His smile softens. "And I'm glad."

I cross my arms. "So, why are we here?"

He gestures at the empty space—a large, open indoor area with fake turf. "This is my favorite place to come when

I need to think, or to work out some anger. I thought maybe you'd like to try it."

I arch one of my eyebrows. "You think I'll hit a few baseballs and immediately forgive you?"

"No." The side of his mouth quirks. "But it's as good a place to start as any."

He picks up the bat and indicates for me to enter the cage. I shift from foot to foot, considering my options. I could still run away. Just turn, leave, and block his number. But he has been a good friend to me over the years, and whether he had an ulterior motive for befriending me or not, I miss him.

"Fine," I huff, rounding the fence and stalking toward him.

He passes me the bat. "Stand over here."

I move to the spot he's motioning at and grip the bat. I'm not sporty, but it isn't my first time hitting a baseball...even if my skills—and my hand-eye coordination—leave a little to be desired.

"The ball will come from there," he says, pointing to the hole in the front of the machine. "If you think you might miss, just step back and make sure you're out of the way. You ready?"

"Sure." Maybe it will be cathartic.

He presses the button again, and a couple of seconds later, a ball rockets toward me.

I scramble backward. "Whoa!"

He grimaces. "Sorry. Forgot to turn down the speed."

He hits the button before the machine attacks again and messes around with a dial. "Take two?"

"Go on." At this point, I'll just be happy to escape unscathed. I'm still not sure what he thinks he'll accomplish by bringing me here.

The next ball is slower, and I swing the bat, making

contact. It thumps into the ground a few feet away and rolls. Another comes at me, and I hit it more softly.

"Nuh-uh," Ryan chides. "Bash it as hard as you can. Don't even think about where it goes. Just swing and hit. Got it?"

I grit my teeth. He makes it sound easy, and perhaps it is for him, but he's been playing since before he could spell. I smack the next ball, trying to ignore the fact it skims the grass rather than traveling a decent distance. Then I hit another. And another. Before long, I fall into a rhythm, and it's oddly satisfying.

By the time the machine runs out of balls, I'm sweating and breathing heavily.

"Nice work." Ryan carefully takes the bat from me, as if worried I might use it against him, and offers me a high five. Reluctantly, I slap our palms together, but I narrow my eyes, so he knows he's not completely off the hook.

I look around and spot his water bottle behind us; I uncap it and drink. When a bitter, slightly salty taste fills my mouth, I sputter.

"What the hell is this?" I demand, outraged.

His mouth twitches, but he manages not to laugh. "Electrolyte solution."

"It's terrible."

"But it's lemon and lime flavor," he protests. "Everyone loves citrus."

"Not when it tastes like that." I wipe my lips on the back of my hand. "I'll have to buy a coffee now to rinse my mouth out."

He rolls his eyes. "You poor soul." Then his expression turns serious. "Can we talk?"

For a brief moment, I ponder the idea of rejecting him, but he's making an effort, and surely, I owe it to the past three years of our friendship to at least hear him out.

"As long as we can get coffee first."

"Do I look like an idiot? Of course I'm getting you coffee."

He takes the drink bottle from me and, together, we pick up the balls and return them to the machine. Then we head to a cafe a block away. It's almost empty, which is surprising so close to lunch time, but when I sip my caramel mocha, I realize why. The coffee is terrible.

"This is so bad," I murmur, not wanting the server to overhear me.

"Is it?" He looks surprised. "Mine is fine. Maybe you're just more of a coffee snob than me."

I glare at him but can't deny it. "Perhaps they make better oat milk coffees than dairy-based coffees."

His face is full of doubt, but he keeps his mouth shut.

"So..." I guess there's no better time than now to get to the point. "I'm glad you invited me to do this. I miss spending time with you. I just have trouble with the fact I don't know where your friendship for me starts and your obligation to Tyler ends."

He wraps his hands around his coffee mug. "Everything I've ever done with you has been because I wanted to. Well,"— he smirks— "everything except that time you made me watch the BBC version of Pride and Prejudice."

I laugh at the memory, and it breaks some of the tension between us. "Yeah, but you made it clear you didn't enjoy that by cringing every two seconds."

He shrugs. "How else was I supposed to react to women in pretty dresses hunting men for their wallets—or rejecting them for the same reason?"

"That's what you took away from Pride and Prejudice?" I shake my head. "I need to get better friends."

"I wish you wouldn't." His gaze is serious now. "BBC

aside, I love spending time with you. I don't want to lose you."

I close my eyes and release a pent-up breath. "Maybe you don't have to."

When I open my eyes again, his face has brightened.

"Really?"

Our conversation reminds me of evenings of laughter, shared study sessions, and confidences exchanged about almost everything.

"We could take it day by day. I don't have many friends, and I don't want to lose you either."

"I'd like that."

We smile at each other, and for a moment, everything feels right with the world, but then Ryan's phone buzzes. He checks the screen.

"Damn. I have to get going."

I frown. "Where to?"

He hesitates, visibly torn. "The hockey game. I told Tyler I'd be there."

"Oh." I deflate a little. It's strange for me, now having to think of Tyler and Ryan as friends. "It's the last game before the playoffs, isn't it?"

"Yeah." He stands and pushes his chair back. "You should come with me."

Excitement flickers in my gut, but I squelch it. "I think it's best if I don't. I still don't know what to do about Tyler, and if I turn up, it might complicate things."

Plus, seeing him will make me want to be in his arms, and that won't help my objectivity at all.

He glances at the time and sits again. "Talk me through everything that happened with him. All I know is that you were together in high school but broke up—it was his fault —and that he desperately wants you back."

So I tell him.

Despite the rocky place our friendship is in, I confess everything. Our secret relationship. Our plan to go to prom together. The way Tyler stood me up and then humiliated me. Even the rape—although I gloss over the details.

No one needs to know that I still have nightmares featuring the scrape of concrete against my cheek and the helplessness of being pinned down.

When I'm finished, he pulls his sleeve over his hand and dabs beneath my eyes. It's not until I see the damp spots on the fabric that I realize I'm crying.

"I'm so sorry that happened to you," he says. "I'm glad that asshole is behind bars. As for Tyler, he has a lot of ground to make up, but I can see what's behind the shitty decisions he made. Can't you?"

Yes. That's what makes this so hard.

"He was trying to protect you," he adds. "Even if it was misguided."

"I know," I whisper, wiping the wetness from my face. "Sorry. I didn't mean to get so emotional."

He places his hand on mine. "You have nothing to apologize for."

When I start to protest, he holds his hand up to stop me.

"No, I mean it. Anyone would be upset after reliving what you just did. I'm sorry if you felt like you had to. I didn't mean to push."

"Actually, it feels good." I'm surprised to realize it's the truth. "It's...freeing...that you know. I'm tired of keeping secrets." And of having them kept from me.

"That's a relief. I'd hate to set you back." Ryan rubs his lips together, and something tells me he has more to add but isn't sure whether to go for it.

"What?" I ask.

He opens his mouth but takes a moment to put his thoughts together. "Tyler always struck me as a bit of an asshole, but he genuinely seems to adore you. I totally understand if you never want to see him again—honestly, that might be the sanest thing to do—but I truly believe he'd do anything for you."

I don't reply immediately. In some ways, he's right. After all, Tyler paid Ryan to watch over me for years, and he put his own happiness aside in an attempt to protect my future, even if he shattered my heart in the process. Nothing has worked out as he intended, but the good intentions were there.

Now, thanks to him, I have a whole lot more to work through with Dr. Rodriguez, but perhaps, with enough time and therapy, Tyler and I could have a relationship again. It wouldn't be like the one we used to have, or even like the one we were building these past weeks. Instead, it would be fresh and honest.

We know all the goods and bads now. All the rights and wrongs we've done. There's no reason we can't eventually try again.

Ryan's phone buzzes, reminding me that he's supposed to be on his way to the game.

I get to my feet, ignoring the slight wobble in my knees. "You need to get going or you'll be late."

"Nah." He stands too, but makes no move to leave. "You shouldn't be alone right now. I'll drive you home and get one of my friends to pick up my car."

My eyebrows knit together. "You can't miss the game for me."

"Of course I can." He sounds exasperated. "It's just a game, Echo. Not even the biggest game of the season. Tyler probably won't even notice I'm not there, and if he does, he'll understand. To him, your wellbeing comes first."

"It does, doesn't it?" I muse. "But who puts him first?"

"Pardon?" he asks.

"Never mind." I wave my hand dismissively. The answer is clear anyway. No one puts Tyler first. As far as I know, he's never had anyone other than his sister in the stands purely to support him. His father attended all his games, but not because he cared about Tyler's life. He deserves better.

"Take me to the game," I tell Ryan, drying away the final traces of tears from my cheeks.

He purses his lips. "Are you sure?"

"Yes." I raise my chin. "I want to be there."

A slow grin transforms his expression. "Then let's go."

Half an hour later, we shuffle into the stadium with half the student body and push through the crowd to seats a couple of rows back from the ice. My stomach rumbles. I should have eaten something at the cafe, but I was tied in too many knots.

The teams are already skating, and I spot Tyler easily. He and one of his teammates are warming up the goalie. Two of them pass the puck back and forth so quickly I have trouble following it, before a third player receives it and shoots it over the line.

They circle around to repeat the drill, and as they do, Tyler raises his eyes to search the stands. When they land on me, they widen, and then light with so much joy that even looking at him makes me feel like a voyeur. He taps his fist over his heart and blows me a kiss.

A few people turn toward me, but the moment wasn't obvious enough to capture much attention.

Ryan nudges my shoulder, and gestures toward the coach. It takes me a few seconds to notice Soraya in the stands just behind him.

"Do you know if she's single?" Ryan asks.

I turn to him slowly. "Soraya?"

"Yeah." He looks down at his hands, his cheeks flushing.

Wow. I didn't see that coming.

"I don't, but I'm sure I could find out."

He raises his eyes briefly, his lips quirking. "That would be great. Only, don't mention it to Tyler. I like my organs being on the inside."

"I won't." I look over at Soraya again. She's completely focused on the ice. She's pretty, anyone could see that. She's also strong and vulnerable at the same time. Whatever his motivation, Ryan has been good for me. Perhaps he could be good for her, too.

We watch without talking as the warm up finishes and the game begins. Tyler is on the ice from the start, along with the same two guys in the front line from last time: Welch and Anaheim. They're absolute magic, scoring in the first two minutes. As soon as the puck crosses the line—directly from Tyler's stick—his eyes find me in the crowd.

Butterflies flutter in my gut. How does a simple look have the power to affect me so much?

The other team comes back strong, whizzing past our front line and taking a shot on goal. The goalie deflects, and one of the defensemen collects the puck on the rebound and sends it winging back to Welch. A few minutes later, there's another goal on the scoreboard.

It's the last one Newbury scores until the third period.

Their opponents make up a goal and then focus on defense, doing their best to make sure the puck never gets as far as the goalie. In the beginning of the third period, their center flies up the ice the instant the puck drops, catching Newbury by surprise, and manages to score.

The home crowd boos. The score is tied now, with only nineteen minutes to go. Tyler doesn't look at me, but there's determination in the way he squares his shoulders and lowers his chin.

The score holds.

With thirty seconds left on the clock, one of the

defensemen gets the puck from the other team, and Newbury's defense line moves forward. Together with the front line, they skate in formation toward the opposition goal, passing rapidly between themselves.

Anaheim takes aim, but the goalie swats the puck away. The left defenseman recovers the puck and shoots it across to Tyler, who slips it past the goalie's skate, into the corner of the net.

The buzzer sounds, signaling the end of the period, and the players stare at the scoreboard for a long moment, waiting to see whether the goal was fast enough. The second it appears in red lettering, they swarm Tyler. Hugging. Back clapping. Cheering.

I smile and clap. Beside me, Ryan hollers his support.

It's official. Newbury is going through to the playoffs.

When the players have finished celebrating, they shake hands with the other team, and someone passes their coach a microphone. He says a few words about teamwork, and how the team will go the distance, and the stands erupt. Honestly, I think he could say anything, and the audience would go wild.

When he's done, I expect the theatrics to be over, but instead, the coach gives the microphone to one of the players.

Tyler.

"What's going on?" I ask Ryan as Tyler strips off his helmet and tosses it to Ruiz.

"No idea," he replies, but the smile flitting at the corner of his lips makes me think he's lying.

Tyler clears his throat, and it echoes through the stadium. Someone cheers. Because of course they do.

Tyler is red-faced and sweaty. He mops his damp hair off his face and raises the microphone.

"Hi, everyone." He sounds surprisingly nervous. Public

speaking has never been an issue for him before, which makes me even more curious about what's happening. "I just have a few words to say before everyone takes off."

His gaze lands on me again, sparkling blue, even from a distance.

"We had a good game tonight, and it was a team effort, like Coach said. It helps that we all wanted to make the play-offs, and that fueled us. It's a nice change for me to be fueled by something other than desperation."

There's a confused murmuring. My stomach tightens. What is he doing?

"My father was an asshole—excuse me, Coach," he adds when his coach tries to snatch the microphone back. "I trained hard to avoid his punishment. But he died months ago, so it wasn't fear that helped me win this game. It was love."

A group of girls nearby make a collective 'aww' sound, and a couple of them glance at me. A guy on the opposite side of the stadium jeers. My heart is beating a rapid rat-a-tat-tat while I stare at Tyler with no idea what he'll say next.

"Love of hockey, my favorite game, but also love of a woman who's as magical as a shooting star." He blows me a kiss and winks, but the slight tremble of his voice belies his nerves. "Whether or not you love me, I'll always love you, Echo Dean."

"Holy crap," I breathe.

This maniac. This absolute maniac.

I can't take my eyes off him as he returns the microphone to the coach and skates off the ice. With this announcement, he's making it clear that I'll never be a secret part of his life again. There's no putting the cat back in the bag. I'd bet at least a dozen people filmed his little speech on their phones and are already uploading it to the internet.

"Did you know he was going to do that?" I ask Ryan.

He shrugs. I narrow my eyes. Of course he did. That's probably why he invited me along. Then he reverse-psychology-ed me into doing it. The question is: what am I going to do now?

"I have to go," I say, brushing past Ryan. He shouts something over the crowd—many of whom are still eying me curiously—but I don't make out the words.

I push through the crush of spectators, making my way to the changing room, but by the time I get there, the team is already inside.

I wait by the door, pretending not to notice the looks I'm receiving from strangers, until the players begin to emerge. The first one out is the winger, Welch, who winks at me and touches two fingers to his forehead in a little salute.

Another guy follows, a big bear of a man I recognize from the defense line but whose name I can't remember. He gives me a thumbs up.

When Tyler finally exits, his hair slicked back and wet from the shower, freshly dressed in dark pants and a button-up shirt with a duffel bag over his shoulder, my breath hitches. Somehow, I always forget how gorgeous he is until he's right in front of me.

When he sees me, a grin spreads across his face. He reaches for me, as if about to pull me into an embrace, but then stops.

"That was quite a speech," I say, far calmer on the outside than I am on the inside.

He cocks his head. "Did you like it?"

"Yeah." I can hardly deny it when he bared his soul in front of so many people. "It was sweet."

"Sweet enough to earn me one last chance?" he asks, achingly hopeful as he steps closer.

I close the distance between us and kiss him. He grips

my hips, his hands hot even through several layers of fabric. I close my eyes and breathe in the scent of menthol and some kind of spicy aftershave.

"One last chance," I whisper as I draw back. "But there can't be any more secrets between us."

He grabs me around the waist and spins me in a circle, then lowers me back to my feet.

"No more secrets," he promises.

26

ECHO

I snuggle against Tyler's chest as the final few minutes of the movie plays. I close my eyes, warm and relaxed in the semi-darkness of his apartment. The room still smells of Chinese takeout, and a few candles flicker on the coffee table.

With him so close to me, his arms around me and his heart beating beneath my ear, I've never been more content.

Tyler kisses my forehead. "You make me so happy."

I angle my face toward his as the credits begin to roll. "You make me happy too. I... I love you, Ty."

His lips part and his eyes light up. "You do?"

"Yeah." I smile as he squeezes me tighter and peppers my face with kisses.

Since we got back together, we've been taking things slowly. He'd told me several times that he loves me, but this is the first time I've been brave enough to say it back.

"I love you more than the moon and the stars, baby girl."

I reach over to switch the movie off and roll in his arms until the front of my body is pressed to the front of his. A sense of rightness swells within me. I'm completely at ease with this man. Sure, he's made mistakes. So have I. But I trust him, and I believe in our relationship and the future we're building together.

I cup his bristled face with one hand and brush my lips against his, drinking in his surprised gasp. His lips are soft but firm. Hard but yielding. My tongue darts out to taste him. A hint of sweet and sour with a deeper richness that's all him. His tongue twines alongside mine and a shiver ripples through me.

I pull away. "I'm ready."

His brow creases. "For what?"

I'm tempted to roll my eyes but grin instead. What a beautiful, clueless man.

"Sex."

His eyes widen, the pupils still their normal size, which means his thoughts are probably clear. That's good. I don't want him making decisions with a fuzzy head.

"We don't have to do that," he says. "I know I need to earn your trust first."

I kiss him again, first on the nose and then on the mouth. "I want to try. I trust that you'll stop if I need you to."

His expression turns fierce. "I will."

I rock my pussy against his sweatpants-covered erection as we melt into another kiss. I'd be lying if I didn't admit I'm a little nervous, but I do trust him, and besides, I've practiced.

I had a session with the dildo he gave me a few days ago. I didn't tell him in case it went badly, but except for being a bit tightly wound at first, and taking a few minutes to relax, it was fine. I even came.

Of course, a dildo has nothing on the real thing.

The kiss deepens, and Tyler's hands settle on my lower back, holding me to him. The embrace makes me feel cherished, and I bury my face in the crook of his shoulder and kiss my way up the exposed skin of his neck.

He does the same to me, and I close my eyes and relish the gentle scrape of his whiskers over my skin. He isn't shaving until after the final championship game has been played, and I'm surprised to discover I'm a beard person. Although perhaps the delicious way it feels against the inside of my thighs has something to do with that.

I lift off him and remove my shirt. He follows my lead and bares his chest. I kiss his pecs, then dust kisses all the way down his washboard abs to the treasure trail that disappears into his sweatpants. Goosebumps race across his skin and his cock bops, bumping my face through the fabric of his pants.

Reaching behind myself, I unhook my bra. I know Tyler would love to do it for me, but doing it myself helps me feel in control. I need that right now.

"So fucking sexy," he groans. "So perfect for me."

He pulls me up his body and into another kiss. He takes my mouth sensually and thoroughly, until I'm languid and needy in his arms.

I rub myself against his hard cock, reveling in the deep groan that vibrates up his throat. He scoots down and licks my nipple, then sucks it into a nubbin. I whimper and squirm against him. He switches to the other nipple and teases it with his lips and tongue.

I reach between us and cup him. His head drops back, and he groans. Our mouths meet again and stay connected as we gradually lose all our clothes, except for our underwear. I've been naked with him before, and he with me, and we've even rubbed against each other a few times, but we haven't gone further.

I end the kiss and maneuver down his body, until my

face is hovering over his groin. I grab the waistband of his underwear and slowly peel them down.

"Echo..." His cock thumps against his abdomen, flushed red and already leaking precum. "You don't have to do anything you're not ready for."

"I know."

Growing impatient, I shove his underwear the rest of the way down his legs until they drop onto the floor, and then I return to his erection. Heat radiates from him, and I inhale his musky scent. His hair is neatly trimmed, and I caress his balls, which are drawn up tight to his body.

Tyler watches me from above, caution and desire warring in his eyes. He wants my mouth on him, but it's not something we've done since we got back together, and he won't push me. When it comes to anything physical between us, he never has.

My mouth waters, and I lick him from his balls to the plump head of his cock. The salty tang of his precum instantly brings me back to the first time we did this. He was so careful with me, and I loved making him lose his mind.

I lick him again, and then circle my fingers around his base and suck him into my mouth. His hips twitch, as if he's desperate to go deeper but is restraining himself. For now, I appreciate it. Maybe one day soon, I'll tease him until he can't remember to be gentle, but today, I need his thoughtfulness.

I swirl my tongue around him, sucking him and working my mouth as far along his length as I'm comfortable with. I cup his balls with my free hand and stroke them gently.

"Fuck, Echo," he curses. "You keep doing that and this is gonna be over real quick."

I grin around him and draw back until his head is the only part of his cock still in my mouth. I flick my tongue over the velvety skin and taste more precum.

Sometimes it's easy to forget that it's been as long for him as it has for me. I still struggle to comprehend that he remained celibate during his college years because he was waiting for me. He must have had so many opportunities, and he turned them all down because of me.

I pull off him with a pop. "I love you."

"I'll never get enough of hearing you say that."

He scoops me into his arms, sits up, and gently places me on the sofa. He kneels between my thighs and pushes my panties to the side. Holding my gaze, he sucks his thumb into his mouth and then dips it between my legs, using it to draw tiny circles around my clit. My lips part on a ragged breath.

"That's it, baby girl." He doesn't take his eyes off me as he wets another finger and strokes down my center while his thumb continues teasing me. Never adding pressure or easing up. Just keeping up the same steady rhythm until I'm ready to scream.

Then, as I'm trembling from his touch, he presses against my entrance.

I stiffen.

"It's okay," he croons, those blue orbs lasered onto me. "Exhale nice and slow and let me in."

Holding his gaze, I breathe out, releasing as much tension as I can from my taut body. He pushes his finger in a little and then ducks his head to kiss my clit. Just one soft, chaste kiss, followed by the dip of his tongue into my wetness.

Bit by bit, he works his finger inside me, keeping me balanced on a sharp edge of pleasure with his mouth. He curls his finger inside me and heat blooms deep within, unfurling up my spine.

"Ready for another?" he asks.

I nod.

"Gonna need the words, baby."

"Yes, please. I want another finger inside me."

"Good girl."

The second digit enters me much more smoothly than the first. He keeps them buried inside me as he leans over and drags me into another breath-robbing kiss. Only when I'm boneless and have completely forgotten my fears does he get up.

"I'll be right back," he promises. "I don't have any condoms in here, so I need to run to the bedroom."

He disappears, and for a moment, my brain tries to click back into gear, but I focus on the flickering orange glow of one of the candles, and the sweet, fruity scent it's giving out. Strawberry, if I have to guess. He's always had a thing about me and strawberries.

When he returns, it's with a new box of condoms. He tears the wrapper off, opens the box, and pulls one out. He hesitates, then passes the foil to me.

"You do it," he says. "I need to know you're completely in this with me."

My heart pulses, feeling too big for my chest. With a dopey smile, I take the foil, rip it open, and grab the edge of the condom. He comes closer and I roll it down his cock, being careful not to hurt him.

He frowns. "Would you rather do this in the bedroom?"

I laugh, shocked that it hasn't occurred to me to move things in there. "No. I like it here."

He sits on the other sofa cushion. "You're on top, baby. That way, all the control is yours."

With that statement, he dispels any of my lingering nerves. I stand so he can spread out along the sofa, and then I climb over him. I draw in a calming breath and slowly let it go. With steady fingers, I position his cock beneath me and lower myself onto it.

At first, I tense slightly, but as soon as I meet his concerned gaze, my muscles relax.

This is Tyler. He would never hurt me again.

I sink onto him, inch by inch, until he's fully seated within me. Rocking my hips, I test the sensation.

"This is definitely better than the dildo," I say.

Tyler's eyes darken and his fingers dig into my hips. "You used the dildo?"

I smile kittenishly and begin to move, just enough to tease. "Only once. I needed to know I could do it before I tried anything with you."

A muscle in his jaw twitches. "Wish I could've seen you."

"Maybe next time."

He thrusts up. "Definitely next time."

We rock together, gradually building the intensity. We're both out of practice, but it doesn't take us long to remember how to please each other.

I ride him with growing confidence, my ass slapping against his thighs each time we meet. He presses his fingertips to my clit but doesn't try to take control of our lovemaking. His quiet grunts and moans urge me on, and before long, my core is liquid fire.

I need him.

I need to come.

I'm so close. So close.

I throw my head back and work my hips faster, spurred on by the slap, slap, slap of our skin. Using the sofa to steady myself, I whimper at the delicious friction between us.

Pressure builds within me, and I meet Tyler's eyes, my lip caught between my teeth, as he grows stiffer inside me. His cock pulses, and he rumbles a low groan. He's struggling to hold onto a thread of control. He's doing that for me.

Pleasure draws taut and then snaps between us.

I shatter.

I'm a whimpering, writhing mess on top of him, but he just keeps his fingers on my clit, rubbing in loose circles as his other hand strokes up and down my back.

When I come back to myself, he's smiling, the expression full of affection.

"All good?"

"Perfect," I reply, and begin riding him again, rolling my hips to prolong each movement.

With a growl, he grabs my hips and—after making eye contact to seek silent approval—takes control of our pace, driving faster, his breath becoming shallow. When he comes, jerking inside me, his mouth open in a silent shout, he holds my gaze for the entire time.

I feel raw, vulnerable, and completely worshiped, because in that moment, his soul is bare to me. He doesn't even try to hide. He wants me to look. To see my name carved on the deepest, most private parts of him.

I kiss him because no words could possibly capture the maelstrom of emotions raging inside me, and then I snuggle against his chest.

Eventually, we separate for long enough to clean up, but immediately return to the sofa. He pulls me onto his lap and wraps his arms around me.

"It's the final championship game next week," he says. "In Portland. Will you come?"

I've been to all of his home playoff games but haven't attended any of the away games yet.

I relax into the warmth of his embrace. "I wouldn't miss it."

27

TYLER

I don't open my eyes after I wake up. Even now, I sometimes wonder if our reconciliation was a wonderful dream and one day I'll wake up alone in my childhood bedroom while Dad yells at me for being lazy.

"Ty." She sounds amused. "I know you're awake."

I crack one eye open and blow her a kiss. "You caught me."

She laughs and lifts herself up on her elbow, her dark hair spilling over her shoulders like liquid silk. "How does it feel to be a champion?"

I pull her against my body and rest my hand on her hip, taking comfort from her presence and the scent of strawberries that lingers in the air.

"It's nothing compared to being the champion of your heart."

She rolls her eyes. "Uh-huh."

She thinks I'm being cheesy. If only she had any idea how much it means to me to have her. Winning the championship yesterday was a blast, and I know it'll look good as I enter the draft, but she matters more to me than hockey.

"Hopefully Matthews is okay," I say.

The defenseman hurt his ankle when he was knocked on his ass during a desperate play by the opposition in the last few minutes of the game. I know he intends to enter the draft too, but if he has rehab to do on an injured ankle, it could hurt his chances.

"We could check in with him later," she suggests. "You could call him during the drive."

We all traveled back to Newbury after the game yesterday and had a celebration at Coach's house, but Matthews didn't turn up.

"Good idea." The drive to Charlesville is far enough for me to have plenty of time to talk to him.

"What about your bruises?" She pushes the bedspread down and scans my body, then winces. "That one on your hip is nasty."

I chuckle. "That's what happens when someone hip checks you into a wall."

She doesn't laugh back, just narrows her eyes. "We should have iced it yesterday."

"It's just a bruise." I draw her down for a kiss. "It'll be fine in a few days."

She grumbles but doesn't say anything else about it. I have to admit, it's nice to have someone worry about me. Soraya has always been supportive, but she doesn't fuss the way Echo does. I kind of like her clucking over me like a mother hen.

Ugh. Speaking of mothers...

"I'm worried about meeting your mom today," I admit. "She doesn't have a very good impression of me from the past."

Echo's expression softens, and she drops back onto her side and cuddles against me. "I've explained everything to her. She knows why you did what you did. I'm sure it will be fine."

"Yeah, maybe." I mean, she's been polite so far, but we also haven't come face to face.

I clutch Echo tighter, unwilling to let her go. I'm far less sure about whether her mom will be willing to forgive and forget than she is. If I had to watch someone I cared about get treated like shit, I sure as hell wouldn't be rushing to forgive anyone.

"I'm going to make pancakes for breakfast," Echo says, kissing my cheek and then slipping out of bed. "Take a nice, hot shower to ease your muscles and by the time you're done, they'll be ready."

"I can help," I protest.

She arches her eyebrow. "I'd rather you put liniment on all of your bruises."

"Fine." Warmth fills me. I never thought I'd find someone who cares for me like she does. God knows I don't deserve it, but I'm greedy and I'm going to take her anyway.

I shower, and then we share pancakes. Hers are drenched in maple syrup and chocolate sauce, while mine are accompanied by blueberries and caramelized bananas. Based on the texture, I suspect she added a scoop of protein powder, and I somehow doubt she did the same to hers.

I love it. She's so thoughtful.

After breakfast, she showers while I pack my bag. Hers is already ready to go because she packed enough to get through the away game, a night here, and the visit to her mom's, knowing she wouldn't be back at her dorm for a few days.

When she emerges from the bathroom, her hair damp around her shoulders with only a towel on, I scarcely remember to breathe. It's like every time she leaves the room, I'm terrified that I've imagined the whole thing—or that she'll come to her senses and run.

I wrap my arms around her, entwining my hands against the small of her back and touching my forehead to hers. "You have no idea how stunning you are."

"And you, Tyler Kinsey, are far too charming. Let me get dressed. We have places to be."

Reluctantly, I release her, although it's a struggle to keep my distance when she strips off the towel. With gritted teeth, I focus on adding the last few things to my bag and zipping it shut. When I return my gaze to her, she's dressed in jeans and a bra, and is in the process of choosing a shirt from her bag.

Once she's fully dressed, we carry our bags to my Audi, which we agreed to take since it's less likely to break down on us halfway there.

I drive and Echo sits in the passenger seat, the window down and classical music streaming from her phone. Violins and pianos aren't my thing, but I don't dislike the music either, and I love how relaxed it makes her. It isn't often that she lets go of all tension and just exists.

But as we draw closer to Charlesville, she grows stiffer, and eventually, she turns off the music.

ECHO

At the beginning of our road trip, my heart was light, but as we drive into Charlesville, my soul grows heavier.

I rarely come back here. I don't like the way the town makes me feel, or the memories that haunt me while I'm visiting. Too many ghosts exist here for me to be happy.

I direct Tyler to my mom's place. She lives in the same small, single-story house I grew up in, although the paint is no longer peeling. The garden outside is neat, in contrast to how it used to be. Mom has taken up gardening in her free time.

"Are you okay?" Tyler asks as he parks outside.

I stare out the window at the cheerful yellow porch, with its cane chair near the stairs, and force myself to nod. He takes my hand and squeezes it.

The front door opens and Mom races out, her ponytail bouncing as she jogs over to greet us. She's smiling widely, and there are more gray streaks in her hair than the last time I saw her.

I catch her in a hug and bury my face against the side of her head, breathing in the unfamiliar scent of hair spray rather than the citrus aroma she used to carry. She must have been in the salon today. She cut down her cleaning hours after I left home and has been working toward an apprenticeship.

I'm so proud of her.

"I love you, Mom."

She doesn't let me go. "I love you too, my beautiful Echo. I missed you so much."

I hug her back, not caring that most people would have separated by now. We aren't most people, and that's okay.

When Mom finally steps back, I reach for Tyler, grab his hand, and drag him forward.

"Mom, this is Tyler. Ty, my mom, Inez."

He offers her his hand, brackets of strain around the corners of his mouth. "A pleasure to meet you, Mrs. Dean."

Mom puts her hands on her curvaceous hips and studies him for a long moment. He squirms beside me. Finally, she smiles and—ignoring his hand—wraps her arms around him. My eyes fly to Tyler's. The hug has clearly caught him off guard, but he doesn't seem to mind it. In fact, he might even enjoy her display of maternal affection.

"Please, call me Inez," Mom says as she pulls away. "Congratulations on winning the championship."

"Thank you." He blushes. "We worked hard for it, and I'm glad we got there, but honestly, I've been more worried about today."

Mom tilts her head, understanding in her eyes. "Come inside. I made cookies. We can eat them while we get to know each other better. Leave your bags for now. We can get them later."

"Okay." He seems relieved she's willing to let him inside the house. He takes my hand as we approach the porch, and Mom presses herself against my side. We've always been affectionate, but we became more so in the aftermath of The Incident.

At the door, Tyler lets me go and bends to remove his shoes.

"Don't worry about it unless they're filthy," Mom says.

He checks the soles of his shoes, then shows them to me, concern creasing his forehead. "What do you think? I should probably take them off, just to be safe."

My heart aches at his uncertainty, which reminds me that not all parents are as accepting as my mom. He's already told me how his dad used to make a fuss if his mom missed so much as a speck of dust.

"They're fine," I assure him.

He takes them off anyway.

The mouthwatering aroma of chocolate chip cookies fresh from the oven permeates the house. Mom leads us down the hall to the living room, where a plate of cookies sits in the center of the coffee table. A mug sits next to it, and I can smell coffee brewing. Mom doesn't have a fancy machine, but she splurges on good filter coffee.

"Do you like cream with your coffee?" she asks Tyler.

He hesitates. "Do you have half and half?"

"Absolutely."

He relaxes. "I'll have that please. Plenty of it."

She laughs. "A man after my own heart."

She heads into the attached kitchen—which is more of a kitchenette, really—and prepares two mugs of coffee. I have no doubt there's already a scoop of hot cocoa and a splash of caramel sauce in mine. Tyler and I sit on the sofa, leaving the armchair behind the coffee mug free. When she brings the drinks over, Tyler thanks her.

We sit, and Mom takes a cookie. I grab one too, hoping that Tyler will calm down a bit if we keep up a non-threatening stream of actions.

He tastes the coffee. "This is really good, Mrs.—uh, Inez. Thank you."

"You're very welcome, Tyler."

I peek at him out of the corner of my eye. A bead of sweat has formed at his hairline and is trickling down the side of his face.

"I appreciate you being willing to have me here." He wipes his palms on his jeans. "First off, I just want to apologize for how I hurt Echo in the past. I know I did wrong by her, and I can hardly believe she's forgiven me. I know what I did wasn't okay, and I don't take her for granted. I'm grateful every day she's with me."

The groove between Mom's eyebrows fades. "Thank you for saying that, but Echo is the only one you owe an apology to, and since she's forgiven you, it would be ridiculous of me not to. Just don't hurt her again, or I'll hunt you down."

No one laughs.

Maybe she meant it to come across as a joke, but we all know it isn't one. Mom would have torn Eric Weston apart if she'd had the chance, and I have no doubt she'll fight for me in the future if it comes to that.

But I don't think it will.

"I won't ever hurt her like that again," he promises. "And if I do, I'll be first in line to kick my own ass. Uh, sorry for cursing."

A glimmer of amusement enters her eyes. "Cursing is fine as long as it isn't at someone. Right, Echo?"

I wince, because I sure have done a lot of cursing at Tyler this year. "Um, yeah."

He raises his eyebrows at me, but I don't mind him silently calling me on the fib because at least it means he's less preoccupied with the idea that my mom hates him.

Mom offers Tyler a cookie, and he takes it, looking at the treat as if he isn't quite sure what to do with it. That's when I remember what Soraya said about junk food being outlawed in his house growing up. I doubt his mom ever made him cookies.

Slowly, he nibbles at the edge. A chunk breaks off and falls on his lap. He stares at it, then snatches it up and shoves it in his mouth.

"Delicious," he mumbles around the cookie.

Mom beams. "I'm glad you like it. And Tyler, back in high school, you were only a kid. You did your best. Plus, Echo tells me that we have you to thank for the attorney. It meant a lot to have that support."

"It wasn't enough," he grits out, glancing at the cookie as if contemplating whether to swallow it whole.

She shrugs. "Then I guess you have plenty of time to make up for it. You are intending to be with Echo long term, aren't you?"

"As long as she'll have me." He gives in and eats the cookie, his eyes almost closing as he chews and swallows.

"I need the recipe," I mouth to Mom.

She nods and gives me a thumbs up.

We talk for a while longer, and then we work together to make sandwiches for lunch. After we've eaten, Tyler tells me to grab my purse and pulls me toward the door. I look around at Mom, expecting her to be surprised, but she's just nodding and smiling.

What's happening?

"Where are we going?" I ask as he guides me out the door and to his car.

"A surprise."

That's all he'll say. I pester him during the short drive, but he refuses to elaborate.

When we arrive at the high school, my stomach plummets.

"Should we be here?" I ask.

I don't want to be here. My last few months of school flash through my mind like a horror film. The taunts and jeering, first because of Tyler's public rejection and then because I'd dared to accuse one of their kings of rape.

As if reading my mind, Tyler takes my hand and raises it to his lips. "Trust me."

He releases me, gets out of the car, and walks around to open my door. I let him help me out, and I cling to his hand even though I know, logically, that I'm not going to encounter Eric or Whitney walking the halls. They're long gone.

"Ty?"

"I've got you," he says, gently tucking my hair behind my ear. "I won't let anything happen to you, okay?"

I nod.

Hand in hand, he walks with me around the administration buildings. It takes far too long for me to realize that we're heading for the school gymnasium. The same building where I watched him kiss Whitney and shatter my heart the night we were supposed to announce our relationship.

My heart hammers. Why is he doing this? Why would

he push me to go somewhere he knows will be painful for me?

"I'm with you," he murmurs. "You'll never be left in the cold like that again."

His words soothe me, but I can't completely let go of the unease as we approach those massive double doors. When we're only twenty yards away, I frown. There's music playing from within, but surely, on a weekend like today, the gym should be empty. I concentrate, but the music is too quiet for me to identify.

We reach the doors, and Tyler takes a deep breath. He pushes the door open and holds it for me. I take a moment to steel myself. Even if all that's inside are a few basketballs and a stereo, this still won't be easy. Finally, I lift my eyes and follow him inside.

I gasp, my heart skittering wildly.

I look around, stunned and bewildered. The gymnasium has been transformed. The lights have been dimmed, and silver and blue balloons hang from the ceiling. The walls are covered with black fabric, and Dua Lipa plays through the speakers. It's an older song, from a few years ago.

That's when it hits me.

"Oh, my God." I whirl around to face Tyler. "It's prom!"

The song changes to something slower.

He shuffles from foot to foot, obviously uncertain. "Will you dance with me?"

I still can't get my mind around what's happening, but I allow him to guide me into a dance. We sway together, our bodies brushing with each movement. He dips me and spins me with more grace than I could have imagined. I hold onto him as tightly as I can.

When the song ends, he stills, and cups my face between his hands. He kisses me, slowly and tenderly. My toes curl and I smile against his mouth. I can't believe he's done this.

He pulls back, just enough to speak. "This is the prom we should have had. I should have danced with you, kissed you, and told everyone how proud I was to be with you. I'm sorry I didn't, but I swear things will be different this time."

I brush my lips against his. "I know they will. You've already shown me that."

"Good." The corners of his eyes crinkle as he smiles. "There's a suit and a dress in the changing rooms. What do you say we dress up and dance some more?"

"Really? You bought me a dress?"

He runs his hand through his hair, his expression turning sheepish. "I paid. Your mom chose it. She's the one who helped me organize all of this."

I shake my head, hardly able to believe it considering how nervous he was to meet her in person, but at the same time, it makes perfect sense considering how they both seemed to be in on a secret earlier. As the school cleaner, Mom has the connections to make this happen.

"Thank you." I wrap my arms around him and rest my cheek over his heart.

He kisses the top of my head. "I'll dance with you every day if it makes you happy."

When I've had my fill of hugging him, we change into our prom clothes. I can't help noticing how similar mine is to the one I wore that night. Mom must have done that purposefully.

We dance and laugh and kiss, and it's nothing like our actual prom was.

It's a hundred times better.

EPILOGUE

TYLER

Echo shifts restlessly on her seat beside me. "When does it start?"

I stare at the stage, my stomach a riot of nerves. "Any minute now."

Conversation buzzes around us, but I tune it all out. My companions understand. They know how important today is for me, and they're here to support me through every minute. I reach over and squeeze Echo's hand. I'm sweating, even though the air conditioning is on.

"You'll get Washington," Soraya says, leaning over Echo so I can hear her. "Right, Mom?"

"They'd be silly not to pick you first," Mom replies, her smile hesitant. "They need a strong center."

I allow myself to be distracted by her momentarily. In a blue dress and makeup a little brighter than Dad would have let her wear, she looks good. She and I have been talking lately, and I'm glad she's here with me. While we haven't mended any bridges yet, we're on the way there.

Echo toys with the necklace she now wears every day. "Whatever happens, we'll make it work."

My gut knots tighten. "I know."

But that doesn't mean I don't have all my fingers and toes crossed for Washington. It would mean the least distance between Echo and me. She's said she'll relocate for her post-graduate studies so she can be with me, but I don't want to take her too far from home.

A hush descends when a man stands in the center of the stage, where a podium is positioned with a microphone to ensure everyone can hear him. I barely manage to pay attention to the words of his introductory speech, but I clap when he calls up the manager of the Chicago Chaos, whose team won the draft lottery.

The manager is still relatively new. He takes to the stage and steps up to the podium. I raise my hand to where I know the moon sits against my chest, even if it's currently hidden by my shirt. I keep my eyes trained on the stage, my ears straining for the name. When it comes, I'm unsurprised.

Cole Trent. Son of Joseph Trent, the team's owner.

Talk about nepotism.

Not that Trent's a bad player. He should definitely be a first-round pick. But it's not a good look for the Chaos. Hopefully the team's public relations teams already have a campaign in place to put a positive spin on the choice.

Trent heads up to the stage and dons the team's shirt and cap. He poses for a photo, then joins them as they leave, making way for Nashville, who have the second pick. I hold my breath as the Nashville manager makes a brief statement of thanks before announcing that their choice is Devin Sanders.

Boston chooses Michael Wilkins.

Then it's Washington's turn.

I grip Echo's hand tightly. On my other side, Inez slips her hand into mine too. I don't even care that one of the many cameras here might be recording us clinging to each other.

The Washington manager seems to speak forever, even though I know it's probably less than a minute.

When he voices my name, my mouth falls open.

I blink in shock. Echo and Inez release my hands and Echo pushes my shoulder.

"Go," she whispers. "Go, Tyler. It's you."

I walk to the stage in a stupor, somehow making my way up the steps. The manager shakes my hand. I thank him, but everything seems to be happening at a distance, as if I'm watching myself from above.

Someone from the small cluster of people with him offers me a shirt with the number 21 printed on it, and my name on the bottom. I raise my arms and it falls over me. I'm guided into position in the center of the group as a woman with a camera snaps photos, and then we leave the stage.

I join my new team at their table, where I make small talk between announcements. Washington chooses another 6 players. Several of my former teammates are selected for NHL teams, including Anaheim and Matthews. When the rounds are complete, we're whisked away to a meet and greet.

It's completely surreal.

Later, when I'm finally free to return to my family, I find them waiting in the hotel room Echo and I are sharing.

They cheer as I enter, and crowd around me. I accept the congratulations, but before they can properly begin the celebrations, I stride over to Echo and drop to one knee in front of her.

Everyone falls silent.

Echo raises her hand to her mouth, her eyes wide.

"Echo. Baby. I love you so much. I've always loved you,

and I want to continue to love you for the rest of my life. Getting picked for Washington is awesome, but it's nothing compared to a lifetime with you."

I reach into my suit pocket and pull out the ring I chose for her several weeks ago. My hands tremble as I open the box.

"Will you marry me?"

She blinks back tears. "Yes. I would love to marry you, Ty."

She offers me her hand and pulls me to my feet. I kiss her, and once she's gazing up at me with glazed eyes, I carefully remove the ring from the box and slide it onto her finger. A perfect fit. It's white gold, and in the center, a cluster of diamonds are shaped into a star.

She studies the ring, and a tear spills down her cheek. "It's beautiful."

I gather her in my arms, cradling her against my chest. "I can't wait to spend my life with you."

My heart is so full, it aches in the sweetest way possible. Once upon a time, my existence felt like a black hole, sucking my soul into nothingness. Now, everything is bright and hopeful—lit by the glow of a shooting star.

My shooting star.

THE END

EXCERPT FROM FIGHTER'S HEART

Lena

Eight words. That's all it takes to ruin my day.

"LaFontaine, I have a special assignment for you."

I recognize the voice without looking up from my desk. It's my prick of a boss, Adrian, and anything he's terming a "special assignment" will inevitably be a nightmare. That's all I get these days. The unfixable cases. The spoiled, self-entitled sports stars who screw up so badly, no one else wants them.

God, one massive win and I become the go-to public relations girl for the biggest jerks-with-abs in Vegas. Why can't I, just once, get a client who's a marginalized feminist with a cause? Sighing, I raise my head and meet Adrian's beady little eyes. This douchebag has my career in his hands, and he knows it.

"What's the case?"

His thin lips curl in a self-satisfied smile. It doesn't escape my notice that he's yet to close the door, which makes me wonder if he's keeping it open as an escape route.

"Jase Rawlins."

Oh. Hell. No.

"Nuh-uh," I say. "No freaking way."

Jase "The Wrangler" Rawlins is one of the bad boys of MMA. I don't even have to ask why he needs our services. Anyone who pays attention to the sports industry knows his ex-girlfriend has come forward with allegations of domestic abuse. I've seen photos of her bruised cheek and read the story in popular magazines. The guy is violent. But I suppose I shouldn't expect any different from a cage fighter.

I know the type. I've *dated* the type.

"There's no way I'm working with that asshole. Absolutely not. Find someone else. I'm not aiding and abetting a jackass who thinks he can get away with hitting women."

The door opens wider, and Jase Rawlins himself steps into my small, airy office, his gaze immediately drawn to the view out the window, which looks over the business district. I know him on sight, and I'm not even sorry he overheard my comment. He deserves all the condemnation he gets, and more. Fuck him.

Adrian's brows draw together, as if he didn't expect me to argue. "Everything is organized, Lena. The papers are signed. It's a done deal."

My teeth scrape together loud enough I'm surprised no one else hears them. I meet Jase's eyes, and a jolt runs through me. They're a strange color. Dark gray, or maybe green, it's hard to tell, and fringed with the thickest lashes I've ever seen. Pretty eyes. Out of place on a man known for choking his opponents into submission. He has high, arrogant cheekbones and plush lips, although the upper one is marred by a thin scar.

This is a face a woman could study forever—if she wasn't too caught up in his body. Because holy shit, he has a *body*. Broad shoulders, tapered hips, and strong legs with muscled calves showing beneath his shorts. Unfortunately, however panty-meltingly hot he is, he's also a brute, and I'm done with men like him. If I have anything to say about it, I'm not touching another MMA superstar—not with a ten-foot pole.

Time to shut this shit down.

"I'm *not* working with you," I tell him, and watch for a change in his expression, but his only reaction is a quick flick of his eyes to the right, where a man in an expensive suit has followed him into my office. "This is *not* a happening thing." I aim this comment at the suit, and he glowers. I don't care. There are some jobs even I won't take, and Adrian wants me to cross a moral line I'm not prepared to.

"Lena," Adrian says in a cautioning tone. "Hold on a moment."

Crossing my arms over my chest, I stare at him, wondering how far he's prepared to push. Considering Jase Rawlins is worth seven or eight figures, I'd hazard a guess that dollar signs are flashing in Adrian's eyes. Too bad. I don't operate that way. Money isn't my driver, and he knows it. So what approach will he take?

Jase

Sometimes, I wish it was legal to put someone in a chokehold outside of the cage. Like this uppity image specialist, for instance. Yeah, she may look like a schoolboy's wet dream in an ass-hugging pencil skirt and V-necked blouse, but it's obvious from the second she opens her mouth that she's already judged me and found me wanting. Nothing I'm not used to, but it still stings.

Maybe it's the fact my dick has some really great ideas about what he'd like to do with those gorgeous red lips, which are currently set in a sulky pout, or maybe it's her instant dismissal, but I want to rile her. To ruffle up her silky feathers and find out just how mouthy she can get.

I step forward before her boss can intervene, and raise a hand. As expected, everyone falls silent, which only seems to piss the redhead off more. Fuck, we haven't even gotten as far as exchanging names before she's mentally convicted me. That's the shitty part of being in the public spotlight. Everyone thinks they know me. They believe every stupid lie anyone tells.

Well, guess what? This girl doesn't know a goddamn thing.

"Calm down, cutie pie." I love it when her eyes chill to an icy blue, silently threatening to cut my balls off. Yeah, I knew she'd hate the pet name. Considering what she thinks of me, I don't give a crap. "Turns out, I don't want to work with you either." I raise a brow at Nick, my manager, and ask, "Is this really the best you could do?"

The redhead gasps, and I want to check whether she's crossed her arms tighter over her chest, plumping her little tits up, but I resist the urge to look.

"We can go somewhere else," Nick says. "I was told these guys are the best for miracles, but I'm sure we can find someone else just as good."

"Now, wait a minute," the stuffed shirt interjects. I wasn't listening when he introduced himself so I didn't catch his name. "Lena is the best there is. You won't find anyone else."

Finally, I succumb to the desire to glance at her and see how she's taking this. I catch the tail end of an eye-roll, and it makes me soften toward her a little. She's not drinking up the flattery the way some might.

Lena. I try her name out. It suits her. Pretty, bordering on pretentious but not overstepping the mark.

"Whatever puppy dog stunts *Lena*"—I emphasize her

name now that I know it—"wants to pull, they aren't going to do jack." I address Nick. "I still don't get why we're here. Give it a couple of days; Erin will decide she doesn't want to act on her threats, and the hubbub will die down."

Lena's face twists into a sneer. "Die down?" she demands. "The only way this shit-nado is dying down is if someone gets proactive about putting out your fires, and fast. Also, have a little respect for your girlfriend."

"*Ex*-girlfriend."

"Whatever." She says it like the "ex" part doesn't matter. As if Erin and I didn't break up more than two months ago now. "She's not some problem that will disappear if you ignore her. Domestic violence is a serious crime, and you can't just hand-wave it away." Her nose crinkles like she smells something bad. "It disgusts me that you're callous enough to think otherwise."

Callous? Me?

I count to five in my head and remind myself she doesn't know me. Her perception of me is based on what she's seen in the news, and I have to admit, it's damning. It also isn't true, but I don't bother saying that because this woman isn't going to believe me. Stuffing my hands in my pockets, I decide the best way to deal with her is to call her bluff.

"Okay, so you say the problem isn't going away on its own. What did you have in mind to fix it?"

"I... I..." She flounders, and I can't stop the smile that tugs at my lips. She's all bluster and no bite.

"That's what I thought." I turn to leave, but her smarmy boss lays a hand on my arm. When I stare at it, he snaps it back like he's been stung, his cheeks going pale. This guy is even worse than Lena. At least she has the balls to say what she thinks to my face. He's the type who'll pretend to be on my side, but all the while he's secretly fucking terrified of me.

"Wait, wait, wait," he says. "Give me two minutes to speak to Lena in private and talk her around. I promise you won't regret it."

Lena looks like she wants to bash him over the head with a paperweight, and I don't blame her. He's a condescending little shit. "Adrian—" she says.

"My office." He snaps his fingers, like he's ordering a dog to heel. "Now."

They leave, her trailing behind, practically dragging her feet, and Nick gives a low laugh. "Good old Jase. Always charming the ladies."

I jerk a thumb at the door. "Can we go? I've had enough of this."

He sighs, his expression regretful. "I wish we could, but what she said is true. Whether you want to believe it or not, this situation has the potential to derail your career."

"How can it, when I have the championship bout so soon? I'll blow Karson out of the water, and everything will be fine."

Nick ums and ahs. "That's if you don't get arrested before the fight."

"Pfft." I shake my head. "Not gonna happen. Erin is full of hot air."

"She also has a taste for the spotlight, and she'll keep spouting this bullshit as long as the cameras are rolling." Damn, he's right, and he must sense he has the winning hand because he powers on. "Not to mention, you promised Seth you'd take this seriously and do whatever you could not to tarnish the reputation of Crown MMA gym."

Ouch. Low blow. Nick knows I'd go to war for Seth if he asked. My trainer gave me everything. He had faith in me, took a chance on me, and he had no way of knowing I'd pan out to be a good investment. I was just a kid from a poor neighborhood with a mother of a chip on my shoulder and a willingness to shed blood to escape.

"Fine," I concede, not surprising either of us. "I'll hear them out."

But I have a bad feeling about this, and my gut doesn't often lie to me.

ALSO BY A. RIVERS

Crown MMA Romance

Fighter's Heart

Fighter's Best Friend

Fighter's Secret

Fighter's Second Chance

Crown MMA Romance: The Outsiders

Fighter's Frenemy

Fighter's Fake Out

Fighter's Mercy

Fighter's Forever

King's Security

The King

The Veteran

The Spy

ACKNOWLEDGMENTS

All Your Pucking Secrets was unlike anything else I've written. It has darker themes, more angst, and wasn't a story I ever expected to write but it holds a very special place in my heart because of that.

Thank you to everyone who has helped make this book a reality. To my husband, for challenging me to stretch myself and try new things. To Mum, who told me this book was hard to read but maybe the best thing I'd written. To my sister, who chatted all things Tyler Kinsey with me during our long (slow) runs. To everyone else in my family, for your ongoing love and support.

Thank you to Kate at Paper Poppy Editorial for bringing that extra shine to my books, as you always do, and for going above and beyond. You're amazing. Thank you to Zero Alchemy, for ironing out the kinks.

Thank you to the team who contributed to my absolutely gorgeous covers. Christopher John, for the stunning photograph. Quinn Biddle, for bringing Tyler to life. Deranged Doctor Design, for bringing everything together into an incredible package.

From the bottom of my heart, the most massive thank you to my Street Team and ARC readers, who spread the word about my books and share the love. You mean the world to me.

Thank you to my readers. Each and every one of you. I appreciate you all. These stories couldn't exist without you.

ABOUT THE AUTHOR

A. Rivers writes romance with strong heroes and heroines who kick butt and take names. She loves MMA fighters, private investigators, hockey players, military men, bodyguards, and the protective guy next door who isn't afraid to fight the odds for love. She also writes small town romance as Alexa Rivers.